Robert Dunn's other musical novels:

*Pink Cadillac*
*Cutting Time*
*Soul Cavalcade*
*Meet the Annas*
*Look at Flower*
*Stations of the Cross*

*To Liz —
miss you every Thursday!*

# Savage Joy

*[signature]*

a novel by
**Robert Dunn**

A Coral Press original novel

Copyright © Robert Dunn 2017

All rights reserved under International and Pan-American copyright conventions.
Published in the United States by Coral Press.
All characters are fictional and bear no relation to anyone living.

ISBN-13: 978-1-935512-36-3
Library of Congress Control Number: 2017905243
Printed in the U.S.A.
1 3 5 7 9 10 8 6 4 2
First Edition

Cover Design and Cover Photo: Beth Bugler

"Memory" © Robert Dunn / First Published by The New Yorker, November 1977

More about Coral Press musical fiction at:
www.coralpress.com

For Pat, who always deserves another one

# 1

IN 1976, WHEN I was 25, I moved from my *Father Knows Best* Los Angeles suburb to FORD TO CITY: DROP DEAD New York. I scored a premium, $90-a-month apartment in the East Village; premium, that is, because the toilet was actually *inside* the three-room, fifth-floor walk-up. The two apartments at the back shared a facility in the hallway, and at night, when I couldn't sleep, I'd hear the occupants pad down the Italian tile floor, unlock the door, splash into the bowl, sometimes even flush. At the rear behind me was a skinny, bespectacled young guy with an old man's name, Wendell (or was it Walter?). Wendell would spend way too much time in the hallway john. He was also tied in with the Church of Jesus Christo, the storefront Pentecostal worship hall next door on East 11th Street run by Mr. Strump, the silver-stubbled, near toothless soul who lived on the second floor and owned the whole building.

Next to Wendell (or Walter) was a retired Eskimo seaman who spoke no English. He peed like a fire hose. All else I knew about him was that he never said hello, just grunted in the hallway, and that he welcomed a bone-thin junky prostitute to his place a couple times a week. After I'd been living there for nearly a year, the worst smell I'd ever come across suffused the narrow hall—so vivid and unexpectedly dark in its implications I gagged and nearly threw up—and later that day the Eskimo was carried out in a heavy black rubber bag by two gray-uniformed men.

Late that night I heard a loud mewling from behind the dead Eskimo's door. I didn't know he'd had a cat, but a cat was sure making a desperate ruckus now.

I went down and knocked on Mr. Strump's door to see if

I could get a key. He was in a yellowy-white nightshirt down past his knees and looked bemused by sleep, but when I mentioned the cat, he fetched a large ring of keys and led me back up to the fifth floor.

Inside the door was a skinny, tight-jawed gray tabby with pale purple eyes and a profoundly wary face. A sharp, hard-knocks New York City cat. I was immediately intrigued, yet when I reached to pick him up, he hissed at me, then swatted at my hand with his paw.

Hungry, I figured. I opened up the Eskimo's refrigerator, but immediately shut the door on the rotten, gassy smell that flooded out. I had fresh milk in my place, and cans of tuna fish—I'd recently read a financial book that said stockpiling cans of tuna when they were on sale was the best investment you could make, and, hey, it was a move I could at least afford—and went and got the food.

When I got back, the cat was settled in Mr. Strump's worn hands, body stretched over his chest, his head turned back, those savvy eyes gazing at me.

I fed the cat, and he immediately calmed down. I found that surprisingly satisfying. The thing was, I'd been seriously allergic to cats since I was a boy, and I told that to Mr. Strump. He shrugged, then muttered, "What would one more matter?" (When I paid my rent, I found his place crawling with cats, probably close to a dozen.)

"You sure?" I said. Part of me wanted to give the cat a try, but I could already feel my nose sniffling up.

He nodded, locked the apartment door, and that was that.

✷ ✷ ✷ ✷ ✷

A WEEK LATER Slater Martin moved in.

The first time I saw Slater he was leaving his new digs. The first thing I noticed was how short he was, a good four, five inches shorter than me (I'm five-ten), and bone-skinny except for his arms and shoulders, which were muscle-bound. He had long sandy hair, cut bowl-like to his shoulders, murky blue eyes, sharp cheekbones. He looked a lot like the surfer dudes I'd grown up with in L.A., but harder, as if ever he went surfing, it would be through a sea of garbage—or steaming molten metal. He had a tight, punchy chin, a hint of a dimple, and when he led with it, his chin gave him the look of a small boat braving angry surf. That, I came to know, was all Slater Martin: Bow first, he sliced through whatever was in front of him.

Today Slater was wearing an oversized leather jacket, studded with metal stars and glittery zippers. Even so, I could make out dusky blue-black tattoos on his neck and around his wrists. I was running out, late to work as always. I smiled at him, he grunted at me (in tones not unlike the dead Eskimo's), then cut me off to lope down the five flights of stairs two at a time.

I was thinking, What a rude asshole, when I got to the bottom of the rickety stairs and found him waiting there.

"Hey, I'm Slater." He held out a hand, thin and more delicate than I expected. I took it. His motion was unexpectedly wan, a ghost of a shake. His voice was surprisingly soft, gentle, though his eyes stayed wary, harsh. "Where you off to, bro?"

"Um, work." I gave my head a shake, surprised to be talking to him.

"Work? What's that?" He smiled, but also looked genuinely puzzled.

"You mean, what do I do?"

"You shittin' me?" Slater threw a shoulder toward me.

I blinked, didn't get what he meant. I felt my chest swelling, though. I'd blundered into the best publishing job in New York, my dream job, and—

"Listen," he interrupted, "why don't ya come with me?"

"What?"

"It's a lovely day, man. May. It's not May that often here, you know." He lifted a hand and waved it into the perfect slate-blue sky, then pointed at the just-budding Callery pears and honey locusts on our block. "It's no day for ... *work*."

"Why're you—"

"Cuz we're neighbors, bro." Slater's eyes lit up. "What's wrong with bein' neighborly?"

For somebody as slight as he was, the wraithlike body in rail-thin black jeans, a torn white T-shirt underneath the smothering studded jacket, Slater had that forceful way about him, like a spinning tornado ready to whisk you up and deposit you God knows where—probably not Kansas, Toto. A lot of it was in his blue eyes, murky yet strong, piercing, compelling. And of course his anvil chin, bursting through anything boring. As long as I knew Slater Martin, I was always surprised by how he could get me to go along with whatever madness he came up with.

But not that first day. I begged off, telling Slater maybe some other time, then headed to Union Square to the subway, taking it uptown to West 43rd Street.

My job was at *The New Yorker* magazine. I'd been there nine months, in the typing pool—Walden's Pond, named after Harriet Walden, the lovely older woman who presided over it—and it was such a great, unexpected place to be that I was still startled that I could get off the elevator on the 20th floor and be buzzed in. I was also not at all the type to play hooky—at least not then.

And besides, I had a lunch date with Emily Prosser, the elegant, ever-surprising girl I had a total crush on.

One of the cool things about working at *The New Yorker* was that literary New York took the job, and thus callow me, seriously. Including Emily Prosser.

Emily was recently out of Yale, with center-parted blonde hair, a Mickey Mouse Club cute nose, and glittering pale-blue eyes (I know, she'll hate me when she reads this), and those chunky black glasses that weren't yet universally sexy on smart girls—just damn sexy to me.

Emily worked at Farrar Straus & Giroux, the book publisher equivalent in prestige to *The New Yorker*, a junior editor, looking for authors (me! me!), and attending every bookish cocktail party in town. That's where I met her, at a soirée above the Gotham Book Mart on West 47$^{th}$, standing there along with tweedy old guys like George Plimpton, Gordon Lish, and Roger Straus. There were other kids my age, but it was Emily who struck me hard as I walked into the party.

She had on a turquoise sweater, perfectly curved, a pleated skirt just above her knees—nice knees—black ballet flats, around her neck a string of genuine pearls, and those thick black frames that set off her delicate blonde loveliness, making her look just a little dangerous. For all her bookish quality she sent off a definite meet-me-out-back sexiness.

I moved up close to her elbow. She was talking to a short man with cuffs two inches too short and a tall, owlish woman in huge lavender glasses I later learned was Joyce Carol Oates. I stood there, smiled—O.K., it was that I-don't-know-anybody-and-I'm-not-sure-I-belong-here party simper I'd yet to turn into mysterious confidence (if I ever did); and even though none of the three looked at me, I was so drawn to the blonde woman about my height, with her wide shoulders and perfect skin ... and those black, in-your-face eyeglasses ... that I stood there, sipping the cheap white wine, shuffling side to side, waiting for—

"No, I think Sontag is brilliant writing about photography," Emily said. "You know, we're doing a collection of her pieces soon."

"I don't like that silvery stripy thing in her hair," the short man said. "Seems pretentious."

The tall woman just rolled her eyes.

"I've been reading her pieces in *The New York Review*," I said, seeing a way in, "and I love them. Learned all kinds of things about photography I never even thought of."

"See!" Emily said, turning to me for the first time, and smiling.

The short guy, who I later found out had published a well-received novel ten years earlier but hadn't done much since but attend parties, shook his head distastefully: these children, these *upstarts*. He took the tall woman's elbow and steered her away, saying, "So, Joyce, how many books are *you* going to publish this year?"

"Hi, I'm Cole," I said as soon as they were gone. I held out my hand.

"Emily Prosser." Emily's gaze followed her former interlocutors. "Pretentious?" she said, making a cute-as-the-devil chipmunk face. "Where does that windbag get off saying that Susan Fricking Sontag is—"

"I love her stuff," I said, and meant it, though I didn't always know what Sontag was talking about. Heck, I'd only been reading the *New York Review* since I'd moved to the city those ten months back.

"I know, I know." Emily shook her head. "Some people."

We stood there, just the two of us for a moment, till in that severe yet curious New York way she looked at me and said, "So, what do you *do*, Cole?"

"I work for a magazine," I said. I'd learned pretty quickly that was the way to start off—just say "a magazine." So who was pretentious? My only defense: What could this former barefoot wannabe L.A. surfer boy do but pretend!

"Oh, which one."

"*The New Yorker.*"

That hooked her, as I knew it would. She gave me a second look, then a slow, easy smile.

"What do you do there?"

"Oh, I'm an editorial assistant." I smiled quick, thinking the faster I smiled, the better chance I had of slipping past my actual job.

"So you're in the typing pool." A sly smile. "I heard they were hiring men now."

I sighed, then laughed. "You know about Walden Pond?"

"A girlfriend of mine from Yale worked there for a while. She moved up to fact-checker."

"Who is she?"

"Annie Gottfried?"

"Oh, yeah," I said. The fact-checkers were the exalted young folk at the magazine. They actually got to work on copy, not just retype it. As a rule, they didn't mix that much with us.

"So, Cole, do you write?"

"Um, yes." I shifted from side to side. "Mostly fiction." Then I held my breath; I knew where this was going.

"That's nice." Emily was still smiling, and I found I was falling harder and harder for that smile, the way her lips held little wisps of joy in their corners, her perfect teeth gleamed. "Where have I seen your work?"

"Well—" I exhaled. That was the thing I was learning about the literary world: It was all points and credits. If you didn't have any...

"You have a novel yet?" she said, a sudden flood of kindness in her eyes. She was not going to cut me off because I had no quick answer to the publishing question. Emily was going to be sympathetic. "I mean, anything close to being finished?"

"I am writing a novel. Working away, and, well, it's already the third draft, and—"

"Want to send it to me?"

I pulled my head back. Farrar Straus, along with Knopf, were my dream publishers. I didn't think I could get close to them without an agent, and I didn't yet have an agent.

"Just like that?"

"Yes, sir!" Emily laughed. "I mean, whenever you're ready, Cole. I want to be the first person to see it." She lifted that fine-chiseled chin. "I insist!"

I stepped back. It wasn't that I hadn't gotten encouragement for short pieces I'd shown one of the fiction editors at work, but an out and out request to see my novel, my day-in, day-out, typing, obsessing, tearing up paper, feeling brilliant one moment, hopelessly stupid and kludgy five minutes later ... my baby, my sole reason to exist ... all this without even asking what the damn thing was about? I was flabbergasted.

Emily kept smiling, but I was self-consciously wracking my brain for some idea of what she might be seeing in me. A guy who had trouble tying a tie well (back in California, a clip-on got me through any event demanding one). A guy who went to a public university. (O.K., it was Berkeley, but they had to let me in with my GPA; I didn't pass any "You're Yale or Harvard material" test.) A guy who still walked around the glorious big city with eyes agog?

"Can we have lunch sometime?" I blurted out, then half-froze. "I mean, talk more about it or ... or something?"

"Yes."

"Really?"

"Cole, please, it's not that big a deal."

"No, I—O.K., that'd be great. Next week?"

"Sure." She was rooting into her purse, pulling out a pen. "Here's my number. Give me a call, I can check my calendar, but next week it is."

So Emily and I became lunch pals. And ... only pals.

I'd decided to hold off on showing her any of my book. If I'd learned anything yet as a writer, it was to *not* show work to anyone till it was ready. But talking about writing and the literary scene certainly gave us a start at that first lunch; and then it was mostly my crushing on her hard, and Emily trying not to acknowledge that—and most definitely not responding.

How bad was I? I thought about Emily a lot (not all the time, she wasn't exactly my first thought in the morning—fortunately, that was still the fortunes of Peter Strohmeyer, the hero of the novel I was writing, *Negative Space*), but I'd daydream at my typist's desk at *The New Yorker* about what Emily was up to, wonder way too much whether I'd waited enough time to call her up again, and plot—fruitlessly yet obsessively—how to make her my girlfriend.

Her just-friends friend, that was easy. We *were* friends; she seemed to really like having me wander the city with her on a Saturday, or meet her in Chinatown for an impromptu noodlefest on a weekday night, then stroll uptown through the then desolate land between Canal and St. Marks talking about anything and everything.

Emily really dug the Bowery. This was true skid row Bowery back then, not much else on the street but winos crumpled into doorways and ragged panhandlers spilling out of the Bowery Mission. Emily pressed coins, even bills into their hands, then turned to me, laughing.

"I love this city," she'd cry, twirling like Audrey Hepburn in some old movie. "I love everything about it."

Everything but me. I could be a fool with girls, for sure, and over the years I'd blundered passes and kisses with more of them than I want to recall, but I knew better than to make a move on Emily. There was just something there, a vibe, a tacit implication, a field of privilege and specialness I understood I'd better not breach. Did this make me want her any the less? Of course not. I panted for Emily, desired her the first moment my eyes sprung open in my lonely bed, and kept waiting for an opening—a way through her force field to what I passionately wanted: to be her boyfriend, her lover.

Was anyone else getting through? Emily was private in manifold ways, and part of staying her friend was not asking the wrong questions or pushing too hard. But still I had my ideas. Her class, her uptown sensibility, the simple fact she could go anywhere—any salon, fancy restaurant, elite gathering—and be right at home made me believe she was looking for a similar kind of Upper East Side guy, someone named Chance or Brock, say. I knew almost nothing of where she was from other than Yale, but my picture of her was of somebody who aspired to an expensive life—an East Coast version I had no understanding of. Polo? Why not? Brock's or Chance's grandmother's pearls? They'd look spectacular on her long, perfect neck.

Still, Emily *liked* me. And I more than liked her, though I did well tamping down that fire I felt when I looked past her sexy black frames into her silky blue eyes. It's just that they were ... rich girl's eyes; Over the Hill eyes—that's the way this San Fernando Valley kid thought of the Beverly Hills/Bel Air chicks he couldn't score with in high school. And if Emily had to keep herself pure to marry a man worthy of her—or with enough old-money worth *for* her—well, that seemed to be the way it was.

To Emily's credit, she never played me or made me feel emasculated. And she did unhesitatingly take me along on her rich-girl adventures, which as an aspiring writer was a godsend. A party at a huge apartment on Park and 71st? At first I felt klutzy and out of place, but she introduced me around and finally I felt almost accepted. I also kept my eyes open and made notes and notes and notes....

So, lunch today. At the Mary Elizabeth Tea House, this old-fashioned joint on East 37th Street right off Fifth, that I enjoyed going to just because for this California boy it was so exotic. Hmmn, lunch today? Sushi, Mexican, Chinese ... no, how about 1940s food?

Emily liked it, too. A cheese-and-olive nut-bread sandwich, with iced tea and cream, and banana royale for dessert? The chow reminded me of my grandmother.

So there we were at the starched-white-cloth table, heavy silverware in hand, dipping into cups of sorrel soup, when Emily said, "I have to move."

"You what?"

"Yes, get out of where I am. It's—" and she gave a pretty-as-a-picture shudder.

"What's wrong?"

"Oh, Cole, it's ... it's em-bar-ras-sing." Emily looked down at the white tablecloth. I don't know if I can remember her looking cowed like that. "Can I just tell you I need to find a new place to live?"

"Sure, I mean—" The thing was, I'd never been to her home, didn't even know where she was living. I'd always assumed it was some fancy Eastside digs at the least. "Anything I can do?"

"Keep your eyes and ears open." She gave me a steady nod.

"Sure."

"Can't be very expensive, you know." Up rolled her eyes. "Lit-er-ar-y publishing."

Was Emily really living on her salary? She dressed immaculately, I'd seen clothes certain to have come from Bergdorf's or Saks. As you can imagine, she fit right in at the Mary Elizabeth Tea House, as she fit in everywhere.

"You know," I said, a most unlikely thought springing into my head, "there's a lot of flux at my building on East 11$^{th}$ Street. A guy on my floor ... well, there was an unexpected opening, though it's taken now." I thought for a second of the short, studded-leather-jacket guy who'd asked me off on his lark this morning, then shook my head.

"Cole, what're you saying?" Emily's voice went up, no doubt noticing my head shake.

"Oh, well, I've heard there's another open apartment." Emily hadn't been to my place, either. Ours was a pal-ship of phone conversations, lunches, and parties. But East 11$^{th}$ Street? It seemed utterly unlikely that she'd have any interest in my tenement building. Still, I added, "At least it's in the front, but I...."

"With a view?" she said quickly.

"Well, it's the third floor. There's a two-story school across the street—"

"So there should be some decent sky, right?" Her enthusiasm startled me.

"Well, um, I can see the whole top of the Empire State Building from my place," I said, nodding, "but I'm at the top. This is on the third—"

"How much is it?"

"I'm paying ninety a month, can't imagine it'd be more than that. I can always ask the old coot who owns the building, Mr. Strump, I mean, if you're really...." My voice trailed off, still laden with disbelief.

"That would make things really simple, wouldn't it?" Emily said. "Have somebody I know right upstairs. In case I need a cup of sugar or something."

"Yeah, I guess—"

"Might be good," Emily went on, giving me her sly smile, "to have somebody around who actually *has* sugar in their place." An eye-sparking wink I had no idea how to take. "You know, if I ever *need* some sugar."

Turned out that was that. Mr. Strump didn't even have to meet Emily, was happy to have the apartment rented, I guess, though he was a genuinely laissez-faire landlord. He didn't even ask if she had a job; most of the people at 340 East 11th didn't.

And so on Saturday, still full of disbelief, I helped Emily move in.

# 2

THE CRAZY THING was, after we lugged Emily's furniture and boxes up the stairs on Saturday, Wendell and another Church of Jesus Christo member helping, I didn't see her for two weeks.

Where was she? I had no idea. There was so much about Emily that just never came up, such as where she was from, and her life before Yale and New York. She did seem to take off every now and then, but I only knew that from leaving her a phone message and not getting an answer for a while. I guess she had a fluid deal at Farrar Straus; probably she took a pile of manuscripts with her wherever she went.

And where was that? I doubted it was home, wherever that was; Emily never spoke about her parents or any siblings. I tried to ask a few times but got nowhere. Was it a secret boyfriend, that Chance or a Brock up in Greenwich or Newport? It could have been, but there was no evidence; and believe me, I kept my eyes wide for everything about Emily I could learn, especially when it came to men. The only thing that mattered right then to me (more than I wanted to admit) was that she wasn't around.

I missed her that first weekend. Sure, we'd just been literary buddies—at least, that's what I told myself—but now we were new neighbors, buildingmates. I truly thought she'd pop in on Sunday for that cup of sugar, and I was ready for her. *Knock, knock ... do you know any good restaurants around here, Cole? Yes, Emily, I was just thinking of getting cheap Indian down on Sixth Street ... want to come?*

Instead ... well, I spent the whole Sunday as I often did, all alone, reading, then when the loneliness crept over me, going out for a long walk—which, with all the brunchers and hand-holding couples strolling through the Village only made me lonelier. Finally, I picked up a turkey sandwich at the deli around the corner—last week it was tuna, if I remembered right—and watched *60 Minutes* on my little black-and-white TV, then read some more till I fell asleep.

That was a hard truth about my move to New York. I might be working at the best magazine in the world, in this startlingly cool job, but I was also less than a year in the city, moving from 3,000 miles away; and the thing was, none of my deep and abiding friends were anywhere even close. I hadn't gone to a nearby school, didn't have parents and old pals up in Westchester; and though I liked most everyone I worked with, they were mostly older and had their own lives. Except for Emily, I hadn't yet found a lot of people to hang with if we weren't at the office or one of the book parties I was able to get into.

Weekends were especially empty. I remember now that sometimes I didn't speak to anybody from Friday evening till Monday morning. As I rule, I didn't mind being by myself, but still....

Saturday morning had been full of the hope and effort of moving Emily in, and then she was gone.

Gone for those two weeks, too. Nobody was around. By the next weekend I was lonelier than usual, and of course once you start feeling that alone, it gets worse and worse; you sink into yourself and can't even reach out ... no, Bill's going to be busy, Larry's busy ... everybody's busy, they're all doing something grand and exciting ... except me.

I even started thinking about Slater, the new guy in the back who'd tried to swoop me up on his hooky adventure, but he wasn't around either.

No one, for two long weeks. I think it was summer and the book parties had stopped. Everyone was up in Maine or Vermont or Long Island, even *The New Yorker* felt half dead except for us drones who actually helped put out the magazine.

This is probably a good time to talk about how I got to *The New Yorker*, since it's central to my story. The job was a total fluke. I mean, I was the suburban Valley boy, I hardly knew *The New Yorker* existed. (I liked magazines though. My mom subscribed to *Newsweek*, which I devoured each week, and I had my own subscription to *Surfer*.) I certainly wasn't the offspring of anyone famous or well-connected, like so many of the people I worked with. Think of it: You want to get into magazine publishing but can't imagine work at *McCall's* or *Salt-Water Angler*. What's your dream job? Maybe *Esquire*, maybe *The New York Review of Books*, but no question it would be *The New Yorker*. A woman I later worked with, a Smith grad, once pulled from the filing cabinets the letter she wrote in as a twelve-year-old saying how much she loved the magazine and hoped to work there someday. Another coworker's father was short-listed for the Nobel Prize each year....

Then there was me.

Here's how I got the gig. First off I had to get to New York City from L.A., a kinda crazy story: postcollege Europe trip, first stop Spain; going for gazpacho with a lovelorn Oxford dropout named Mary (living in my *pensíon* in Madrid) and hearing how much she missed her anti-Franco beau, up in the hills working on the revolution; a later meeting with Mary and her mother in England (she had dropped the boyfriend, decided to return to Lady Margaret Hall) and an offer to "come be a writer" in their guest house in Connecticut; a three-day stoned drive across the country with a guy I found on the UCLA ride board; two months in the country outside Hartford, then displaced by relatives; finally down to New York City all on my own. (July 3, 1976; the next day was the Bicentennial. I wandered the city, took in the Tall Ships on the Hudson, crowned the evening hearing Leonard Bernstein conduct for free in Central Park.) I lucked into a sublet in the East Village (celebrated video artist off for two months in Europe; silver-lamé shoes in the closet, first Donna Summer LP I'd played); then a latent desire for a "serious writer's" typewriter sprang up when I saw an ad on a board at St. Marks Books offering an IBM Selectric for a mere $100.

No phone number, just an address: 340 East 11th Street, apartment 15. I still remember walking into the tenement building (no lock on the downstairs door), thinking, *Wow, people actually live like this?* Knock on the door, no answer, then leaving a note. A phone call from the guy a couple days later, loping up the five flights of stairs, a quick deal on the Selectric, and ... "Oh, by the way, my boyfriend and I are moving to Miami. Think you might need an apartment?"

So there I was, living in New York City. August, hot and humid, my ambitions flying, but no work. I did get a job entering backed-up insurance forms into a primitive computer, but that was only temporary. Somebody I worked with recommended an employment agency. Who knew? I signed right up.

So there I was checking in with my rep at the agency from a phone booth on Fifth Avenue and 46th Street when she said she had a really good one for me. "Hold tight, Cole. It's *The ... New ... Yorker!*" To my eternal shame, I simply shrugged; remember, as a dumb L.A. kid, I'd never read it. Still, it was a job, the rep was enthusiastic, and I was more than ready for anything other than insurance forms.

An opening in the typing pool. (August, somebody probably quit the magazine because there was no air-conditioning.) Mrs. Walden, tired of hiring only the offspring of the famous and well-connected, had reached out to the employment agency, and they were recommending me.

I promptly called Mrs. Walden, set up an interview, then came down with the worst stomach flu I can recall. I didn't dare leave my apartment. (Summer of '76, fortunately the Olympics were on the tube.) I called back Mrs. Walden, who shifted right into mom mode and asked how high my fever was (104), if I was getting enough fluids (trying to), then said not to worry, we'd reschedule—just call her in a week.

A week later I was mending but not whole, able to go a block or two for food before having to scamper back to my place; and when I called, Mrs. Walden again made sure I was taking the best care of myself I could, and rescheduled my interview for a week later.

I tell everybody I got *The New Yorker* job *because* I'd been sick; that Mrs. Walden hired me since, well, she was Mom Walden. It certainly wasn't my typing. When I finally made it into the magazine's offices, Mrs. W and I chatted for a bit, then she asked me to go type—no formal test, she only had to listen to the clacking of the keys.

I clacked away. When I was done, she looked at me with concern and said, "You *will* get faster, won't you, Cole?"

I assured her that I would. (I did.) And got the job.

Thus starting my thrilling, lonely, exalted, miserable, striving, lovelorn first year in Manhattan.

# 3

SLATER WAS BACK.
I was in my apartment alone on a Saturday night, getting ready to watch *The Mary Tyler Moore Show*—not all Tolstoy all the time—when I heard a lot of banging and crunching in the hallway. When I opened my door, I saw a guy and a girl both in leather jackets—it was June and getting hot—lugging big black cases up the stairs, crashing them into the sea-green stucco walls, then piling them outside Slater's door. Stenciled on the boxes was BONY MARONIE.

"Is that it?" the girl said. She had red-bronze hair, cut in a sleek bob, bangs just over her eyebrows, the sides following the nicely sculpted curves of her cheeks. It was an immediately arresting look, like an old-time film actress. She had large eyes, set just a whiff too far apart; she had a touch of gamine about her, yet something far more intense also. She wore a short salmon skirt, and under the black jacket she had on a KLITZ T-shirt, the V-neck stretched and tattered. I caught a flash of a black bra against creamy pink-white skin.

"No, there's one more load downstairs." This I saw now was Slater. He looked even shorter than I'd remembered from our one encounter those few weeks back when he'd asked me to play hooky. His dirty blond bowl of hair was pulled back in a tiny ponytail, held tight in a girl's scrunchy. He too wore a worn T-shirt, reading CLASH—a band, like the Klitz, I hadn't yet heard of.

"Shit!" the girl said. She turned, saw me looking at her, then flinched, mostly in her eyes. It was a curious move, not the startlement of just anyone being there, but something more personal.

"Who're you?" she said, sharper than she needed to. She looked oddly flustered.

"Um, Cole," I said. I gave a half-hearted smile. I was feeling curiously caught out, not because I had popped out to see what the noise was, but a feeling deeper in me, things moving, shifting. The sensation was so unexpected I totally ignored it. "I live here," I added, as if I needed to. Of course I did. I'd been lying around on a hot summer night, wearing shorts and my own favorite new shirt, a navy-blue NEW YORKER T I got for playing on the magazine's softball team in Central Park.

"Cole," the girl said under her breath, then nodded to herself.

"Hey, Cole, you wanna help, bro?" Slater's voice was always loud—I'd soon find out he was the lead singer, well, the *former* lead singer of Bony Maronie—and it rang down the hall.

"One more load?" I said. "Sure."

"That's great—that way Sailor don't have to stick around." He nodded at the sleek redhead. "You've been a honey, babe. Thanks."

"Least I could do, Slater," the girl said. It was taking me a moment to process. Her name was *Sailor*? She didn't look at all like she was a boat person (and I'd recently met a few yacht guys through Emily). But that was clearly the name I heard.

This was also the first time I'd heard Slater's name, the odd thing being that when the girl said it, it seemed like I'd known his name all along.

They left the boxes where they were in the hallway, then the three of us clattered down the stairs. There was a black panel truck, also crudely stenciled with BONY MARONIE, parked on 11th Street. When we got to the truck, Slater and Sailor embraced—I was watching, and it was hard to tell just what it meant, not an actual kiss but a close hug, their cheeks bussing—and then she took off. I watched her head down the street, her cotton skirt flouncing as she walked.

"Hey, Cole—it is Cole, right?" Slater said, staring at me hard. "Over here, buddy. Over here!"

All that was left in the van were two microphone stands, some small plastic mike boxes, and ropes and ropes of cable. We both loaded up and made the climb to our fifth-floor apartments.

I had the mike cable looped over my shoulders as Slater opened the lock on his door.

"Want me to bring this in?" I asked.

Slater considered a moment, then shook his head.

"Nah, I got it from here, bro." He lifted his narrow chin. "But big thanks." Then he looked hard at me. "So, Cole, what you doin' home on a Saturday night?"

I tensed. Not a happy question. But there was only one answer: "Getting ready for *Mary Tyler Moore*."

Slater looked intensely at me almost half a minute, then burst out laughing.

"Tomorrow, brother, tomorrow you're comin' with me." He sent out a huge, winning smile. "That trip we didn't take that while back, you know. Y'up for it?"

Tomorrow was Sunday, of course, and since I was deep in a terminally lonely weekend, I had nothing planned—nothing at all.

"What time?"

"Musician's time. Morning ... which usually works out to be about one or two?"

"We're not having brunch?" I said. I slit a thin smile as I said it.

Took Slater a moment, then he got that I was goofing.

"Nope, not this Sunday, brother. No Eggs Benedict Arnold for us. Just Eggs Slater Martin—you know, scrambled. To-tal-ly scrambled!" He looked hard at me, then chuckled. "Think you can handle that, Cole?"

I shuffled back and forth. For a moment there, I recall now, I wondered what I was getting into agreeing to go off with Slater. He was far, far from what I was used to, at least in my aspiring literary sophisticate in New York moment.

"No problem," I said, smiling.

I headed back to my place. It was just time for *MTM*. Rhoda was up to something, and Ted Baxter brayed dopily all over the place. I didn't really laugh out loud at the show, but I smiled through it. Then I read for awhile and easefully fell asleep.

# 4

WE GOT GOING at noon, evidently early for Slater. He knocked on my door loud, like a prisoner trying to get out of a trap. He was wearing a yellowed-out wifebeater, scrawled across it in red Magic Marker, I FOUGHT THE LAW—the title of a favorite Top 40 song from my high school days—tight black jeans, a thick black belt, engineer boots, and over it all a well-used knee-length mid-'60s poplin black raincoat. It was shirt-sleeve weather, but Slater looked cool enough standing there.

"You ready, bro?"

"Sure." I was in shorts, sandals, and my NEW YORKER T-shirt. "Where are we going?"

"Roamin'," Slater said, then shot me one of his subtly vulpine smiles. "Following our *blood*."

We hit the train at Astor Place, hopped a 6 uptown. It was crowded, and we stood there holding on to the straps, swaying as the train rushed along. Almost every spot was covered with grubby spray-painted graffiti, like every other subway car in the city back then.

"Where do we get off?" I said as we headed past 42nd Street.

"Man, that's *not* the right question," Slater said. "You're in my hands, man." That smile. "Kick back, enjoy the ride."

Slater seemed perfectly content to just hurtle along in silence, but it was making me a little anxious. Looking for something to say, I asked, "So what do you do?"

"What do you mean, what do I do?" Slater gave me an odd look, as if he were talking to a child.

"You're in a band, right?"

"In a band?" He looked at me hard. Why was he being so difficult?

"Yeah, that's what I was picking up on, you know, the truck, the microphones, all the stuff you were un—"

"Was," he said abruptly.

"Sorry?"

"I *was* in a band." He brought his long fingers to his thin mouth, then went "*Phffft!* All gone."

"What happened?"

For a second, a dark cast came over Slater's face. Strangely eerie; I saw bones and muscle and hollow gray cheeks—a lot of miles. Then he shook his head.

"What always happens, man. Thing broke to shit."

"You've been in—"

"All my life. I been playin' music all my friggin' life."

"Rock and roll, right?"

He gave me a hard look right then, a little scary.

"What do you mean, rock and roll?" he said.

"I mean rock and roll." I shook my head. "You know, what's on the radio, everything I grew up with." I pointed to his chest. "Like the Bobby Fuller song you got written there."

"Back in the last decade."

"I guess." I wondered then how old Slater was. I was twenty-six. He looked to be about the same age.

"And you dig the Bobby Fuller Four?" he asked me.

"Yeah."

"Then maybe you can get it." He was almost glowering at me. The subway kept roaring uptown, and there he was, throwing attitude at me.

"I hope so—"

"No, I mean, *really* get it. What do you think about ELO, brother? Boston? Foreigner?"

"I don't listen to them," I said.

Slater glared at me again, though I had no idea why. Did he listen to these big, overblown bands clogging the radio? Couldn't imagine it.

"So what *do* you listen to?"

I took a step back. His dark, sharp features had a hatchet edge.

"Truth is, these days mostly classical music. I—I kinda got sick of rock and roll after all the good stuff ended or got wishy-washy. You know, Beatles, Kinks, even the Stones. I loved them, then ... well, let's just say I bought McCartney's *Ram*, played it once, and immediately started listening to Bach and Mozart."

It was that hard, sharp glare Slater kept on me, whistling wheels cranking in his head, not sure what he was thinking, when he let out a big laugh.

"That fuckin' makes sense, man!" He slugged me on the shoulder, a couple knuckles popping my skin through my NEW YORKER T-shirt. "In fact, that's positively genius. Mozart, he the man!" And leaping to his feet, Slater did a hornpipe right there on the subway, his knees lifting, engineer boots kicking out, heels clattering against the floor, shuffling joyfully side to side. Ol' Wolfgang would've been proud. I just sat back and watched it happen.

Slater kept up his spirited dancing longer than anyone would've thought. He had most of the eyes on the 6 train on him, though he paid nobody any mind. Kicking and clattering all the way up to 116th Street, where we got off and climbed the stairs to the sidewalk.

"A Hundred and Sixteenth Street?" I said. Slater had calmed, and now we were walking across Lexington.

"Got a little errand I gotta run."

"Up here?" This was East Harlem, a part of town I hadn't been to yet. I looked around. Not much other than worn tenements and old five-and-dimes and tire shops.

"Just be a minute." Slater nodded toward a candy store with an outside magazine rack. He reached into a pocket and pulled out a rusty metal Sucrets box, took out a hand-rolled cigarette from it, then fired it up with a metal Zippo lighter. "Hang here, I'll be back in five."

"But—" I called out to his receding back. Took him eight minutes, he came back whistling. I put down the *Rolling Stone* I was looking at and said, "Now what?"

"Back to the subway."

Slater swept me through the turnstile, tokens dropping into their slots, and we waited silently for a downtown train.

"Is this it?" I finally said. "We're just riding the subway?"

Slater was half turned away from me, bent over and peering down the track for a train light. When he turned back to me, he said, "Something wrong with that?"

I didn't know what to say, so said nothing.

"Just fuckin' with you, Cole," he said with a laugh.

Yet when the downtown train came, it turned out that was just what we were doing.

I had more questions, and as we switched to the express at 86th and found places to sit, I asked them.

"So, O.K., your band's kaput—"A look at him, a quiet nod. "So how do you get by?"

"Get by?" Slater looked puzzled.

"Yeah, like food, for instance. Like pay the rent on your place at 340. I know it's cheap, but—"

A quick laugh. "You don't want to know, bro."

"No, I do." I leaned toward him on the subway bench.

"No, man, you really ... do ... not." Slater sat back, folded his skinny arms over his bony chest. He looked curiously smug.

"Hey, come on!"

Slater slowly turned to me. His face went dark, purposeful.

"I do what the fuck I can, man." The look he threw me was the hardest one yet. His jaw line tight, his chin up a whiff. A very hard look. "Whatever I have to."

"And that is?" Why was I so insistent? The whole trip up to East Harlem, the way Slater got dark and moody like that, his knife-sharp chin.... I probably should have left it alone.

But my neighbor was so different from me, and I wanted the whole picture. Also, I liked to think I could read people, but I was not reading Slater Martin.

"Listen," leaning in on me, "you sure you want to keep asking this shit?"

There was something in the way this came out that sent a shiver up my spine. Here we were, rattling on the 4 train out of Manhattan, to Brooklyn, right now under the East River, a flood of water above our thin tunnel ... and Slater was daring me to ask what he did.

"Yeah, I do." My quiet, dead-on answer. "We're neighbors, I guess I want to know—"

"O.K., well, for one I sell blood."

"Sell blood?" I'd heard of this, of course, but nobody I knew had ever done it. That was what street urchins did, down-and-outers. "Like what, go to a place, they put a needle—"

"Yeah, long friggin' needle, tourniquet, plastic bag. You lay there, drip, drip, drip." Slater shot me a ghoulish smile, then went on: "Drip, drip, drip, drip, drip...."

"And that's enough to get—"

"Of course not. They got rules, you gotta wait two months, officially, but, you know." He held up his arm, puffed out his hard muscle. "If you got a lot of blood ... ser-i-ous blood...." He laughed. "Plasma's faster, but they don't want that so much."

"So what else?" I said, nodding.

"Cole, baby, you sure you want the full guided tour of Slaterville?" He looked relaxed now, enjoying himself. "You know, the gold ticket?"

"Why not?"

"Well, you asked for it." A sly smile. "Pictures sometimes, these rags up on 48th Street, you know."

"Pictures?"

"Photos."

"Oh, photos!" I was starting to imagine something, not yet clear. "Like of what?"

"Me."

"What, for catalogs?" I knew a couple girls in college who had gone into San Francisco for catalog shots. Christmas ones.

"Absolutely, yes, this lovely face—" he stuck out his chin, lifted it smartly. In truth, Slater was definitely good looking in his tough way, sharp features, high cheeks, fuller lips than you'd think. His bowl of thick blond hair, while often dirty and scraggly, had a certain buoyant glory to it, too. Yet there was also that emaciated thing, not to mention his tattoos and pale skin. I couldn't quite see him wearing dress shirts in a Penney's catalog.

"Hey, come on."

"O.K., bro, we're talking less fancy, you know. More … active."

I shook my head.

"I look pretty good, I don't got a lot on." Slater wiggled his torso, smiled. "Sometimes it's not just me, capiche?"

"Oh." I blushed. I'm sorry, I was so, so innocent back then. "That, um, pay well?"

"Not like it should, but nobody's stickin' a needle in you—and it don't take two months to get, um, re-plen-ished." He bounced down each syllable of *replenished* as if down the flight of stairs in our building, then cracked up when he hit bottom.

"And that's it?"

"Boy, you're nosy, Cole. I thought you wrote *fiction*. You wanna be a reporter or something? *New York Post?* You got big eyes?"

"Just curious."

But it was more than that. I was truly intrigued. Wasn't meeting people like Slater part of why I moved to New York City? Not just those tweed-jacket types up on West 43rd Street? Maybe even then I was seeing Slater as someone to write about, so far from my world, yet right there down the hall. Also, he had this way about him—charisma, if you like—where you just wanted to know more.

"Hey, bro, I tell you anything else, I might have to take you out."

*"What?"* burst out of me

Slater thinned his lips, truly spooky, then leaned back and chortled. His laugh rang through the subway car.

"Just saying."

"O.K." I nodded. Not that stupid, I figured he was talking about illegal stuff. Even I wasn't sure how much I wanted to know about that.

But he was revved up, kept going.

"You see me in my long coat?" he went on, patting what he was wearing, more enthusiastic than I expected. "This is kinda my bus-i-ness attire, bro. Get it?"

I nodded. Easy to throw cans of tuna fish, tomato paste, whatever into those big pockets, right?

"And I got me some new shit happenin'." A faint smile to himself. "Tryin' it out, you know." A deep nod. "Might get pretty damn lu-cra-tive." That was Slater's way with any three dollar word, as it tripped out of his mouth he enjoyed every nickel of it. "Kind of right up my alley, you know what I mean?" He waved his hands, did something with his fingers, then smirked at me, knowing, probably, that I would have no idea what he was talking about; and I didn't.

"But it's all so I can play fuckin' music." Slater let out a quick huff of breath, silent nod, downcast. I thought back to helping him and that girl Sailor with their equipment. "Music, man, that's my whole fucking life."

"Your band? Something happen—"

"Shit, man." Slater gave his head a harsh shake. "I keep believin' different, but it's always the same damn thing. Music, she's a fickle bitch. That lady kicks your ass, then breaks your fuckin' heart."

That was all he said. His mood rushed to darkness, and after that he clammed up.

We were into Brooklyn now, heading past Borough Hall. The train grew emptier but we stayed on it. Were we actually going somewhere again, or was it what he first said, just riding the subway for kicks?

The thing was, it wasn't that bad. I used to run the L.A. freeways sometimes just because I was bored, and it was the same with the subway. I truly dug it, and often on a weekend I rode out to some part of town I'd never been to, getting into just watching all the different people on the train—this crazy, huge, jumbled city I was calling home.

Slater was watching people, too. I followed his gaze. We were just approaching Atlantic Avenue when he went up to two Hispanic women in tight halter tops and short shorts. He had both hands in the pockets of his black raincoat. He was facing the girls, away from me, so I couldn't see exactly what happened, just that the girls threw their hands to their mouths and shrieked.

Slater cackled, grabbed my hand, and as the doors slid open, tugged me out of the car.

"Run, Cole, run you son of a bitch!" Slater took off, the heels of his engineer boots ricocheting in the tiled corridor. We dashed up stairs, turned down corridors, finally burst out into the Brooklyn streets. Slater had his head back and was crowing.

I didn't know what to think. I was in a kind of shock. This was fun? But in a crazy way it was... wild, startling fun. What had he done back there on the train? I had a good idea but pushed it away; it was enough simply to pick up on the adrenaline running through his—through both of our—blood.

We got a bunch of Nedick's hot dogs, mustard and red onion sauce dribbling down our chins, then headed back to the subway. We pushed onto a crowded 4 train back to Manhattan. Slater kept his face tight, features focused; he didn't look like he wanted to talk anymore, which was fine by me. I'd gotten a lot out of him, a lot to noodle around.

We stayed on the 4 all the way to the Bronx, up to right before Fordham Road, where Slater went up to a couple of nuns—in full habits, sweating it out on the subway train—and with his back to me, did his raincoat thing again, and ... well, before I saw any reaction on their faces, he'd grabbed my hand again and pulled me onto the platform.

"Slater, are you fuckin' crazy, those were nuns!" I cried as we dashed up the steps. I was laughing but not as much.

"Not all's what it looks like, my friend," he said when we'd crossed the street and were heading back down to the subway. He threw another of his slicing smiles at me.

This time heading downtown, well, the thrill was gone. Not just in me, in Slater, too. We were deep into Sunday afternoon, and Sunday afternoons are almost always a crash. So we settled into the plastic seats and let the train hurtle us back to the East Village and home.

# 5

EMILY WAS BACK. As Slater and I climbed to the fifth floor, I saw her door was open, a fan in the doorway blowing in air, the radio loud, playing a disco song that went, over and over, *"You sexy thang"*; and through the opening I could see my friend in just a black bra and very small white shorts dancing to the music, kicking out her long legs, shimmery blonde hair shaking, bopping her shoulders—Emily looser than I'd ever seen her.

It kind of blew my mind, seeing her like this, my proper, buttoned-up, Mary Elizabeth Tea Room pal; and I was hustling away from her door when she heard us in the hallway—Slater's heavy heels?—and called out, "Hey, Cole, is that you?"

"Um." I pulled up on the landing. Slater was right behind me.

"Oh, good, I've been hoping I'd catch you." Emily was at the door now, and she'd pulled on a thin white cotton blouse, buttoned a few of the lower buttons. It was a little sheer, and her black bra shone through. Her legs in the tiny shorts were longer than I'd ever seen them. "It's really good having a neighbor who's a friend. I mean, I went up and knocked on your door, I need to borrow a ... oh, who's this?"

I guess she'd been seeing only me, but Slater came over from down the landing, hands in his black raincoat, and stepped to my side.

"I'm Slater," he said. His voice had dropped a few tones, lower than his wild cackle on the subway. "And I guess I'm your neighbor, too."

Emily simply stood there, silent a moment. What crossed her face? It was hard to tell. Her lips pursed, her eyes lightened, and a thin smile bowed her lips.

"Well, then, maybe you can help me, too. Cole ... Slater ... what I need is some chicken bouillon. Not a *lot*, but I'm making this soup, and, well, it really, really needs *something*."

Emily was still looking past me at Slater when I heard him laugh.

"Sorry, *Mademoiselle, mais je n'ai pas bouillon*," Slater said. He winked. No, of course, the rock and roller would *not* have bouillon. And yet he spoke perfect—

Emily's eyes grew. She'd been taking in Slater, his rough, handsome face, slippery grin, torn T-shirt, ratty raincoat, stovepipe thin pants, and here he was speaking French to her?

"Um, I think I have some," I told her quickly. "You know, I have a lot of basic things like—"

"Great!" Emily buttoned another button on her thin top, then came out into the hallway. "So I can just come up and get a few cubes?"

We were all on the fifth floor when Slater peeled off and headed toward his apartment in the back. Emily followed toward my door, then called out loudly, "You boys hungry? It's just soup, but I'll have a lot of it. What do you say?"

Slater turned, and I felt my heart clench.

What he said was, "I'm famished. What time?"

"Well, um, Cole will get me the bouillon, um, but we'll need some bread—you boys will want bread, won't you?" Emily's voice pitched curiously higher than usual. She kept bringing her right hand to the open top of her blouse.

"I can do that," Slater said. "I know a great li'l place on Ninth Street."

"So let's say forty-five minutes from now." Emily turned to me. "That O.K. with you, too, Cole?"

My stomach was sloshing around, but of course I told her it was just fine.

\* \* \* \* \*

THE SOUP WAS DELICIOUS, a creamy orange Moroccan concoction, made with squash, Emily told us. Raisins and almonds as condiments. The soup was thick and satisfying even on this warm night. Slater's long baguette, crisped in Emily's oven, along with slabs of sweet butter made everything perfect. (Butter was still exciting to me; I was raised on Day-Glo margarine.)

Slater had brought back a couple bottles of white wine, already chilled—Emily called out, "Sauvignon blanc—I love Sauvignon"—and as we sat at her four-seat table, we plowed right through them.

"You look hot," Emily said to Slater as we were finishing up dinner. "I mean, that raincoat? You always wear that?" She had her head cocked, a slanting wry look in her eyes. "Some kind of trademark thing?"

The deal with Slater was I never saw him sweat except later, when I caught his band playing out; onstage, he was a whirligig of streaming sweat. In Emily's roasting apartment his sallow cheeks were dry.

"You think?" he said. He'd been quiet through dinner. We hadn't chatted a lot, mostly Emily telling me about a couple of new manuscripts she was reading for FSG.

"It's sure not going to rain in here, buddy boy." Emily laughed.

Buddy boy? She'd never called me anything but Cole; never called anyone anything but their proper names.

"Are you sure?" Slater shot me a look. "Maybe Cole's left his faucet running."

"Funny." I shifted, side to side. The wooden chair was surprisingly well-built. It looked old and felt solid, handcrafted. My furniture and those of my peers were either from Goodwill or were rickety things picked up off the street.

"Well, if you insist." Slater threw out his right arm, then his left—sharp jabs into the air, as if he were Mick Jagger. Then he slithered both arms back so that they escaped the black raincoat. He didn't remove the coat from his shoulders, just wiggled his arms till it dropped to the floor.

Slater was wearing that yellowy wifebeater with I FOUGHT THE LAW on it, no sleeves, his arms just sticking out there. And though his arms—his whole body was stick thin—I was surprised to see muscles popping just where they should. To my surprise Slater was ripped.

I wasn't the only one to notice. Emily actually swallowed; her eyelashes batted fast, eyes went large. Then she wrinkled her brow.

"That's a dis-gus-ting T-shirt you're wearing," she finally said.

"Yeah." Slater, a beaming triumphant smile.

"So what's the deal?" Emily was leaning forward, and I knew she wasn't all that disturbed by what she was seeing.

"You mean the shirt?"

"I mean the whole rigmarole. What gives, boyo?"

Slater didn't say anything, just sat back, twiddling his full wine glass between his thumb and fingers. His dark lips slit thin, and the longer we sat there, the clearer it was he wasn't going to say anything. One thing I can say about Slater Martin, he knew how to wield silence like a rapier.

"He's in a band—was in a band, I mean," I finally piped up. The silence was really grating at me.

"Was in a band?" Emily raised her fine chin. "What happened?"

"What always happens." Slater shrugged, said nothing further.

"You really like to play the silent dude, don't you?" Emily leaned over the table. "You just have a whole James Dean aw-shucks thing going." And she nodded as if she were seeing straight through him.

Slater didn't answer right away, but the focus was strong on him. Emily bearing down from across the table, and me turned in my seat next to him.

"You spend long enough in a van, well, sometimes you don't come back the way you took off." Slater spoke slowly, resonantly—hitting that thrilling tone level that made him so good onstage. It was also clear he was purposely saying nothing. "So, *phffft!*" He kissed his fingers, sent them swooping into the air.

Not enough for Emily.

"That's it?" she insisted. "We ask you a friendly question, and you just go—" And she perfectly mimicked his hand floating dismissively into the air.

Slater, silent, simply smiled at her. The silence held, built, ballooned, then—

"What the fuck!" Emily let out, loud. She jumped up. "I mean, we're all flatmates here, right? Getting to know each other bet-ter." She was glaring at Slater. "So why so cagey? That part of your shtick, too, boyo?"

I couldn't account for this outburst and doubted Slater could either. I felt him dig his elbows into his sides, a quick flinch at Emily's explosion. He was all tense, and I felt the moment could've gone a couple ways: Slater simply getting up and dragging his skinny butt out the door, or he'd drop some of the attitude and tell us what was what.

Definitely could've gone either way. But Emily started laughing, giddily, like a teenage girl, then saying, "You're not what I'm used to, buster. You're a whole other kettle of fish." She sat back in her chair, leaning across the table and staring straight at Slater. "So I'm curious. I got the curiosities. I got the wanna-knows. Ser-i-ous-ly!"

It took Slater a long couple minutes, but he got it. He had to crack. Emily was too tough, and we all lived here, and he had to crack.

"It was called Bony Maronie," he said softly. "Four of us. Guitar, bass, I sang, chick drummer—"

Oh, I went to myself. That girl, Sailor. She's a drummer.

"We were on a tour from Maine down to Washington, a lot of small clubs. Last gig was in Trenton. Something happened there, I still don't understand it." Slater shrugged. "When we got to the Holland Tunnel, the band was over."

"So what're you going to do now?" I said.

Slater turned to face me; it felt like an effort. "Get a new band together." He gave me his slit smile. "That's what I do." Weight of the world shrug. "You know any players?"

"Not my scene." I shook my head.

"Mademoiselle?"

Emily took far longer to react, but she, too, shook her head. At least she half-shook it.

"Thing is, we got a gig booked at CBGBs in a week."

"We?" I said.

"Oh, yeah, you met her. Sailor. She's my drummer. *She* is still in the band—'cept there ain't no friggin' band."

"And you can't simply go out with a … a chick drummer?" Emily said deadpan.

"I could with a guitarist, but … oh, you're fuckin' with me, ain't you?"

Emily laughed, triumphant. She'd gotten Slater to let his guard down that far, that she could slip one in and get him. She chortled again.

"Glad you're having so much friggin' fun, Em-i-ly." That way Slater had with fancy words, tripping down the syllables, though what was fancy about my friend's name?

"Let me see what I can do," she said, standing again, this time to gather up our dishes. "You know, I might have an idea or two for your band."

"Really?" I went.

"Cole, you truly don't know much about me, do you?"

I was silent, but Emily was right. I've already written that she was most definitely right.

"Well, the gig's in a week," Slater said.

"What's CBGBs?" I said.

Slater's jaw slackened; he looked at me as if I'd just asked who Reggie Jackson was.

"It's a club on Bowery," Emily said. "A real dive, but with some great new groups."

"You've been there?"

"Um, let's just say I know about it." She shrugged. "I keep up."

O.K., so I was the lame-o. The aspiring writer so besotted to be in old Manhattan that he got a thrill from stumbling on Edgar Allen Poe Street or heading downtown and seeing not Wall Street but taking in Herman Melville's 19th-century shoreside wanderings ... and maybe missing what was right in front of me?

"Well, maybe I'll drag you there on our *next* adventure," Slater said. He leaned back in his chair, swallowed off his wine, then burped.

I was thinking cheerily: Well, I can't be too much of a stiff, there'll be a "next adventure." Emily was looking a little curious what the *first* adventure had been, but I wasn't going to say anything and neither did Slater.

"And maybe you'll come, too." Slater, direct to Emily.

A slight pause, then, "Oh, maybe I will," direct back to Slater. A little fizz in Emily's eyes, then her homemaker voice again: "So, boys, dessert?"

She got up, went to the kitchen.

"What is it?" Slater said.

Emily paused, looked back.

"Oh, it's this orange cake my grandmother makes, you have not known anything like it." She drew her tongue over her full lips. "One taste of the frosting, going to make you boys cra-zy! Make your tongues hang out. Make you start panting. Going to make you *dizzy* with lust!"

# 6

THE NEXT DAY it was back to work, for all of us ... well, except Slater, of course.

I bumped into Emily on my way out, and she said I should walk her over to Union Square, where her office was. I could catch the subway there.

I was already a little late to *The New Yorker*, but—well, sure.

After her grandmother's orange cake, unexpectedly intense, even fizzy, out came another bottle of white wine, and we kept talking. We learned that Slater's mother was actually French, a war bride, which accounted for his facility with the language. He was from Ohio, which I'd never been to. Neither had Emily. And where *had* she been for the last two weeks?

Curiously, that question never got answered.

"You hungover?" she asked as we headed west on 11th Street.

"Not really." I shrugged. She shot me a look. "O.K., maybe a little. How about you?"

Emily shook her head, though now that she mentioned it, I recalled she had plowed through at least a full bottle of wine. I looked at her closely. She looked just the tiniest bit askew, hard to pinpoint, though maybe her light mascara was caked just a tad in a corner, her hair not exactly parted perfectly. She was dressed as usual, though, in sensible tan linen pants and a flowered silk blouse. She looked terrific, as always.

Then I remembered her from the night before, that perfect body through the doorway, dancing in just her black bra and those tiny shorts. I felt myself swallow.

"You O.K., Cole?"

"Of course," I said quickly.

"So what do you think of that guy, what was his name?" Emily looked at me closely.

"Slater."

"I kept thinking of a wooden fence, this odd thought. Slats. I kept thinking of *slats*."

I shrugged, didn't know what to make of that.

"I kind of like him," I said carefully. I thought back to our subway wanderings the day before. "He's different."

"Yeah," Emily said after a moment. "At least different to the likes of you and me."

"What do you mean?"

"There's stuff going on out there, Cole," she said. "A *lot* of stuff. If we only chase Marcel Proust's ghost, we don't always get it."

"Sure," I said, though I wasn't quite sure what she meant. A quick thought: That club they were talking about, the jumble of initials, what was it again?

"So I'm glad to get to know him." She nodded.

"Why?" I said, sharp even to my ears.

Emily looked at me oddly.

"Well, since he's in the building and all...."

"*And all?*" The two words jumped out of me, and as they left my mouth, I wished I hadn't uttered them. But I had.

I waited for Emily to respond, but the thing was, she didn't. At least not then.

"Oh, here were are," she said cheerily. FSG was on the western side of Union Square, Number 19 if I remember right, but the subway entrance was well before that.

I was tempted to walk her to her door, then continue on to my offices on West 43rd, but a glance at my pocket watch— yes, the Valley boy fresh in the Big City was into pocket watches—told me I was already late enough. I said goodbye and headed down to the train.

✳ ✳ ✳ ✳ ✳

SO HERE'S MY JOB in the typing pool.

As I said, I was supposed to show up at ten, which in truth meant I could leave my apartment at that time and get there twenty, thirty minutes later—well within tolerance for magazine publishing. (On this day after walking Emily to FSG, I made it in at 10:40; nobody said a thing.)

Here I am at my desk, my IBM Selectric turned on—this is way before personal computers—and humming away. I'm ready, eager for work. And ... well I just sit there.

What did we do in Mrs. Walden's typing pool? Not much. There were five us, all older women but me—I was the second man hired, a profound breakthrough of the, well, the glass floor—and pretty much, day in, day out, on average we each did an hour of actual work.

What was our work? Well, we typed responses to letters to the editor. Around three in the afternoon Mr. Shawn's secretary brought up a stack of letters, responses quick-typed on cheap paper, and we retyped them onto proper *New Yorker* stationery. That took a while, but the letters were divided among five of us, so not that long.

We also helped out some of the writers. One was Ved Mehta, this blind Indian who somehow had bamboozled Mr. Shawn into letting him publish whatever boring family history he came up with. (Years of typing the dreck speaking here.) And how did the blind guy actually write? On staff was a personal assistant to him, a truly thankless task, sitting in Mehta's small office and taking down every pointless word he said.

These were all young women, sweet, smart, wasted on Ved Mehta. (With all sympathy, I called them Vedettes; later—*ouch*—I dubbed them Seeing-Eye Girls.) Sometime late in the afternoon they'd bring up that day's transcriptions, usually big scrawling words that we would type out triple-spaced, which would then be sent back down to Ved's office, where he'd rewrite by having his amanuensis cut up our typing, then paste it on new sheets of papers along with new transcriptions. Such was the intense labor that led to such timeless Mehta classics as *Papaji* and *Mamaji* and *Vedi*—evidently being blind and Indian set him up to fill volume after volume.

Budding wit that I was trying to become, I called this "Give us each day our daily Ved"; and each day, typing up the daily Ved took another half hour or so.

Oh, and whenever Andy Logan's City Hall column was ready to go, we had to retype that. But only her column; nothing for any of the other writers. Why? Ms. Logan set the margins on her Royal typewriter too wide and the pages wouldn't go through the mojo wire to the typesetters in Chicago.

Ask Ms. Logan to reset her margins so her political analysis didn't have to be retyped? That was distinctly *not The New Yorker* way.

No, *The New Yorker* way was to let the illustrious city chronicler Joseph Mitchell show up for work every day around 11, dart into his office just down the hall from Walden's Pond, shut the door tight, then head out around 4:30. What was he doing in there all day? Nobody knew. His final piece in the magazine had run in 1965—twelve years earlier.

Oh, and we typing poolers would fill in at the reception desks at lunch or when people were on vacation. (In 1978, I wrote a poem about sitting at the 20$^{th}$ floor reception desk, and it actually got published in *The New Yorker*—but I get ahead of myself.)

That was about it. Day in, day out, an average of an hour or so of work.

Not a bad gig.

During all the downtime some of us did the *Times* crossword puzzle, others gabbed on the phone, others just disappeared.

I wrote.

I sat at my Selectric and pounded out stories and poems.

(The novel I was working on, the one I dreamed Emily would recommend FSG to buy, I only did at home in the mornings.)

I was kind of a writing fool in those days. (I still recall that later, when a story of mine was being published about a character named David, the editor asked who Peter Strohmeyer was. "Oh," I told her, "he's the main character in my novel; guess I got the names mixed up.")

For now I was that worst of all things: *aspiring*. I aspired twenty-four hours a day, but I only wrote six or seven. And when I finished a short story, well, the first place to submit it to was a no-brainer: the most prestigious magazine going, *The New Yorker*.

Lucky me, I'd simply march it down the hall on the 20th floor and hand it to one of the fiction editors, Dan Menaker.

Here's how *that* went. I'd drop the story off with a smile, then not think about it for the rest of the day. The next morning I'd wake up buzzing with the notion that Dan had read it with unmitigated delight and was eager to show it around to the other editors. (That day at work I'd tiptoe about, not looking any editor in the eye, hoping not to jinx my hopefulness.)

Day Two was all hope. Day Three ... pretty much the same, though the longer I didn't hear anything, the more certain I was that *this* story was going to be bought.

Day Four ... or maybe Five? Well, I was starting to think—against my judgment—about how I'd spend the payment for the story (*The New Yorker* paid more than anybody else for short fiction), not to mention deal with my suddenly looming large in the literary world. Ah, sweet success—

And here's how *that* worked, every damn time. Whichever day it was when I was absolutely certain the current story was going to be taken, Dan would call me down to his office and (very generously) tell me that he was sorry but "this one" wasn't going to work out. He'd tell me why. It was criticism and advice, always genial and considerate, and always followed with a most definite: "But, Cole, they're very good. I'm sure one will work out for us soon."

It was like the old saw, soon as you wash your car, it rains. The moment I envisioned my name in print in *The New Yorker*, my story was rejected.

*Ugh.*

Back then there were lots of other places that published short fiction, and immediately I'd send the story off. I had my own system, and I was proud of it. The time being way before PCs, I used good old index cards. I had a green metal card catalogue on my desk, and for each story or poem I wrote, I made out a new card. I'd write where and when I was mailing the piece off, then pack it into an envelope, carefully addressed to *The Atlantic* or *The Paris Review*. I'd also carefully address another envelope back to me. This was the legendary SASE, self-addressed stamped envelope (joy of writers everywhere before e-mail submission).

Fortunately, there was a post office on the ground floor of 25 West 43rd Street, and down the elevator I'd go, my manuscript inside one manila envelope, the other envelope in hand. Like a gambler playing a narrow range of odds, I'd have the post office guy weigh both envelopes and the manuscript, and then weigh just one envelope with my story—and sometimes I'd hit the jackpot and there'd be a full ounce discrepancy, and I could save myself all of thirteen cents postage.

A small but genuine triumph! With more triumphs to come. After plugging away for what felt like forever, sometimes instead of my own hand-scrawled SASE plopping back on my desk with the afternoon mail, I'd get a slender envelope or even a phone call—the story or poem had been accepted for publication!

But not then. Not in the months of this tale. That initial year in New York all I did was write, and submit, and get the fist-in-the-gut *ooof!* of being rejected. That was the word always used, *I got a rejection slip*, *my story was rejected*, and seeing those SASEs on my desk after lunch was as grim and ambition-crushing as the word *rejected* sounds. How to keep going? I found that if I had a lot of stuff out there, any one rejection wouldn't hurt that much. (I once came back from a weeklong vacation to find four stories waiting on my desk. That wasn't one punch to the gut, it was butterflies floating, then bees stinging; and, yeah, I can still feel *that*.)

This is where another old saw came in: The horse bucks you off, you immediately get back on. That's what I'd do, take the rejection—the punches to body and spirit—then immediately stick the story back in a new envelope, make a note on the right index card, and march down to the post office to send it out all over again.

That first year at *The New Yorker* I sure had a lot of success and joy in my life. Oh, yeah. I wrote *all* the time and *every last thing* got sent back. (O.K., often with "encouragement.") I'd become totally obsessed with a girl who was ... just a good friend. Now Emily lived in my building. My great fear was that I'd be on my way to work and bump into some guy leaving her place; to my amazement *that* never happened. Also, for someone with a regular job, Emily seemed to disappear a lot—a week here, two weeks there. Still, we stayed lunch buddies, book chat pals, and now good neighbors. We even instituted a regular Sunday evening barbecue up on our roof.

Of course it wasn't just the two of us. When we first got the idea, Emily made sure that Slater was invited. Burgers and chips and lots of beer—the whole deal usually Slater's treat. Turned out he was generous that way; if he had any money, he'd pay for everything.

Then, our third Sunday barbecue, Slater told us he was inviting the drummer in his group, Sailor, the girl with the sleekly bobbed red hair. That night everything changed.

# 7

Y ES, THAT THIRD BARBECUE, a cooler summer evening, light wind lifting off the East River, Emily's special minted iced tea going down easy. Slater's surprise: a raft of smoked sausages he'd gotten from someplace (via his magic raincoat?), all lined up ready to go onto the coals of his grill. Sailor wasn't there yet but expected any minute; and so we were asking Slater what was up with his band.

"Don't ask," he said, blowing on the coals. He'd just fired them up with his thick metal WWII Zippo; the air was acrid with fumes from the lighter fluid.

"Oh, come on," Emily said in that gruff, take-no-prisoners way she had with Slater.

"Well, if you have to know, we're having a hard time finding players."

"But you had that gig at ... what's the name of that club you were booked at?" I said. Once it was set we'd be having regular grillings up here, Slater scrounged up a few half-broken beach chairs and fixed the webbing himself. I was deep into one of them, sinking into its lime-green and yellow ribs.

"CBGBs. On the Bow-e-ry, *New Yorker* magazine boy." Slater shrugged. "Played it with just me and Sailor and her drums."

"You said that couldn't work, right?"

"Hey, you make do," he said across the grill. The gray smoke was dying down and that thrilling crimson glow was streaking the black coals. Slater held a tall can of Schaefer beer, from one of three twelve-packs he'd brought. He also held a lit hand-rolled from his rusty Sucrets pack.

"Really, just you and the girl?" Emily was poking the ashes to get them hotter.

"No so bad, not so bad. Down there, everybody ... I mean, that's the scene, you make it up as you go along. None of that ... that bom-bas-tic shit." Slater smiled at his big word; he seemed to like that about hanging with Emily and me, that he could drop in words he'd picked up somewhere that nobody else he knew would get. "You play, and you play your friggin' heart out." He pumped his arm muscles. "It's all kickin' in the blood, man."

"Not even a guitar?" I was trying to see that, just somebody pounding away on drum heads and a skinny guy wailing. I didn't really know Slater's music—he'd made it clear that Bony Maronie had died with the ill-fated van tour, and there was no new name—but I imagined it loud and cacophonous, with, if nothing else, lots of guitar feedback.

"Brother," Slater went, annoyed, "as I said, Sailor and me, we did it ourselves, best we could. What the fuck else can you do?"

That was still startling to me, how casually Slater cursed. It wasn't like later, when *fuck* and *shit* were published in *The New Yorker* and dropped all the time into everyday conversation; there was still a thought back then that you didn't talk like that "in front of the ladies." I glanced over at Emily, but of course she was nodding cheerily in agreement.

"I think it's gutsy," she said. "You gotta love it: *The show must go on.*"

Slater lifted his beer high, drained it, then popped another one.

The way you got onto the roof, you went out an apartment window and up the fire escape. There were fire escapes front and back of the building, though the one in front of my apartment seemed awfully rickety. (I kept thinking that if I had a fire, maybe the iron contraption would slowly, gracefully, bend me to the ground.) To get to the roof, I always used the one in the back, as did everyone else. But we'd moved off from that, camped at the right front, facing toward the river, so when our first guest arrived, he took us by surprise.

"Hello," we heard, a high male voice. "What're you guys doing?"

I spun around. It was Walter Wendell, or whatever his name was. He was dressed the way he always was, today in too short mustard-colored pants and a long-sleeved pink crew neck shirt that was too large, both likely from the Salvation Army on Fourth Avenue. He also had on this crazily long black leather belt. It was tucked through a silver buckle shaped like a cross (I noticed later a small, embossed Jesus stretched across it), yet the belt was so long the metal tab at the end hung down at least another foot, almost banging his knee. A fashion statement? I doubted Walter or Wendell *did* fashion statements. He was just there, in all his slopped-out glory, sporting the hangdog grin he always carried, his hand-cut sandy hair lifting in the light breeze.

"Oh, hey, Wendell," Emily said, "we're gonna be grilling up some sausages. You want to join us?"

Wendell Walter ... yes, that was his name. I'd had it totally backward. If Emily knew it correctly ... well, from then on I made sure to get it right. Wendell followed by Walter. Wen-dell Walter. *Wen-delllll* Wallllll-ter....

Wendell looked surprised and said quickly, "Does Mr. Strump know you're up here?" His voice went even higher pitched as he said this.

"Does he?" Slater said. He flicked off cigarette ash. To my surprise, our landlord and Slater had hit it off. There was something shared in their past, as if they'd both been Marines or something.

"I don't think he'd be very happy," Wendell said. He saw me, nodded. "Hey, professor."

That's what Wendell always called me, professor, because I was a writer—or wanted to be—I guess.

"Hey," I said back.

"So, Wendell," Emily said from her own chair, with pink

and chartreuse webbing. "We really do have a lotta meat here. You in?"

"It's a fire, on the roof. Isn't that dangerous?"

"Brother, we've taken *all* precautions." Slater got up and put his arm around Wendell's shoulders. "How 'bout a brewski?"

We only had the three chairs, but there was a discarded white-slatted iron bench on the other side of the roof, and after Wendell took the can of Schaefer, Slater lifted up the bench and brought it over. It was a heavy sucker, and though the veins in Slater's neck went taught beneath his bowl of blond hair, I was impressed he could carry it himself, especially so easily. A glance at Emily: Her round eyes said she was, too.

So Wendell joined the party. He didn't look that comfortable, fingers twitching, playing with that long belt hanging down; though that was the thing with Wendell, he never looked comfortable. You could just read his mind: *Do I really belong here? Probably not. Then what am I doing here? Should I leave? Oh, my.*

Still, it seemed right that our odd housemate was with us, and I kept throwing Wendell genial smiles to try to make him feel welcome.

Even though Sailor hadn't shown, Slater decided it was time to throw on the sausages. They sat cold and pink for a minute, then started hissing on the hot metal. The air went tangy from grill smoke. Emily took over the cooking, rolling the sausages to keep the browning even, poking them with the long fork to let out steam. Lovely glistening fat burst out and dribbled down their crisping sides.

This was the first time Wendell had been part of our nascent little family up on the roof, and he didn't say much, just sipped his beer and watched Emily turn the sausages. Suddenly famished, that's pretty much all I did, too. Those boys were getting nice and brown. Dark blisters on their skin popped.

Since Slater's apartment, rear, top floor, was the closest to the fire escape, Emily had left a pot of beans and boiling corn on his stove. One more poke with the fork and she told Slater it was time to bring them up.

"You want the watermelon now, too?" he said.

"Why not?" She handed me the long fork. "Cole, give 'em just a minute or so more, then pull 'em off." A nod at Slater. "Come on, help me get everything up here."

Slater stood, smiled. Then they were gone.

I did as Emily asked, sticking the fork into each sausage when I was sure they were ready, watching the clear juice ooze through the cracks in the skin. I set them carefully on the platter. That's where they sat. We gave Slater and Emily six, seven minutes, but they weren't back.

"Whadda ya think, Professor, should we eat them?" Wendell's eyes had gone wide. "Used to have sausages like this all the time back home, you know, with grits and gravy?" A quick, satisfied nod. "They look dang good."

I glanced over at the fire escape, trying to will their appearance. Nothing.

What could it be? The corn not quite ready? A problem in Slater's kitchen finding a bowl big enough for the beans? Trouble negotiating the fire escape with all that food?

I was thinking all kinds of things, and getting a little worried, but with the tingly gut feeling it wouldn't be a good idea to go see what was holding them up. Instead I asked Wendell how things were at the church.

"Oh, blessed, Cole, truly blessed." He brightened.

"What does that mean?" I guess I was mostly making small talk until Slater and Emily reappeared.

"What do *you* mean?" He looked distinctly perplexed.

I was never religious, had a thing about churchgoing even though I was raised a Congregationalist; and I could tell from the way Wendell came back at me that if I kept talking to him this way, we'd fall into some odd rabbit hole of doctrinal misapprehension. That was not what I wanted, certainly not then. I just did not want to think about what could be happening in Slater's kitchen.

So Wendell and I sat there, silent each in our own way, staring at those perfectly crisped sausages and smelling the heady, lusty scent of greasy grilled meat.

Until finally I heard, "You'll never guess who we found?"

Emily's voice, then her head popped over the edge of the roof. She held a pale blue bowl full of golden corn.

"What happened?" I asked.

"Oh, um, we had a little, um—" Emily was heading toward us now, then turned and gestured to the fire escape. "But look who turned up!"

And over the rooftop's edge Sailor's dark-flame bob appeared.

\* \* \* \* \*

SAILOR WAS IN a jolly mood, giving me a quick smile and a friendly wink, and shaking Wendell's hand before taking a seat next to him on the iron bench.

"This smells great!" she said. "I can't believe I lucked out. You do this often?"

Nobody said anything till I spoke up. "We're shooting for every Sunday."

"Well, it's a beautiful night," Sailor said, taking a Schaefer. "And a beautiful thing."

We'd finished eating and were just talking when Slater looked at Wendell and said, "Hey, you play guitar, don't you?"

Wendell looked surprised to be addressed head-on. He'd been quiet so far as our chat about books and movies and bands ricocheted around the roof.

"I've seen you, you're up in front there in your little church, playing away." Slater leaned forward. "Nice looking Gibson SG, if I know my axes."

"I … um, I accompany the hymns," Wendell said. His face, usually pale, had gone a faint red.

"But you do it well. I've heard you, you got a nice rhythm thing going." Slater stuck out his hands and mimed playing the guitar, going, "Chunk-a-chunk, chunk-a-chunk, chunk-a-chunk," with his mouth.

"I do what the Lord asks of me," Wendell said. He slipped out a thin smile; closer to home turf, I figured.

"And what if the Lord asks you to rock-and-roll, son!" Slater leaped up and windmilled his right arm like Pete Townshend.

"Slater?" Sailor went. I'd been surprised how easily she fit into our evening party. The presence of both her and Slater had kept Emily and me from talking too much book biz shop, but our being there probably kept them from talking too much rock and roll shop, too. But something else was going on now.

"Think you could play something ... something less ec-cle-si-as-ti-cal?" Slater asked Wendell, ignoring his friend.

Sailor kept staring at him. I did, too, always surprised he'd pulled another big word out of his butt.

"I ... I don't know," Wendell said. His face was growing redder.

"Listen, where're you from?" Slater said. "Some place like Milwaukee? Detroit?"

"Kentucky," Wendell got out.

"Kentucky?" Slater thought a second, then said, "You got Bill Monroe from there. That dude's a motherfucker!"

Wendell was fully blushing now.

"Slater, what're you up to?" Sailor said.

I took a look at Emily. She was smiling deep to herself, enjoying this, whatever it was.

"We need players, babe." Slater shot her a look. "Need fresh ones, somebody without an a-gen-da." A turn back to Wendell. "You got an agenda, Wendell?"

He shook his head, then mumbled, "Just the Lord's."

"See, he'll be perfect!" Slater crowed, his smile as curved

as his bowl of hair. "I've heard him, he really can play, you know."

"And *I* don't have a say in this?" Sailor was looking at him furiously from under her copper-red hair, her fine '30s plucked eyebrows.

"Wendell, friend, here's how it's gonna go down. This is Sunday—I know, it's the Lord's day—so, say, you free for an audition tomorrow?"

Wendell didn't move. He looked paralyzed in the face of Slater's offer.

Slater took his blankness as a yes, of course.

"Perfect. We'll try you out with just the two of us, some of our original stuff, see how you do—though I know you're gonna be awesome." Slater beamed. "Then we'll just need a bass player, and, shit, any asshole can play the fuckin' bass!"

And Slater hooked an eye at me.

"What?"

"Cole, hey, *you* ever play bass?"

I shook my head. I did play guitar some, inspired by the Beatles twelve years back, but it was pretty rudimentary. All I had was the Yamaha acoustic my parents got me in 1965.

"You sure?" Slater leaned in.

"No, no, really I—" Join a band? While I was trying to become Scott Fitzgerald? That was nuts.

Slater turned to Emily.

"O.K., how about you, babe?"

"You know, I played ocarina in my sixth-grade play." Emily threw out a big smile. "I also used to be great on spoons." A quick laugh. "And, well—" a modest glance down "—I sang with the glee club at college."

I hadn't known that, wait, Emily was in the Yale Glee Club? I filed that away, one more mysterious piece of the puzzle.

Slater was holding Emily's gaze for a long while, a long, unreadable look. I thought again of all those seconds tick-ing away when they'd disappeared to get the rest of dinner.

A glance at Sailor, but before she could respond, Slater said, "Hey, might be a place for spoons and ocarina." A laugh. "Or maybe some singin'. You willin'?"

"I'm up for anything."

"That's the spirit, darlin', that's the spirit." Slater lifted his head as if a thought had just winged in on the evening breeze. "Actually, you're just what we need. Good to have a looker up front, right? You know, a whole Velvets-Nico thing."

He was saying this to Sailor, who kept glaring at him.

"Hey, O.K., babe, I love it, it's all coming together." Slater rubbed his hands. "We'll get us a bass player somewhere else, or just fuckin' not have one like the Doors.

"But babe—" he turned to Sailor, who kept looking like she was going to speak out but hadn't yet "—ain't you feelin' this? This night, the sky, the building tops.... I don't know, it's like we're bein' born again. Gonna get Bony Maronie— no, fuck, enough with that shit-ass name. We need a new fuckin' name!"

Slater swung on me again.

"Mr. Pro-fes-sor, you got a name for us?" Give Slater credit, he'd like that picked up on Wendell's moniker for me. All I did was shake my head.

"Nothing you've been carrying around inside you, man?" He flicked quote marks: " 'Wouldn't it be cool to have a band named—' What, Cole, whatta ya got?"

I didn't know what to say. I was feeling the Slater whirlwind, of course I was—that whisk you up, drag you along thing like when he took me riding the subways—but nonetheless I didn't have an idea right then.

"Ah, but you will," Slater said, as if reading my mind. "I got this feeling—this pre-mo-ni-tion." He swung on Wendell. "You get those, brother? Those feelings like the ... the Holy Spirit is with you? Like it's just fallin' down on you and gonna lift you up to ... to something glorious?"

It took a second, then Wendell smiled. Invoking God must have done it. I felt it, a click ... and Wendell was in. Who needed the audition?

The crazy thing was, we were all in. Even Sailor couldn't resist. Her and Slater's new band was born that night—its name actually would come from me, but not for a few more weeks—and even Emily had a part. Oh, Emily had a big part.

That's how you did it in 1977, you whipped up a band out of people sitting around a sputtering grill on a rooftop on a Sunday night. Manifest talent? Years of practice? Actual musicianship?

Hey, those days in the East Village, all that never even came up.

# 8

Turned out Slater actually did have talent, ability, and musicianship. More, he had strong musical ideas, even vision. That came clear once the new band got going, and—to my surprise, and with deep complications—I became a fan.

It was amazing how quick the whole thing came together. Turned out with a little guidance Wendell Walter was a whiz at rock guitar, slamming the right barre chords when needed. And his cheap too-short pants and sweated-through Salvation Army shirts fit Slater's group aesthetic perfectly. Put the Lord's dummkopf on ax? Wendell was in with flares.

Good thing, too, since Slater and Wendell went to work on Mr. Strump, and the Church of Jesus Christo was there for rehearsals anytime they wanted. I'd hear them banging and thrashing away on my way home from work.

Emily was a tougher fit. Her voice was truly lovely—I stopped in one evening, and the way she climbed the scale was thrilling—but it was also way too pretty. She was used to singing Bach cantatas. But Emily was, if nothing else, determined, and she seemed to be spending all day there in the church, FSG be damned. (What *was* her arrangement at the publishing house?) It was fascinating how quickly her singing stopped being a problem. The next time I heard them she was wailing, a little Janis Joplin, a little Grace Slick, but also floating lovely colors all around Slater's taut-vocal-cord screech. Still, Emily kept looking the way she always did: well-raised, proper sheath dresses and Peter Pan–collared salmon blouses. Maybe the Bowery club look would take a little longer....

The only thing missing was bass, and with a little of Slater's mojo up turned a big, taciturn guy from Queens named Chet who was actually pretty good.

A week later, another gig at CBGBs was booked. This was for Tuesday night, and we were all going to go.

* * * * *

IT WAS ARRANGED for me to take Emily to the gig. I knocked on her door at ten, and after standing there for minutes and minutes, it swung open. Back flew my head. This was Emily as I'd never seen her.

First off, she was wearing the tiniest white miniskirt I'd ever seen, her long legs encased in white-patterned stockings (my first thought: exactly the stockings a young girl wore to church). She also had on the same heavy black boots Slater wore. (Turned out the miniskirt came from Slater; no telling where or how he picked it up.) On Emily it was tight, revealing, overwhelming.

"It's something, isn't it?" Emily said with a giggle as I stood there. "Wasn't sure I could fit into it."

"Um, looks like you, um, do."

"Thanks, Cole." She gave me a slitted smile. "You look good, too."

I nodded but knew she was just saying this. I was wearing what I always wore in summer ... well, not always. I wasn't as bad as I could have been. I'd left my chinos home, had on a well-worn pair of Levis and a Madras-patterned cotton shirt loose over a black T-shirt.

"It's truly stunning," I said, an excess of spirit. This might sound odd, but I think this was the first time I'd ever complimented Emily's appearance like this—I mean, big, obvious, not just trying to appear polite.

"I'll take that." And she giggled again.

We headed west on 11$^{th}$, then turned south on Third Avenue toward the Bowery. The thing was, when I went somewhere, it was most often uptown to work or across town to the Village. Emily and I did like walking around the nearly empty, desolate Bowery and what's now known as Soho, but we almost never went down there at night, so I was surprised by the horde of people outside the club at 315 Bowery. I'd been living in the East Village, of course, so the sight of people heavy in leather, studs, and dyed pink hair wasn't new to me. I just wasn't used to such a concentration. Something new was going on outside this CBGBs club, that's for sure. Even on a Tuesday night.

Slater's makeshift group still didn't have a name, and I just saw SLATER 10:30 written in chalk on a board with half a dozen other bands. Each one had forty-five minutes, which I learned included load-in and load-out; in truth, about twenty-five minutes onstage.

I was to learn damn quick that if you played fast enough, hard enough, that was sure to be enough.

There was a buck-and-a-half door charge, but no particular line. I learned later that on Tuesdays and Wednesdays pretty much anyone could play at CBGBs. Slater's old band, Bony Maronie, had held coveted Friday and Saturday night spots, but of course Bony Maronie was kaput, and Slater was starting over, without even a name.

After Emily and I got in, I bought us a couple cheap beers from the long wooden bar on the right. In front of the bar there were tables, only half filled, and then at the end of the bar a slight decline down to where the stage and pit were. Playing as we walked in were a group of guys with long, stringy black hair, sallow skin, and all leather suits stained with sweat. There might've been air-conditioning, though it was July and there was sure no evidence of it.

I was already sweating, too, as we went down to check out the band. Up close, they were so loud I stuck my fingers in my ears, which got an immediate contemptuous look from Emily.

"Cole, behave!" she cried over the thrashing guitars and drums.

I laughed, a little giddy, a little on the defensive. That was the thing: How *did* one behave at CBGBs? This was not a book launch party at the Gotham Book Mart. Nobody in tweed coats here. This was loud, compressed, and full of kids in the strangest garb. How did anyone behave, especially a girl like Emily?

She sure didn't seem to have any problem. The band—I think the name was Tunnel—wasn't very good, just a lot of incoherent noise and pounding and shrieking from the lead singer, who now that I was closer I could see had long hair on half his head, a buzz cut on the other. How odd! It was like looking at two different people depending on my angle; that, or a before-and-after in some old-time psych experiment.

You couldn't make out a word, just the singer's wailing at pretty much the same pitches as the insistent, two-note guitar riff; and yet it didn't matter at all to Emily. There she was next to me, bouncing up and down, throwing her arms out, half clogging about in her black boots, half simply leaping into the air.

I don't know what kind of dance it was, from my teenage days I was used to steps with names like Watusi and Swim; and what Emily was doing really wasn't much like dancing anyway, just amped-up jumping up and down, as if she were on a pogo stick; and yet she fit right in! Everyone else was doing it, too. Bouncing and waving and twisting and gyrating.

Emily still held her beer bottle, and every time she threw her hand out she sprayed me with it.

I caught a full blast of hops in my eyes, and when I'd wiped it away with my sleeve, I shot her a look, which she caught.

Over the din she shouted, "Cole, I meant it, fuckin' behave!"

Then Tunnel slammed their last chord, which ran and ran with feedback through the long room.

Now I'd never seen Emily sweating before (hadn't heard her curse much, either). She was one of those cool blonde chicks whose skin only glistened from natural radiance; but she was sweating now, all over, pouring down her forehead, hair matting, arms shiny ... and then as Tunnel's noise finally faded, she threw herself into my arms.

"Boy, that was great!" she cried into my ear. Even without the band playing, the club still seemed loud, and I almost didn't hear her. "That was fuckin' amazing!"

"You liked them?"

"Fuck yeah!" She shouted into my ear from inches away, and I can still remember how that felt. I'd imagined her body entwined in mine for so long, the hot nights in my apartment and Emily only two floors below; and how smooth and silky she'd be, those long legs stretched out beside me, entwined around mine ... and yet I'd never been closer to her than a light, Continental hug.

At CBGBs for that moment Emily Prosser was all over me. Her arms slippery against mine. Her damp hair brushing my cheeks. Her full body, electric, abandoned, so tight....

I breathed it all in, held her close.

Then she was gone. A step away, only a couple feet, but it was an ocean. I put my fingers, dripping with both our sweat, to my forehead and let the wetness slither down my face.

Slater tapped me on the shoulder.

"We're next, brother," he said. He was almost smiling but not quite. Mostly, he just looked intense, wired. I didn't know it then, but Slater took all this truly seriously; life and death for him, as I came to know all too well. His blood aflame, as he often put it. He turned to Emily. "You ready, babe?"

"You better believe it!" And my friend threw her most radiant smile Slater's way.

Yet Emily didn't join the band on the stage. I wasn't sure what was going on, but she stood right next to me, glistening, as Sailor went up to the house drums and settled in. On Tuesdays bands used house drums, and Sailor, her copper hair brushed tight and wrapped in a flowered scarf, went up behind them. She was wearing a miniskirt, too, longer than Emily's (she did have to play drums). Hers was carnation pink. Over it, she wore a loose black camisole, and she also had on a pair of black filigreed cowboy boots, halfway to her knees. With her fiery hair and high cheekbones Sailor was also totally striking.

Wendell Walter joined them on the stage, looking exactly as he did every day I saw him at our building, the same too short pants, a green-and-tan-checked thrift shop sport coat, this one too long in the sleeves, and that slappy-flappy black-leather belt hanging like something unnoticed and embarrassing down his leg.

This time he held his Gibson guitar. The strap was as short as his belt long, and the instrument sat high up on his chest. It reminded me of Gerry and the Pacemakers a decade or so back on *Ed Sullivan*. The new bass player, Chet, stood next to Sailor in the back, and Slater took stage front.

"We don't got a name yet," he shouted into the mike, "but that don't mean we ain't gonna rock your fuckin' socks off!"

Down went Sailor's sticks. She was pretty much only hitting the bass and toms, a little snare, no cymbals—a rumbly, train-a-rollin' sound that chugged along incessantly, doubling in force as Chet joined in. His bass boomed a powerful, insistent riff, only three notes, but evidently they were the right ones ... a holler went up from the crowd, and everyone started that pogo dance again. The sound pounded through the long, narrow club. It was loud, tribal, not foot-tapping but gut-punching.

Then Walter slashed down a battery of barre chords and Slater jumped at the mike, baring his teeth.

That was it, as slight and ashy as he was, on that stage that night Slater was an animal. He wriggled and shimmied and bit at the air; threw his head back and let long, guttural cries emerge: shrieks, garrumphs, yowls, hisses, yelps. His face contorted, lips pulled back, teeth gleaming under beaming colored lights.

Wild, rampant, and more than a little scary....

I have to admit I didn't get it all then. There'd been garage bands when I was growing up in L.A., like the Music Machine and the Seeds, and I loved hearing that stuff on KFWB when friends and I were driving the freeways. But with that music, also pure energy, I'd heard lyrics and some structure; it made sense to me. Of course I was fifteen, sixteen. Maybe that was the difference. To my ten-years-older ears, what I was hearing now did not make much sense. At least not right then. It was clamorous and rowdy, but I couldn't hear notes or even a rhythm that caught me; I just heard speed and brutality, rawness and hysteria.

Still, the music was superfast, and it was ferocious; and the crowd kept with it. They'd been bouncing like crazy for Tunnel, but that was nothing to their reaction to Slater's new group.

Sailor's pounding stayed steady but grew louder, and everyone around me jumped up on their heels, then their toes. Some leaped as if they too were chewing the air.

Slater shrieked. Over and over. Not really singing as I thought of it, but the longer the band played, the more I heard him as powerful and compelling, a tiger's low-beam growl. Here I am, look at me. LOOK THE FUCK AT ME!

Next to me Emily was bouncing along with everyone else, at least as wild, carefree. She threw her hands into the air. She cried out herself at the band's crescendos.

Why wasn't she up there? I leaned toward her to ask but the band was too loud and she was moving too frenetically.

Then I got my answer.

Sailor kept the drums going but everyone else stopped playing. Slater ran a hand through his bowl of hair, then moved up Sinatra cool to the mike. "I'm glad all you souls are digging us, that's righteous." A wink, a nod. "We got one more song we're gonna do, and we're gonna need a friend of ours to help." A finger up, pointing right at me. I blinked, startled. Then Slater said, "Emily, you ready, dear?"

And there she was up on the stage.

Emily went to Slater, who flourished a huge tambourine, as if he were a magician—I had no idea where it came from—and handed it to her; she took a place a few feet to his right, almost in front of Wendell, her usually perfectly coiffed blonde hair now sweeping before her face, her miniskirt hugging her hips ... hips already picking up Sailor's chugga-chugga beat.

A slightly different beat, in it a touch of Reggae, still a new style of music to a lot of us, and Emily did a fine job of hitting the tambourine on the right offbeat and carrying the song along. It was more tuneful than the rest of Slater's music, and his voice was almost a croon—lighter, airier, but still with that deep guttural crackle that made it not so easy to take. I could almost make out the lyrics—everything he'd sung so far came at me as just a slurred blur—something about *no woman, no cry*; and, wait, there Emily was, leaning into Slater's mike on the chorus and singing along.

That great voice I'd heard at rehearsals. Floating like spun glass around Slater. Making the tune heart-clutching, lovely. Up there in her tight white miniskirt, slapping the tambourine against her thigh—she'd have a yellow bruise for days, she later told me—and singing perfectly.

You can't say Emily was harmonizing with Slater, because the way he put words into the microphone, well, I couldn't call it singing; but Emily did sing—over him, and under him, and, finally, right along with him.

Voices blending, filling the room. It was ... almost sweet.

Then they were done.

I applauded, of course, and everyone around me did, too. There were even loud huzzahs and cheers. Slater pushed his bowl of dirty blond hair out of his eyes, gleamed at all of us, then took Emily's hand and raised it over their heads. It was a curiously show-biz gesture for this band, and I think Slater did it involuntarily; a moment later, he glowered at the audience, a fierce, back-alley challenge sparking his eyes, tightening his jaw; and with Emily in hand, they left the stage.

Immediately a lot of chattering, people elbowing me as they headed to the bar, the next group pushing right through the crowd as they dragged their guitars and amps to the stage—oof, a guitar case hit my back. Asshole! I lost track of things for a moment, and when I got my eyes back, I couldn't find Slater and Emily.

"Hey, Professor!" Wendell was by my side, beaming. "Whattaya think?"

"Not bad," I told him, in cool mode now. "Better than I would've—"

"Oh, it was soooo amazing," he said. His eyes shone bright. "I never thought I would—"

"I just loved that, Wendell!" I heard, and turned to see a short, thin kid with a shock of dark hair, wearing a very tight red-striped French sailor shirt and blue-black bell bottoms. "I'm Aubrey," he said to me, but he was really all eyes on Wendell, who at the intrusion had pulled his elbows tight by his side. "You really rocked that long guitar in your hands, you know."

"Oh," Wendell said. He was standing very stiffly. The smile on his face was gone.

"Yes, you guys were the best!"

With a sharp blush, and without a word, Wendell walked away.

The kid, Aubrey, shot a look at me, his mouth dipping into a moue, his thin eyebrows arching up.

"Well, you never, ever know, do you, sweetie?" he said, more to the air than to me, then walked quickly away.

I kept looking around for either Slater or Emily. I didn't see any special exits to the club, though there was a dark area in the rear left with what looked like some small rooms. I was pretty sure neither Slater nor Emily had gotten past me, but I just couldn't find them. CBGBs wasn't that big, though it was more and more packed. It was also getting rank: the sweat, the unbounded energy, not to mention an acrid piss smell floating out of the toilets in the back that filled the whole room....

Up on the stage the next band had set up. I saw three guys, all with lanky dyed-black hair, and then a tall, astonishing woman took the mike.

I'd been surprised by Emily's and Sailor's miniskirts, that glam-sexy look I hadn't seen with them before, but the woman standing onstage now was a whole other order of crazy style. For one, she wore the skimpiest dress I'd ever seen, not just a miniskirt but one with the hem truly only a few inches below her waist, and higher up, most of her breasts lifting out of the top. The dress was flimsy, made of a light black lacy material that swayed even if she wasn't moving. She had on black fishnet stockings, ripped along her inner thighs and cut off at her ankles. Oh, and she was barefoot, white toes painted fire-engine red picking up the light.

But it was what was above her shoulders that hit me hardest. This woman had black hair, like her bandmates, and it was curled and curved to the hilt, waves of shimmery cobalt around pale skin. She was Marilyn Monroe pretty, yet dark, very dark. But what was hardly '50s movie star–like was her face. White, sallow like Slater's, yet with fierce makeup: eyes surrounded with what I guess was a mass of liner and heavy shadow, flaring out like cat's whiskers; lips pouty in blood-red; and the longest, blackest false lashes I'd ever seen.

She was compelling, this kewpie-doll-cute devil chick, and the longer she stood there, one foot up on the stage monitor, a long black-sheathed leg extended, those teasing flashes of bare skin through the ripped stockings, the band silent behind her ... well, I kept looking and looking.

A looping shriek, and they were off.

At first it didn't sound that different from what I'd heard with Slater, loud, fast, a lot of drums and bass, no clear melody, crazy intense ... but with this woman, even more than with Slater, you couldn't take your eyes off her. She stomped and prowled the stage, growling into the mike, the boys behind her beating and pounding away, laying down thick, fizzy ground fire she strafed with yelping, chirruping words ... yet every now and then this wild-child chick singer's voice hit an arc of clear, pure notes that actually floated lightly above the din ... a lovely voice like Emily's but with more force.

It was those silver-bell notes that made me stand there and gape. Yes, like Emily, but more certain and all her own. The singer looked a little like Emily, too, a similarly shaped round face, just more extreme in her glamor-girl hair and cat's-eye makeup. Yet looking at her made me think of Emily—where *was* my friend?—and that breathless moment when she'd thrown her hot and excited body against mine; and that was exactly what was on my mind when I felt a tap on my shoulder.

"You want to fuck her, don't you?" This was Sailor, all big eyes, standing right in front of me.

"Huh? What?" The words came out quickly. "What are you—"

"Damn obvious, Cole." She was smiling, lips cut saucily. "*Damn* obvious."

"Um—" I got out. I blushed. "Um, um—" Hearing such a question from Sailor—from any woman back then—was startlingly abrupt. Could she actually be reading my mind so well? My eyes darted about. I blushed hotter, had no idea what to say.

Then Sailor did a huge double take, silent movie style, actually throwing back her blistering hair.

"Oh, you think I mean—" She let out a large laugh. "Oh, Cole, Cole, Cole. No, I'm talking about *Cherry*—on the stage, Cherry Kruntz. With her band the Klitz."

"Oh, yeah, she's—I mean, just look at her, I mean, what guy.... Wait, who do you think I was—" I said this quickly, and just as quickly regretted it.

Sailor, kind woman, simply gave me a sweet smile, then threw her gaze back to the stage.

"*Everybody* wants to fuck Cherry, that's her shtick. And not just guys." Sailor shrugged, then laughed. "She scares the shit out of you, but you *still* want to fuck her."

"Um, I—"

"You know, Cherry does porn to make a living." Sailor leaned in, touching my shoulder, whispering loudly over the music.

"Really?" I felt her fingers light on my shirt.

"*Absolument!*" She lit right up again. "Mostly mags: *Stag*, *Raunch*, that kind of thing. You want *more* of her, Cole, you can head over to St. Marks, one of the news shops."

"I think the live, um, Cherry's enough."

At that moment Cherry Kruntz was down on her knees, torn stockings ripping farther, burying the mike in her capacious mouth.

"'Fuck me! Fuck me! Fuck me!'" Sailor let out, pursing her lips. "Hey, we'll see how well it sells."

"For the record," I got out, more together, "I'm not admitting anything one way or the other." I showed her light eyes, that I was getting the joke, that whatever else she thought I was thinking wasn't true. "But, you know—"

"You're just another red-blooded American boy."

She said this coolly, but it still surprised me. Her words and tone were either flippantly dismissive or ... flirtatious. I honestly couldn't tell.

The band kept going, Cherry again on her knees, her patterned stockings spread, her short dress rising past her intriguing thighs, bleating and blaring ... I didn't hear more of those clear notes, and in truth maybe she wasn't much of a singer. Maybe I'd been tricked. Not that it mattered.

After the song ended, I echoed Sailor's words back to her: "Be interesting to see how well it works."

She gave me a long, mysterious look, then said, "Just so you know, I'm sticking with my drums, Cole."

I nodded quickly, believing her, whatever she meant.

She immediately frowned at me, a deep pout.

"What?" I got out.

A long pause, then Sailor said, "Listen, CBs has house drums, you know." She lifted her shoulders. "So I'm done. Don't know where the fairy-dust couple are—" She looked with exaggeration around the crowded club. No sign of Slater and Emily, or Wendell Walter or the bass guy, for that matter. "But *I'm* starving. Want to go get a slice with me?"

I looked at Sailor, her tight bobbed auburn-bronze hair, fine features, her powerful energy, and ... I hesitated. There I was with this intriguing woman—a rock drummer, no less—standing in the middle of CBGBs, another punky band wheeling black amps onto the stage, even me now hot and sweaty and pulsing with a rare excitement I didn't know what to do with ... and I hesitated. I felt I should wait for Emily. I'd come with her, right? Just take off now with Sailor? The idea of oven-hot pizza was awfully tempting, and the way this sleek-haired woman beside me seemed to get me—or at least play me—was intriguing, too.

But still I hesitated. Long enough for Sailor to read it in my eyes.

"See ya, Cole," she said abruptly. She gave me a dismissive tap on the shoulder, then turned and left the club.

I waited another half an hour, feeling more and more like an idiot. I did see Wendell again. He looked recovered from that kid who'd come up to him.

"Hey, professor, whattaya think?" He gestured to the stage, and I guessed he meant his playing with Slater.

"You guys were great," I said, though at that moment I felt so lonely and stupid I don't know how it came out.

"Yeah, I know," he said softly. I barely heard him over the band, but I did. "That's the freakin' problem."

He grabbed my upper arm and pinched, hard. I flinched. I don't think Wendell had ever touched me before, and there was something unsettling about it, his guitar-strong fingers, yet slippery, unearthly. Then he took off.

Five minutes later, I did too. Without Emily or even Slater.

It was well after midnight. I went by the pizza joint at Second and St. Marks, but Sailor wasn't there. Though the air was fired with tomato sauce and bubbling mozzarella, and I was kind of starving, I didn't stop for a slice. Just kept going. Back to 340 East 11th Street, alone.

# 9

I BLEW INTO *The New Yorker* the next day a lot later than usual, fortunately nobody seemed to mind; and though I thought about spilling it, I didn't tell anyone about my adventure the night before. CBGBs and black-haired porn stars and guys with huge safety pins through their noses ... in the morning light at my Selectric typewriter that didn't fit my idea of myself as the young littérateur. (Sometimes I wonder whether, back then, I could have stood being around me; I like to hope I wasn't, in truth, as precious and pretentious as I'm making it sound.)

Still, my true ambition was to join the literary firmament, and in my day job I was walking the same halls as E.B. White (who I used to see walking dazedly about on visits between winters in Florida and his fabled home in Maine), J.D. Salinger (who showed up for lunches with Mr. Shawn from time to time, though I never did glimpse him), and the great John Updike.

That day after CBGBs was one of the high points of my *New Yorker* days. Sadly, the great Vladimir Nabokov had died in Switzerland, and on Wednesday afternoon while I was at my desk, there was an unusual hubbub in the typing pool. I was going to do something I'd never done before: take phone dictation. Mr. Shawn's secretary came in and plugged an earpiece into my telephone, and then John Updike himself was on the line.

He had written an obit for Talk of the Town on Nabokov, and I was to take it down.

Updike introduced himself, seemed pleased for my help, then asked if we could get right to it. I said sure, and there was his light, small-town Pa. via Harvard accent in my ear, speaking mellifluously.

Here's what I typed:

"*Vladimir Nabokov's most recent novel, on one of its last pages, invites us, 'Imagine me, an old gentleman, a distinguished author, gliding rapidly on my back, in the wake of my outstretched dead feet, first through that gap in the granite, then over a pinewood, then along misty water meadows, and then simply between marges of mist, on and on, imagine that sight!' This man had imagined death so often, from Luzhin the chessmaster's fall into a chasm of 'dark and pale squares ... at the instant when icy air gushed into his mouth' to Cincinnatus C.'s false beheading ('A spinning wind was picking up and whirling: dust, rags, chips of painted wood, bits of gilded plaster, pasteboard bricks, posters; an arid gloom fleeted') and to the reported demise of Mrs. Richard F. Schiller, née Dolores Haze, yclept Lolita, while 'giving birth to a stillborn girl, on Christmas Day 1952, in Gray Star' and on to the death by gunshot of the poet John Shade and by 'time-and- pain' of Van Veen—Nabokov had imagined death so often, so colorfully and variously and searchingly, that we felt him to be exempt, having already passed through, into that Switzerland he inhabited as a chocolate-box province of immortality, the last and most playful of his exiles. His death, at the ripe age of seventy-eight, comes too soon, too coarsely—an ugly footnote to a shimmering text, reality's thumbprint on the rainbow.*"

Can you imagine. John Updike dictating his own stunning prose, then quoting Nabokov's perhaps finer, into my ear. The above is what actually ran in the magazine, but the great thing I recall is that Updike was editing himself as we went along; he'd scintillate a sentence to me (oh, now I'm doing it), and I'd type it, and then Updike—through a speaker seemingly installed right in my brain—would rewrite himself. "Let's try '*province* of immorality,' forget 'state.' And, Mr. Whitman, do you like 'chocolate box' as a metaphor?"

"Um, yes, Mr. Updike, I do."

So that was Wednesday at work. Having John Updike compose prose right inside my head. Ah, so this is what revision is, I remember thinking. You just take each key word, clip off a tiny bite, let it sit on your tongue, its flavors radiating ... and then either keep it or spit it out for another. Sweet!

Bookish dreams swam around me for the rest of the day, and then I went home.

Emily's door was open a crack, and as I walked by, she pushed it open.

"Oh, Cole, it's so good to see you!" erupted out of her.

I stopped cold. Emily was wearing only a loose sea-foam T-shirt and tangerine terrycloth shorts, and definitely no bra. Her blonde hair was messed up, like it had been last night thrashing beside me at CBGBs, again falling tangled to her shoulders and half over her eyes. She looked bleary-eyed and trashed, like Sue Lyon at her most Lolita-ish. Which made what she next said that much more of a surprise.

"My God, that was soooo much fun last night!" Emily twirled there in her doorway. "Come on in, here, you want something?"

"Um—"

"I took the day off work, I was ... wasted. Totally fucking wasted." Emily gave me an impish smile. "Looks like you're doing a lot better."

"I spent the day talking to John Updike," I told her, trying not to sound too brash and boastful.

Emily took this in, gave me a *hmmn-hmnnn* sway of her head, then said, "And how *is* Mr. Updike?"

I told her about the dictation, and by the time I was finished, I was sitting in the middle room of her railroad apartment, drinking a beer from a long-necked bottle.

"It's like we're leading two distinct lives," she said. She was deep in an old stuffed armchair I'd helped her drag up the stairs, the soles of her bare feet waving off the side. She jittered her own beer toward me giddily.

"I don't know."

"Well, maybe not *you*, Cole." Emily laughed. "Me, I feel like I'm living five or ten."

That was the moment to ask her where she'd gone last night after playing with Slater, but something held me back. She seemed awfully happy, carefree; not exactly the Emily I thought I best knew. Maybe I was worrying what was making her so cheerful.

"So, Cole, where *were* you last night?"

I did a double-take, my hands moving so much I ended up shaking my beer so it started foaming up the top. I caught it with my mouth.

"Where were *you*?" I said, the question popping out after I'd gotten down the brew.

"Around." A light shrug. "But, really, I *missed* you." Another impish smile. "Did you like the show?"

I kept looking hard at her. What was she asking? What was she really telling me?

Finally, when the silence got too much, I muttered, "Yeah."

She looked at me as if she hadn't heard me.

"After full consideration, I think I did like it," I told her.

"Cole, what the—" She gave me a tough look, as if I were disappointing her. "Come on, we were fuckin' amazing! Don't you think so? Wasn't your mind totally blown?"

So that was the game, total agreement. I was annoyed that she'd bugged out on me last night and I still didn't know why or where. But it was clear there was no good path in *that* direction.

"Absolutely," I got out. I said this quickly, mostly to make a sound, then thought how much cooler Sailor was using the same word in French.

"Slater and I worked the whole thing up—wanted it to be a surprise."

"It was, it was." I lifted my quiet-again beer bottle toward her. "You fit in well, I wasn't sure you would."

"Why not?" Emily looked distinctly miffed at this.

"I don't know, Yale Glee Club, it's not the same—"

"Oh, Cole, Cole, there's soooo much about me you don't know!" And there Emily was, laughing giddily again. I wondered how many beers she'd had before I showed up.

What she said was true, of course; and right then I had no idea how much there actually was to know about her. All her secrets were to come out later. But for now there was one question I believed I deserved an answer to. My courage, or frustration, was that rampant.

"So where *did* you go?" I said again, looking at her sharply.

"What do you mean?" Emily looked genuinely unsure what I was asking.

"After the performance. I ... we'd gone there together, I waited around, I thought we—"

"What are you *asking*, Cole?" Emily was still flopped over the chair, the swell of her breasts clear beneath her green T-shirt. Yep, totally Sue Lyon in *Lolita*, curled up and being coy.

"I mean, there you were, and then ... there you weren't."

"But I asked *you*!" She shrugged. "I guess we must've just missed each other." A very quick nod. "You know, so crowded and all."

I kept looking at Emily as she slowly disentangled herself from her Lolita position, sat straight back up in the chair and took another pull on her beer. She wasn't going to tell me anything, was she?

"Hey, did you see the band after us?"

"Um, yeah—"

"God, the Klitz!" Emily laughed. "Can you *believe* their name!?!"

Can you believe their na—. Oh, God, what an idiot! I hadn't gotten it, hadn't thought twice about it ... till right now.

"Slater knows the chick singer, Cherry. They were in some

band together a while back, but, you know, she wanted to be out front." Emily leaned back, shook her upper body under her sea-foam T, and giggled. Then she leaned forward, spoke conspiratorially. "Hey, I just realized, maybe *I'm* supposed to be the next Cherry Kruntz. Hmnn. Just need a different name. "How about Peach Melba?" Emily put a slender finger to her chin. "Or maybe Melba the Peach?" A light laugh. "Or ... Waffle Cones—I can call myself Waffle Cones!" And Emily lifted her fine breasts and thrust them out.

Emily was having her fun but it wasn't catching. I truly didn't know what to say, so I just sat on my hands.

"So, Cole, hey, *did* you like them?" Emily said when she was finished laughing. "What'd you think of the Klitz?" Just saying the band's name, she started giggling again.

I took a long breath. My head was kind of spinning. For a moment, Sailor's question from last night came back to me, about whether I wanted to have sex with Cherry Kruntz. I mean, um ... but what I said to Emily was a simple: "They sure had a lot of energy and—"

Emily, a swig of beer in her mouth, blew it out, a comedian doing a spit take. Silver drops sprayed through the room.

"*Energy?* Jesus, Cole, I don't *know* about you, I just *don't*."

"What?" I was alarmed, as if something important to me were slipping away.

"Oh ... oh, nothing. Don't pay me any—" Emily dug deep and tried to give me a serious smile, but she couldn't. She was too drunk or giddy or just fired up from the night before.

"Listen, I'm sorry, you'd better go."

"What?" I actually did want to leave, Emily's mood was making me unsettled, but of course I didn't want to be told to go.

"I have to get ready."

"For what?"

"Oh, Cole, the questions, the questions!"

"So get ready." I said this hard, harsh.

"But Cole, I have to get *dressed*." She ran her hands over her loose T-shirt and tangerine shorts, then looked around the room as if thinking of what to wear. "Have to become one more distinct version of Emily Prosser."

"Why?"

"You really want to know?" she said. I thought I heard a threat there. Did I? If so, I still needed to.

"Yeah."

"I have a date."

"A—"

"You see!" Emily was up now, moving toward her closet. Like all the apartments in the building, there was no built-in anything; she had two wardrobe cases pushed next to each other. "But yes, I'm going on a date. With a very proper young man, dear Cole." She started giggling again. "You do not have to worry at all!"

"Who is it?" I was fearing the worst.

"Nobody you know."

"Oh, secrets, secrets. Emily, is that all I ever get, *more* secrets?" I leaned into my words.

"Come on, Cole, it's just Harper."

"Harper?"

"Harper Hart." A shake of Emily's pretty head. "Haven't I told you about Harper Hart?"

"No."

"Harper Hart's a proper boy." This came out a little like Blanche Dubois, Emily's ironic spin. More giggling. "And we're going on a proper date." She pulled a sleek, expensive sheath from her wardrobe, then turned to me, back to her own voice. "Come on, Cole, I do have to get ready. For real. Harper's going to be—well, he won't actually come this far south—but I'm going to meet him soon. Russian Tea Room." She whirled the patterned fuchsia dress in front of my eyes. "Do you think this will look good at the Russian Tea Room?"

# 10

Who *was* Harper Hart? Well, *proper* did do a pretty good job of describing him, especially if you disregarded Emily's *Streetcar Named Desire* voice. *Proper* if she meant inherited money and the Hart name, which was a celebrated one here in the East. *Proper* if she meant tennis whites and polo lessons and private schools and some rich-people college I'd never heard of, Hamilton, in upstate New York. *Proper* if she meant he lived on Gramercy Park in one of the original houses ... with his mother, though as Emily explained, "Harper has his own floor." *Proper* if she meant predictably tall, square-chinned, dusky blond hair (with perfect sun highlights!), dressed out of a Sunday *Times* men's fashion insert....

Here in the city Harper worked at the Whitney Museum. The way he made it sound, he was a junior curator or something, but later I found out he was mostly involved in helping run the information booth. His other brothers sold bonds, but Harper evidently was arty. Which meant Emily might've been funning me when she said he never went below 14th Street. Or that he was really serious about her. One way or another, I first met him a few days after their date at the Russian Tea Room right outside Emily's door.

I was on my way out to the Korean greenmarket around the corner to get dinner provisions. It was about seven, and there was this spiffily dressed fellow, sporting a straw hat and a large grin, waiting on the grubby landing. I gave him a friendly nod but got nothing back; then I lingered down the stairs till I heard the door open and Emily call out, "Oh, Harper, it's you!"

My hand clutching my grocery bag, I dawdled on my way back down 11th Street till I saw them come out. Emily was wearing a loose, swingy, peach-colored sundress and strapless white heels. She looked happy, carefree. Harper walked briskly to keep up with her, and when they were halfway toward Second Avenue, he reached out and took her hand ... and she let him.

It looked patently innocent, though, two kids off to the stable to ride horses, at worst to make out. At least that's what I wanted to think. Far as I could tell, and I was trying hard not to obsess about it, Harper Hart wasn't spending the night at Emily's. The only time I saw him around was in the evening, on the way to or from a date. (Drinks at the Plaza? More blintzes at the Russian Tea Room?) And every time I saw him, he was as crisp and proper as ever. He might be venturing downtown, pursuing a singer in a CBGBs band, but not a speck of the East Village was rubbing off on Harper Hart.

Was it serious? I got no indication from Emily. She was as hard to figure as ever. I wouldn't see her for four, five days, then I'd hear she was playing with Slater's band at CBGBs again, and there'd she be in her fierce rock girl getup. The next night? Out with Harper. Then the next afternoon she'd leave FSG for lunch at Mary Elizabeth with me, which was where we were when I had a chance to finally really talk to her.

"So, Harper Hart," I said, not able to resist. We were waiting on our nut bread, cheese, and olive sandwiches.

"Yes, darling."

"You're seeing a lot of him?"

"I wouldn't say *that*." A light shrug. Emily was perfect book gal today, red silk blouse, tan slacks, hair combed back tight but for a few strands teasing her neck, fingers ditzying her black sexy-librarian glasses.

"I'm just wondering."

"My secrets, Cole?"

"No, no, I'm just—

"It's all right. Listen, I appreciate it, the way you try to look out for me."

This came out straight, proper even, though from Emily, I couldn't tell if she was being patronizing or what.

"No, I *mean* it," evidently catching my look. "That's one thing I love about you, boyo." A sincere smile, though it held something back. Emily *always* held something back.

"And really, Cole, it means a lot to me, it does." A tight, rich smile. "You're one of the ... well, one of the few souls I know I can truly count on."

She was saying something here, wasn't she? Her declaration was coming out of the blue. I could feel her checking with a part of her hidden deeply within as she said it, so I wasn't sure at all what she meant. What did I do? Well, I took a deep breath. Telling me I was one of the few people she could count on wasn't exactly what I wanted to hear from Emily, but still ... she got to me. I felt warm, stirred up.

"You do," I said. "You do have me."

"Thanks." A slight, wry smile. "But that doesn't mean you'll get my secrets."

"I don't—"

"Come on, I'm messing with you." Emily laughed. "And truth, boyo, you really *don't* want all my secrets." A wink. "Might not like what you see."

She said this as lightly, as playfully as she could, and that's how I chose to take it. Though there was no way to ignore the darkness floating there, too.

Fortunately, right then our ridiculous old-lady cream-cheese-and-olive sandwiches came and we began to eat.

✴ ✴ ✴ ✴ ✴

SO FAR I HADN'T been mugged in the city, though it seemed like everybody else had. I'd go to a party, that was half the conversation: muggings, car break-ins, robberies, the occasional knife flourish or brandished gun ... scary times in New York town. Not long after I moved there *Taxi Driver* came out;

turned out the street corner (11th and Third) where Jodi Foster plied her trade was a couple blocks from my apartment, and I usually passed it on my way to my job. One morning a working girl sidled up and said, "Hey, wanna go out?"

My answer? "Um—" looking around, I was standing on a street corner, under the sun "—I'm *already* out."

Jeez, what an idiot I was!

Still, I pretty quickly developed enough street savvy—eyes constantly moving, looking for patterns, odd congregations of people, surprise gestures—or at least possessed enough good fortune not to be robbed or mugged ... yet.

Not so much my neighbor down the hall.

It was a Monday night, about nine, and I was home alone reading some tome I hoped would make me a better writer—I recall it was Balzac's *Cousine Bette* (in translation, in translation!)—when I heard boots knocking slowly, heavily outside my door.

"Slater?" I said when I opened it up. "What the hell?"

He was in his usual yellowed wife-beater, tight black jeans, and engineer boots, but this time his shirt was scuffed and dotted with burnt-orange spots—drying blood, I realized, startled—and his tough face was way the hell worked over. I threw my head back as I took him in. Slater's left eye was already blackening, his nose was a bruised yellow, there were cuts on his jaw.

"Cole, hey, since you're here, man, hey, can I come in?" Slater's eyes shone narrow and frantic. His fingers were twitching swift, as if fingering a violin, but nervous, out of control.

He didn't wait, just started moving past me, slowly, haltingly.

"Of course, of course," I said, stepping aside. "Jesus, what happened?"

"You got any first-aid shit?" Slater looked around with his hopped-up eyes.

"Um, not a lot. Soap and water, maybe a bandage or two somewhere."

"That can't hurt." He pulled himself into the kitchen and halted by the tub, leaning against its metal cover.

"Don't you think you should go to the ER?" I saw the cuts on his jaw were still letting blood out, dribbling down his chin and onto his shirt.

"No can do, bro."

"But—"

"Hey, you think Emily's around?"

That hit me, what, wasn't I good enough to help him? Still, he had a point. If I'd ever been worked over like that, I'd probably want Emily in there, too.

"Um, I can call her."

"Yeah, two heads and all, you know, you know."

Emily was home, said she'd be right up. A minute later she walked in.

"Slater, what the hell!" she cried.

I smiled. See, not that different....

"You think you can patch me up, babe?" Slater's eyes softened as Emily stood in front of him, looking intently, lightly fingering his rough skin.

"Cole, soap and wash cloth. Pronto."

I fetched them, and she daubed Slater's chin and around his eyes. He immediately looked better. Then his nose opened up, more blood, and Emily said softly, "Ice cubes." I pulled some out of my freezer, and she had Slater hold them against his nostrils.

The bleeding stopped, he looked almost human.

"So what was it?" Emily said. We'd moved into the living room, Slater holding tight to the wall as we walked there. I'd gotten us all tall glasses of ice water, and Slater, who never drank water, had already emptied his. I filled it right up.

"You don't got a beer, Cole?"

I didn't think I had any in the fridge, certainly not a

Schaefer's; and with all the hubbub I didn't feel like looking. I shook my head.

"Slater?" Emily said again.

"Hey, life in New York City, babe."

"And?"

"I'm going to be fine, right? Cole thought I should hit the ER, but—"

"Just some facial bruises. Yeah, you'll be just dandy. Peachy dandy." Emily took a sip of water, then zeroed in on him. "So, what the hell happened?"

Slater shrugged and wouldn't tell us. Emily kept after him but got no further than a begrudged, "Wrong place, wrong time."

"You know, Slater, sometimes you're a total asshole," she said. I was looking hard at her, trying to read her tone. It wasn't angry, more annoyed but with definite concern.

"That, my dear, is one thing that is *not* in dispute." And for the first time since I'd heard him outside my door, Slater threw back his head and laughed.

When he tried to stand, his legs went out from under him. He wobbled a second, then pitched shoulder-first to my floor.

I threw Emily a startled look, but she didn't look worried. I reached down and helped Slater up from where he'd collapsed on my rug. He thanked me.

"What the hell's that, Slater?" Emily said as we got him into a chair.

"Um, not just my face, babe." He grinned, but it was weak and distracted. "My friends went to town, you know."

"Friends?" I said.

"Well, ac-quain-tan-ces—that word suit you better, Cole?" He chuckled, low, harsh. A glance at Emily, shrugging, What're you gonna do with this guy? She ignored him, then with a lift of her hands got me to help her get Slater to his apartment.

We got him settled on a hideous orange easy chair, tufts

of innards puffing out. Emily bent over and worked to pull off his boots and black jeans. As the clothes came off, we saw bruises and contusions and heavy welts up and down his legs. You could only imagine what was under his shirt. Slater was a mountain range of hurt.

"You're not going anywhere like that," Emily said. "Probably smart for you to lay low anyway." A warm look at him. "You ready to take it easy for a while, boyo?"

I doubt Slater was ready, but he had no choice. By the next day he was bandaged and spending most of the time on his mattress on the floor. Sailor came over with a pair of crutches she'd dug out of somebody's trash, and Slater used them to get down the hall to the bathroom. But anything else, he needed help. Slater was laid up, and that was that.

We all took care of him when we could. I'd stop in before work and go get him something from Veniero's, the Italian pastry joint downstairs, then check in when I got home. Emily would also drop by when she wasn't working. Sailor had a job driving a cab and was working double shifts, so she stopped by when she could, at odd hours. Slater was getting by, though he was grumpy and silent a lot.

What did he do all day? He actually had a couple stacks of paperbacks and he read from them: Aleister Crowley, Jean Genet, William Burroughs, even some William Blake. (The latter was the only one of his faves I was into; I'd done my Berkeley senior thesis on Blake.) The rest of the time he had his small black-and-white TV on, watching soap operas and *Price Is Right*. And he spun records, new bands from England every bit as loud and chaotic as what I'd heard that night at CBGBs.

Slater was down for days, still not able to make it up and down the five flights of stairs. I was getting worried—what if there were internal injuries we didn't know anything about—but everybody else was sure what he'd gone through was just your basic beating, and that Slater, while in pain, would heal up.

Then he got what he really needed. Wendell Walter, with no work but at his church, started helping, tentatively at first, bringing up sandwiches and coffee from the deli on Second, slices from Rosemary's Pizza around the corner, but then he seemed to be there all the time. Emily even brought it up one day while we were walking to work: "I guess we're not needed anymore, eh, Cole?"

"You mean with Wendell?"

"Something's going on, yeah." She nodded, half to herself. "It's like he's moved in with Slater."

"Maybe they're working on the band."

"The band?" Emily shot me a look. "You think?"

"Sure, why not?" I said. She was getting at something, but I as usual had no idea what. "By the way, what's up with that?"

"Our group?"

"Yeah." We were almost to 14th Street, where Emily would peel off to FSG and I'd take the train to Grand Central.

"Nothing without Slater." A tight nod. It was an early fall day, that first hint of crisp in the air. "Had to kill a few CBs gigs."

"You're not happy?"

"I wouldn't go that far, Cole."

"Meaning?"

"Oh, Cole, it is what it is. Slater's what *he* is, the band's what *it* is—it's all just what it is."

"Em, you all right?" The way she sounded, more fragile and angry than I was used to, well....

"What?" She looked distracted.

"I don't know, you sound kind of—"

"I'm sorry. A lot on my mind, boyo, a lot on my mind." With that Emily gave me a quick, shoulders-only hug, then headed west to the Farrar Straus offices.

* * * * *

YES, WENDELL WAS THERE all the time. Hanging in Slater's apartment doing whatever Slater needed, trudging up the stairs with all the twelve packs of beer he wanted, knocking on my door from time to time to borrow some aspirin, out in the hallway with Slater's arm around his shoulders on the way to the toilet. With Wendell's help, Slater was also making it up and down the stairs well enough. He and Wendell would walk over to Tompkins Square and sit in the sunshine. It was the Christian thing to do, Wendell told me once when I bumped into him in the hall. He was glad to be of service.

The Christian thing to do. That phrase flew into my head with what came later.

Once I even saw Slater in the back of the Church of Jesus Christo in a wooden pew while Wendell played through an early-afternoon service. I heard *Closer to Jesus* chiming off Wendell's Gibson. This was just a glimpse from the corner of my eye as I was going out to a cocktail party, and I couldn't be sure that it was Slater, but it sure looked like him.

Slater was mending, apparently with no further medical issues. His mood had also vastly improved; at times he seemed downright jolly. He was itching to play out again, and a new gig at CBGBs was set up. The club was a pretty forgiving place, I guess. The show was in two weeks; plenty of time, Slater insisted, to get the music back together.

Rehearsals in the church, the sound of the band—Slater and Emily, Wendell, Sailor, and Chet—pounding out on the streets. A good, loud sound. Cheered me to hear them going at it whenever I passed by.

Things were back to normal. Turns out I'm the kind of guy who almost always likes things back to normal.

Still, there was one scene around that time I still vividly remember. One evening after work I was stopping by with a fresh bottle of aspirin; I wasn't expected and just knocked on Slater's door. No immediate answer, but I heard a loud record playing and pounded harder.

Finally, Wendell Walter opened it up. The first thing I noticed was how steamy it was in Slater's apartment, a billowing white cloud fogging up almost everything. I guess they'd been running the bath hot as could be, but why I had no idea.

Wendell was in his underwear, just droopy yellowed briefs. This was the first and only time I saw him without a shirt. His chest was concave; he looked more skin and bones than ever.

When I stepped inside, I saw Slater was only in his underwear, too. His were tight, high-riding dark-gray briefs. His barrel chest looked like a lumberjack's; his skinny white legs extended like bowling pins. For the first time, I saw his efflorescence of tattoos in all their glory, stars and half moons up his arms, intricate brambles on his chest, and across his back a spread of filigreed angel's wings from shoulder blade to shoulder blade.

The curious thing: Wendell Walter also had tattoos. Only two, both on his upper arms: on his right, a curling green and red snake, tongue and fangs bared, grasped in a wizened fist; on his left, smudgy black figures, letters and numbers. I made out MARK 16: 17-18—a Bible verse, right? Though which I had no idea.

Slater's record player was blasting. I didn't recognize the music, just loud guitar screeching and thrashing, and over it a shouted cringing voice, like a demented Mick Jagger. Tipped up against the player was the record cover: black background with four slightly distorted heads (all with bowl cuts like Slater's) and in a lowercase script the words THE STOOGES. I didn't know the band.

When Slater saw me, he leaned over and brought down the volume, then took a pull from the tall Schaefer open in front of him. There were easily a dozen other beer cans stacked on the table.

"Um, I got you some aspirin." I smiled at him, even though I couldn't help but feel very odd and discombobulated standing in this white-steamy room with two men only in briefs. "So, you know, you don't always have to come by and—"

"That's really, realllllly kiiiiind of you, Cole," Slater said, drawing out each syllable so it sounded comic. Then he laughed, his worst cackle, snotty and insidious. "Sooooo thoughtful."

"O.K.," I said. I backed up a little. "Everything good?"

"Just peachy dandy." Slater snickered. I recalled Emily's phrase from a week or so back.

"Well, good, good, fine, good." I kept backing up, toward the door. There was something unsettlingly private there, and I knew to my deepest bones I didn't belong. "If you need anything, just holler. You too, Wendell."

"Sure, professor, sure," Wendell said quickly. It was strange to be addressed the way Wendell always did when he was sitting out on the street with Mr. Strump, because that was normal, and everything about Slater's apartment now was anything but normal. The thing I most recall was how Wendell was looking at me, or more accurately, *not* looking at me. Usually his gaze was laser straight right at me—a vivid, pulsing God look, something out of Flannery O'Connor, the way I took it—but now his eyes flitted about, anywhere but on my own. For a soul so simple, so Jesus-inspired, it was memorably furtive ... and I recalled it oh too well later on.

So, that was that. A few days later Slater was able to go up and down the stairs on his own, not even needing Sailor's crutches. It was a surprising recovery and I was glad to see it. That steamy night in Slater's apartment, I don't know what that was.

I also never heard what laid up Slater in the first place. I wanted to think he'd been mugged, but after his riff about "acquaintances," I guess it was more than that.

More likely, the beating came from something to do with whatever it took for Slater to keep going. It wasn't like I was some uptown rich guy—a Harper Hart—with no curiosity in even recognizing that world; I was simply a suburban L.A. kid his first years in the big city, eager for knowledge, but with so much I just didn't see or understand. That Emily didn't take seriously whatever happened to Slater suggested I shouldn't either. One of those things that happen, I guess.

Except that I was trying so hard to learn all I could, uptown and down, and whatever led to Slater's being beaten felt like knowledge I needed. So I stayed wildly curious. I just didn't find out anything more, at least then.

Later, though, I was to get a lot clearer picture.

# 11

A FEW DAYS after that Sailor called up and asked me out to lunch.

"Lunch?" I said. In that word I put all my startlement. Safe to say I was surprised to hear from Sailor, didn't think she even had my phone number. This was a Sunday evening, and I was home and feeling crushed by another lonely weekend.

"I come uptown, meet you at your fancy magazine." A pause, and I saw her sly smile underneath that fierce red bob. "You know, an adventure for me?"

"Sure," I said. "That would be—

"An adventure."

"Exactly." I laughed. Lunch as an adventure? Well, if we could make it one, who knew?

We set it up for the next day, Monday, seemed like Sailor didn't want to wait. I was about to ask her what she had in mind when she said, "So, Cole, I'm looking forward to it. What time should I get to West 43rd Street?"

So she knew where I was. Well, any *New Yorker* mag devotee probably knew the famous address. Did Sailor actually read the magazine?

"One, one-thirty?"

"How about one-thirty. And you'll pick a place?"

"*Absolument!*" The word just popped out of me. Sailor laughed, no doubt remembering that night at CBGBs.

"Does that mean we'll go French?"

"Don't know if I can afford—"

"Hey, Cole, I asked *you*. Pick any place you want, it's all good. I'll see you at one-thirty outside your office. Twenty-five West 43rd Street."

Then she hung up.

So where should I take her? The Mary Elizabeth Tea Room seemed, well, not exactly the place for Sailor ... and then I remembered I didn't even know her last name. I liked it that she was just Sailor, wild downtown drummer, but if we were having lunch ... and why were we having lunch? ... well, I should ask her more about herself. It wasn't that I wasn't curious.

I decided on this Japanese place on West $45^{th}$. Sushi was still somewhat new in the States, and I never knew it existed till I moved to New York. Raw fish? The first time I gritted my teeth. Now I stopped in almost weekly for *chirashi*, a bed of rice lovingly topped with an array of fish and egg.

When Sailor showed up, I almost didn't recognize her. She was wearing a cotton powder-blue skirt and a salmon blouse over it. We were into September now, a slight chill, and she had on a white cotton sweater. Her red-bronze hair, still in its Louise Brooks bob, looked less sleek and intense up here in the daylight.

"Sailor?"

"Hey," she said. She bounded up with a smile. Interesting, for the first time I noticed her height, just an inch or so shorter than me. "Tell me, what floor are you on?"

"Oh, twenty."

"That's the one above the main floor, right?"

I nodded. "How do you know so much about—"

"Oh, I grew up with *The New Yorker*. My mother loved it, and I read every issue—at least what I could understand as a kid. Those Cheever stories, wow!"

"Really?"

"Cole, there's a lot you don't know about me." She smiled. Oh, great, another mystery woman; wasn't Emily enough? But Sailor quickly pushed us along. "So, where're we going?"

Turned out Sailor loved sushi, it was her favorite food, and even though my place was just a midtown lunch joint, it passed muster. We took a two-person table in the back.

"I have to say," I said, sipping green tea, "I was surprised to hear from you."

"Why?" She looked straight at me with her large, wide-spaced eyes. That was a thing with Sailor, I was starting to realize, she always acted as if she knew me far better and longer than was actually the case.

"I don't know—"

"I *did* ask you to have some food with me that first time we were together, you know?"

I winced, thinking back to my turning down that post-CBGBs pizza slice.

"I was an idiot."

"Hey, thought I'd give you another chance." The waitress came by and placed chopsticks and little ceramic soy sauce bowls on the table.

"So that's why we're here?"

Sailor simply lifted her chin and smiled. She had a pretty smile, ripe with just a hint of upturn at the corners; and it hit me totally differently now that she was in, how can I put it, more midtown clothes.

"I almost didn't recognize you."

"Why?" Again, that look straight at me, so forward; yet the word spoken abruptly, as if in offense.

"Last time I saw you, um, you were banging drums at CBGBs. Now you look—"

"Like Little Miss Manners?"

"Closer, yeah."

"Some people can find *a lot* of girls in me, Cole." She lifted her chin. "A way lot." This was odd. Hadn't Emily said almost the same thing to me? Sailor lifted an eyebrow, as if she were reading my mind, then added, "But, really, there's only *one* of me."

"One Sailor?"

"Well, one girl." A nod, bright, brisk, jolly. "Just one." A wink. "But *which one*?"

And that's when our sushi came.

"So, actually, Cole," Sailor said, adroitly lifting a piece of salmon, "there *is* a reason I asked you here."

"I figured."

"Why?" Another growl of that word! This time I ignored it.

"Well," she went on, sweet again, "I've been thinking about your being a writer and all."

"I'm trying to be—"

"I hear you're pretty good."

I held still, wondering who could have told her that. I couldn't think of anyone Sailor knew whom I'd showed my work to. Not Slater, for sure, or Wendell. I really didn't show anything to anybody much, just Emily and editors of magazines or journals that might publish it—or turn it down.

"Come on, Cole, I can tell just being around you." Sailor nodded, her red hair moving. "You have an air of . . . of lit-er-a-ture—"

"Oh, yes, I've cultivated that for years." I laughed to myself. "Ever since I was wearing wide-striped surfer shirts and riding skateboards back in the San Fernando Valley." I lifted my arms, mimed keeping my balance rolling down a cracked sidewalk.

Sailor looked at me curiously a moment, as if what I'd said hadn't quite computed, then shook it off and leaned toward me. "Listen, I want you to write for our band."

"Write for—" I shook my head. I never saw *that* coming. "What do you mean?"

"The words—listen, I'm no idiot. I know you think I'm just some Avenue A snipe who's pounding away in a punk band slapped together with duct tape, but that couldn't be further—" She caught herself there, laughed a moment, then with that spark in her eye went on, "I want this to be good—I *need* it to be good."

"I'm becoming a fan, but, you know, it's not really my—"

"The thing is," Sailor said, rushing along, "Slater, you can't hear what the fuck he's singing anyway, but *I* know what it is—and it's drivel. I want something good."

"Even though he'll just shout and mangle and—"

"He wants it, too." Sailor gave me a tight nod. "We've talked about it."

"Why didn't he ask me him—"

"Because Slater doesn't *like* sushi, Cole." That light in her eyes, she was playing a move or two ahead of me, wasn't she? Sailor always kept me disarmed. I didn't know if I was ready to get used to that. "That's why."

"So what, um, do I do?"

"You're writing poems, right?"

"Well, mostly short stories—and I'm ... attempting a novel." I lifted my eyes, my usual hopeful petitioning of the gods. "But, yeah, I've been trying a poem or two."

"Well, we just need lyrics. Something interesting, intelligible, but, you know, with some flair. Some *poetry*." She hit that word hard. "You know Patti Smith?"

I shook my head.

"You don't!" Harsh, accusatory.

Another shake of my head. What was with Sailor? It was like she kept expecting something from me, unvoiced and not even what we were talking about, and somehow I kept disappointing her. Or? I don't know what I thought. But she seemed to always be attacking me. And, what, how well did she know Milton? Keats? William Blake....

"Patti's this amazing ... amazing *everything*!" Sailor paused a second, and I understood she was showing genuine respect. "The lady's a poet, but she also has a band, they play CBs a lot. She has these—well, she'll start reciting a poem, and then she's singing it, and the band's wailing, and—"

"I love Dylan, of course, and—"

"Yeah, Patti's like that, but *different*. Way different. An original."

"Well, I'll, um, keep my ears open." I swallowed. That sounded lame. "But I still don't know what I can do for—"

"I want you to *work* with us. Scribble something down, it can be loose. Scribbledehobble, you know." That smile in her eyes, then another wink. "You've heard us. We pound and pound away. But there's a bit of melody there, and we can hang lovely words on that." Her wide, quirky eyes deep on mine. "You can see it, right, Cole?"

I wasn't sure I could. My writing, chasing Faulkner and Joyce .... wait, had Sailor just made a reference to Joyce? Scribbledehobble—the so-called Ur-Workbook for *Finnegan's Wake*? What? Just like that, dropping an obscure Joyce allusion? Did Sailor even know she had? But how could she not; who else would make up such an odd portmanteau word?

I pulled back, looked at Sailor totally differently then, not sure who or what I was seeing. My sudden flush of confusion swept my whole body and rendered me silent.

"It's what you do anyway. I'm just saying we'll work it in with *our* stuff. It'll be easy, Cole. You give us somewhere to start, we'll work on the music, the *sound*, and then you can come back and tweak the words." Sailor leaned back, face bright. "I *know* it's going to work."

"You ... you have that much faith in me?"

"Yes." She let out the word just as intensely and abruptly as she had all those *Why*s before, followed by another quick laugh. "*Absolument!*"

"Um, O.K., why not?" I still didn't quite see how I'd pull this off, was trying to think, fool that I was, what T. S. Eliot would have done in the same position. My gut instinct: Even Banker Tom would've gone for it. Why not? Pull him out of his normal life and have him working with this ever-surprising red-haired woman. "Wait, sure, I *will* do it. I'm not—I mean, I don't have any idea what I'll write about, but—"

"It doesn't matter. Or, well, it *does*. But Cole, that's easy.

Write about what *everyone* writes about. Sex, life, freedom, death—you know."

I slowly nodded. I, well, maybe I did know. Or maybe just sitting with Sailor and really talking with her, I was seeing how much I truly *wanted* to know.

"So, good," Sailor said. "How long do you need?"

"How long?"

"We have our next gig in a *week*." Oh, that crisp, focused, always-expectant look from Sailor. "How about I come by tomorrow to your place, see what's going on?"

"To-mor-row?" I bobbled out. That was awfully soon, wasn't it? Didn't Eliot take three or four years just to write *The Waste Land*?

"I have faith in you, Cole," Sailor said, lifting her last piece of sushi with her chopsticks, then giving me a smile. "Nothing but faith." Yes, that lovely smile. "So, hey, I'll see you tomorrow night."

# 12

So, O.K., LYRICS for Slater's and Sailor's (and Emily's) band. Often I had my best thoughts in the middle of the night, jumping up and writing down notes—if I didn't get things down right then, at least a few pregnant words, I couldn't get my idea back in the morning—and that night two words came to me: *savage joy*. They rang and clanked through my head as I lay stark-eyed on my mattress and wouldn't go away, so I fumbled around, flicked on a light, dashed them down on the back of one of those blow-in cards from an *Atlantic* magazine. Then, back to sleep.

In the morning I sat by my Selectric, looking down at the two words: *savage joy*. This was a work day, it was 9:05, I had to jump on the subway by 10.

I sat there, staring out the window. And sat there.

There's a famous story about one of the first times Paul McCartney smoked dope (provided by Bob Dylan, the first time the Beatles met him). After a number of tokes, McCartney evidently saw the meaning of life flash before him. He commanded the band's roadie, Mal Evans, to write down his profound thoughts. The next day Mal showed him the paper: "There are seven levels!"

McCartney's response: "What the fuck's that mean?"

My response to those words *savage joy*? Not exactly "What the fuck?"; in truth, more of a long *hmnnnnnn*.

Problem was, the words weren't taking me anywhere. Those four a.m. glimpses were usually a slender rope into the next section of whatever I was working on; grasp it right, and it would pull me through the next pages. But *savage joy* wasn't taking me anywhere at all.

I began to think it was because it wasn't about *my* writing. In effect, I'd given myself—or Sailor had given me—

an assignment, even a deadline, and I wasn't that good at deadlines.

But there was more to it: I was being asked to put words into Slater Martin's head. My first thought: Who knew what the fuck was going on in there! Slater, hardhead he was, was also hardheaded in that way that when he swooped you up, you'd just follow him, with no idea what he was thinking or where he was taking you. That power was one of Slater's gifts.

So how could *I* become Slater Martin? Deep breath. At 9:15 in the morning, well, I just couldn't get there.

I tried, though. *Savage joy*. The two words felt right for him and his music, a brutal force leading to something exuberant and wild. But where could *I* take them?

O.K., approach Sailor's assignment another way. She wanted lyrics, which meant ... rhymes! I wasn't bad at rhymes, and quickly jotted down "boy, coy, alloy, ravaged toy...."

Hmnnn. They didn't take me anywhere either, so I half-cheated and hit a beat-up paperback rhyming dictionary on my shelf; but that didn't give me much more: "ploy, soy, altar boy...."

A flash to Slater draped on the pew in the back of Wendell's church. Like that startling glimpse of the two of them in Slater's steam-filled apartment, the vision had taken on an almost mythical tone: Had I really seen it? Or merely dreamed it?

And what did any of it have to do with savage joy?

This was going nowhere. I tried to call up Slater's songs from CBGBs for context, but all I recalled was the shouting and flailing; I'd had no idea what he was getting on about. Thought about Sailor onstage, but all I got was her fierce drumming and intense bob of brass-red hair flung side to side. *Savage*, yes, and *joyful*, and....

Maybe *that's* who *savage joy* spoke to: Sailor.

I sat pondering that for a long moment, and thinking about her, the way she'd surprised me at lunch (and kept surprising me), and how I knew so little about her—not even her last name—yet how eagerly I'd taken on her charge about the lyrics, and—

But I wasn't writing a song for Sailor, was I? Only for Slater. I sat there another twenty minutes, trying, yes, I tried, but it was time to head to work, so I shut off my Selectric and bounded down the stairs.

\* \* \* \* \*

ON MY DOWNTIME in *The New Yorker* typing pool—downtime, as I've said, being almost all of my time there—I kept working on my own stories and poems. That day I gave *Savage Joy* another shot, but surrounded by the venerable almond-colored walls of *The New Yorker*, I got absolutely nowhere with it. Instead, I started back on a story I was working on called *Hopeless Acts Performed Properly, with Grace*.

My stories kept flowing, I was getting pretty professional with first one draft, then another, then a third. Finally, on a dizzying prayer, I'd type a final version and immediately send it out, hopes flying high.

Was I any good? Deep breath, Cole, deep breath. Here's the deal: I had an understanding with myself that I could keep this writing thing up till I was twenty-eight, but I'd have to have a pretty good sign by then. (Jump ahead a couple years: A poem of mine was accepted by *The New Yorker*, and the issue came out to the day on my twenty-eighth birthday; I celebrated at the Algonquin Hotel across the street, and.... O.K., I know I promised the story, but think it should still wait.)

Anyway, at this point nothing was happening. Out would go the stories, back they'd come. Those SASEs sitting there on my desk after lunch. Boy, that was a good *chirashi* I just had, and I'll make it through the afternoon at work, fun-sounding cocktail party coming up, and ... ugh, there's another manila envelope on my desk, another story re-jec-ted....

*Ooof!* Each time I saw my scrawled address on those self-addressed stamped envelopes, it was like a punch in the stomach. Another deep breath, rip the envelope open … O.K., right, nothing but a form rejection letter this time, nobody even bothering to take the time to....

Damn, this writing life was hard!

Fortunately, I knew two things. One, I *was* good (at least I believed this slightly more than fifty percent of the time). Second, that a writing career was nearly impossible. I knew what the odds were. All I had to do was walk down the hall to *The New Yorker*'s fiction department and see the eight-foot-high, twelve-foot-wide shelves of submissions, plopped into wire baskets. Each story would sooner or later be looked over by an assistant, almost every one immediately sent back (into someone else's SASE), to be replaced with a flood of new stories the next day....

Lucky me, I began to take rejection as encouragement! I really did.

A couple years later, when I was getting things published somewhat regularly, it turned out it was *acceptance* that was disarming; I was so used to getting those damn rejection slips—and vividly steeled for just that result—that when somebody actually wanted to publish something, I was totally thrown. I was like a balloon blown up with failure, and when a little success came, the air rushed out all at once and I zoomed about like a crazy thing, untethered, all sense of myself blown away. Crazy and confused until, inevitably, another SASE turned up on my work desk a few days later.

Quick, send it off again. Failure was constant, but hope always bloomed. Get the story out there again immediately and just know for certain that for *this* story at *this* new magazine, it would all work out.

Now that I think about it, I was like that with Emily, too. My hope never died. Just stay her friend, keep sending out missives of adoration, make sure I put enough return postage on them, and … well, my love was bound to be accepted sooner or later....

Sure, these were simply stories I told myself; but writing stories was my life. Stay faithful to my writing, all will work out. Stay faithful to Emily, that will work out, too. Sticking to things was all I knew: inflated with fascination and desire, swollen with determination and rejection, yet oh so ready at every moment for all the air to rush out of my frustrated, hopeful soul.... Yes, yes, yes. Emily, *accept* me! *Make* me crazy! Embrace me, confuse me, bedizen me, sweep me away....

*Whew!*

Anyway, there I was, back at my work desk, no Daily Ved yet to type, thinking: *savage joy, savage joy, savage joy*....

This was Tuesday. Sailor was coming over tonight ... and, oh, I just remembered, I had a lunch planned today with Emily.

She met me at 1:35, twenty minutes late, at the good ol' Mary Elizabeth Tea Room.

"Cole, I'm so sorry," she said, rushing in. "There was something at work and—"

"Are you all right?" I said. Emily looked different, ruffled, unstrung. Her eyes had a raw jumpiness to them I wasn't used to. It was so unlike her, all I saw was that she wasn't herself.

"Sure, of course, why not?" She spoke quickly, brushing loose hair out of her face. Yes, that was it, she looked unusually harried, far less put together—not the smooth, classy Emily I was used to at our lunches. It was an interesting dishevelment, though, hair unbound, skirt uneven ... wait, was her red blouse buttoned wrong? I looked closer. No, I guess it was correct, but it sure seemed as if it were buttoned up in haste. Interesting. I found the whole picture strongly attractive. "Maybe I should've canceled," she rushed on, "but ... well, we did have our usual date." She sat down, put her purse on the floor tight between her shoes. "So, Cole, *what's new*?"

That's how we started every lunch, catching each other up; oddly, our lunches were more regular than seeing each other at the apartment building. Today, I told her about work, nothing special, and that as always my stories and poems were out there somewhere—Emily always seemed surprised my stuff kept getting rejected, which from an editor at FSG was nice to hear—and then I mentioned my assignment from Sailor.

"Really?" she said. She brushed back her blonde hair. "Sailor wants you to do *what*?"

"Get involved, I guess." I shrugged. "Write something for Slater and—"

"No kidding?" She was looking at me intensely. There was something about her eyes. I kept wondering if she was getting enough sleep.

"That's what she said, yeah." Emily's gaze was so strong I looked down at my sandwich for a second. "You're O.K. with that, right?"

"I guess."

"Emily?"

"No, of course, Cole, of course. That's the beauty of the group, the way it just comes together higgledy-piggledy." Emily chewed out that last word, enjoying it. I did, too. "Hell, if you'd told Slater you played bass, even though you don't, you'd probably be playing with us now."

"You know, Emily, it all blows my mind, that you're so into this ... this crazy band. It doesn't seem at all like—"

"Blows your mind, Cole? Ooooh, trippy!" Emily made floppy psychedelic fingers. "You know, Slater *hates* hippies."

"I'm not a hippie." I said this straight out, though back in L.A. when I was fifteen, sixteen, hanging on the Sunset Strip on weekends, the Free Press bookstore, listening to the Beatles, Love, Donovan—well, I *tried* to be a hippie. But that was ten years back, and I was just a high school kid.

"I'm not saying he hates *you*, Cole." A laugh. "He thinks you're great, by the way—in your Cole way, that is."

In my Cole way? What did that mean? And how did we

get onto Slater when I was trying to get at what made Emily Emily?

"But, yeah," Emily said, "who would've thought I'd be in a downtown band with—"

"People who hate hippies."

"Yeah." She giggled. "Hardcore hippie haters!"

"Emily, tell me," a moment later, when we both stopped laughing. "What do your folks expect of you?" I said this softly, seriously. That was the thing with Emily, I still had so little idea where she'd come from.

"What do you mean?"

"I'm just curious, you know, what everyone *did* expect of you. Was it working in publishing? Getting married? Harper Hart? I can't believe they thought you'd end up in a downtown band playing hippie hate mus—"

"What did my fam-i-ly expect?" She interrupted me, her syllables clipped, tight. "Is that what you're—"

"Yes."

For a moment Emily looked at me hard, eyes funneled down, pupils dark.

"Oh, Cole, you have no idea. They ... they wanted the world." A blithe wave of her hand, yet forced. "Nothing less than the whole goddamn world."

I was turning that over, what it could mean, when our food came and we started to eat. With Emily showing up late, we had to get our sandwiches down fast, and we didn't talk much more.

I was paying the hostess when Emily asked, "So have you come up with anything?"

"Come up with—"

"Sailor, *the lyrics*?" Emily angled her chin, a little like a female James Dean in one of those movies, then giggled. It looked like talking about the band cheered her immensely. "Hey, big boy, you *got* anything for us?"

"Um, I don't know." I shifted back and forth. "Not really."

"Which means?" Emily, standing now, distinctly interested.

"Well, I came up with a couple words, but ... but they're not taking me anywhere."

"What are they?"

"What?" I knew what she was asking but felt suddenly shy about my late-night inspiration.

"The couple words, boyo." We were heading out of the restaurant, Emily walking backward to keep talking to me. Yes, walking backward. As always, she moved with grace.

"Oh, um, *savage* and *joy*."

"*Savage joy?*"

"Yep."

Emily stopped a second, puckered her lips, let the two words settle there.

I waited for as long as I could stand it, then said, "What do you—"

"Very interesting." A quick nod. "I like 'em. They've got a ... a lot of *feel* to them."

"They pretty much just popped into my head last night," I said, speaking maybe too quickly, the way you do when somebody unexpectedly praises your work. We were outside the restaurant now, facing each other. "I sat there all morning and, well, I don't have anything else yet, like I said, but they—"

"Savage joy, eh?" The way Emily said it, the two words immediately sounded better to my ears, sexier. "The more I think about them, the more I—"

"There's something there?"

"They seem to capture what we're doing." She nodded. "I mean, I don't know if I could explain it, but it just feels like what the band is about."

"You think Sailor and Slater will—"

"Yeah, I do, I do. *Savage joy*. There's definitely something there, Cole." She clapped her hands. "Bravo! Good job."

I did a cheery thank-you ditz with my head. We were standing on East 37th Street, midtown New York hustling by.

"Sailor's coming over tonight, she's going to—"

"Sailor's coming to your *apartment*?" Emily looked startled.

"Yeah, her idea. She wants to—"

"Really?" Emily took a step back, almost crashing into a gray-suited businessman rushing past.

"Excuse *me*!" he threw over his shoulder.

I reached out to steady Emily. This was strange, from backward-prancing grace inside Mary Elizabeth's to lurching about on the sidewalk.

"Yeah, Sailor wants me to show her what I have." I lifted my hands in faint frustration. "Maybe I can get something more going at work this afternoon." I shrugged. "You know, except for that stupid blind-Indian copy, I probably won't be doing much of any—"

"Right," Emily said, slipping away from my steadying hand. She was back in full self-possession again, no doubt: tough, focused Emily. "So, Cole, hey, you'll say hel-lo to Sail-or for me, *won't you*?"

# 13

SAILOR HADN'T SET a time, but I'd cooked spaghetti for dinner and made sure I had enough for two just in case. Tossed up a nice salad, too, and opened a bottle of red wine.

I waited till about 7:30, when I got so hungry I ate half the pasta. The buzzer by my door went off just as I was finishing up.

"Are you hungry?" I said when I let Sailor in. She wore a red-purple blouse, tight black jeans. She looked rock and roll, but also stylish. The top played nicely off her sleek brass-copper bob. She also carried a small, white paper bag next to her purse.

Sailor hadn't yet been to my place, and I saw a thin smile on her lips as she walked past the door right into my tiny bedroom. Good thing I'd made a point of making my bed up crisp as I could.

"Oh, you're eating—"

"It was … well, I didn't know when you'd come, but I thought … it's just spaghetti, but I made enough for you, too."

"That's so sweet, Cole!" We were through the bathtub-in-the-kitchen and into my third room. I had a table right by the open window between the kitchen and the far room. (Yes, there was a huge, framed glass window in the middle of my apartment. I'd learned it was part of the 1901 Tenement New Law, passed right before my building was built, mandating a window in *every* room—hence this ridiculous indoor window.)

"I'm not sure you'll like what I cooked, it's just—"

"Oh, I know it'll be great." Sailor took a seat at my table. "Oh, look, wine, too."

"It's nothing special, but—"

"Hey, this is a total treat. I was driving a day shift today, got off an hour early, and came here as soon as I could. I would've called but I don't have your phone number."

"I'll give it to you," I said. I dished up a plate of the red-sauced pasta, put the salad in a bowl, and passed them both to Sailor through the open window from the kitchen.

"How elegant!" Sailor giggled. "I've never been served through an open window before."

"Only the best here on East 11$^{th}$ Street."

"Yeah, it's better than my place," she said through a bite of pasta. "Oh, it's good! I didn't know you could cook, Cole."

"Well, just a few things, but I get by. It's great there's the Korean greengrocer right around the corner, love picking up fresh whatever I'll make for dinner on my way home. Could never do that in California."

"Got it." Sailor kept eating the spaghetti, sipping the wine. I came around and took the seat across from her.

"If you still have an appetite when you're done, I can go get us a couple cannolis from downstairs at Veneiro's."

"That's a great idea, except that—" And she held out the paper sack.

Inside? Two cannolis—the white cream ones I liked best.

"You're O.K. with the plain ones, not the choco—"

"*Absolument!*" I shot out. Sailor smiled with her eyes. "The white ones are my favorites."

"Mine, too. We can get to them soon as I finish your wonderful pasta."

"Wonderful?"

"Anchovies?" Sailor lifted her fine nose, sniffed comically.

"Yeah," I admitted, wincing. "Buried deep in the sauce, though. You're not supposed to—"

"But I *love* anchovies!" Her eyes lit up. "I come from generations of anchovy eaters."

"Well, I made it all thinking of you," I said deadpan.

We both laughed, and Sailor kept eating. It was nice having her here. She seemed in a true good mood, lighter, airier than I usually thought of her. She wasn't wearing her uptown Miss Prim clothes, but she wasn't in a ripped T-shirt and studded pants, either. She felt like herself, or whatever self I guess I thought she was. No question, though, she looked pretty as ever, her styled red-bronze hair pulled behind her ears, her arcing eyebrows accentuating every smile and laugh.

After her final bite of spaghetti, she got up and went into the kitchen.

"Want me to make some coffee?"

"Sure, but ... well, I only drink tea, and—"

"Oh, tea sounds fine." Sailor was already rummaging through my cabinet. She fired up the burner under my kettle. "Two teas coming right up."

We were mostly through the tea and her delicious cannolis when she said, "This is such a treat, Cole!" She reached out and tapped her wine glass. I started to pour, and she waved me back when it was halfway full. I nodded, then poured myself half a glass, too. "You know, I thought I was just coming up here to hear some ... some po-e-try."

"Ah, that."

"Yes?" She lifted one of those well-plucked eyebrows.

"Harder than I thought." I forced a grimace, you know, the artistic burden and all.

"You don't have—"

"I have a title," I said. I made a moue. "Just two words."

"Well, let's hear 'em." Sailor lifted her wine glass as if making a toast.

"I don't know if they'll hold up to that level of—"

"Oh, come on, Cole, come on!" And she threw a saucy smile at me.

The thing was, right then I was suddenly freaked over sharing my writing with Sailor. Being a writer, that boundless pool of uncertainty, despair was always swirling below; you never knew when you'd catch a singularly vertiginous glimpse. Even with her enthusiasm—maybe because of it—my confidence was swirling down into that dark pool. I swallowed, saw her expectation, then blurted out: "Um, Emily liked what I came up with."

"Emily?" Sharp surprise.

"I had lunch with her today. We have lunch almost every week, and, yeah, I told her about the project."

"Emily, eh?" Sailor held her wine glass before her, looking over it at me intently. "And what did Em-i-ly say?" She broke her name in just that way, syllable by syllable.

This is the first time I'd known there was any bad feeling between Sailor and Emily, and I didn't know how to take it. It went to band dynamics, didn't it? And what did I understand about that?

"I think she liked it." But it was true: The air in the room had turned, just like that. "Like I said."

"O.K." Sailor said. I was half expecting her to say, *Well, then I'm sure I will, too*, but that's all I got, that clipped *O.K.*

We hung silent. I went to pour more wine but the bottle was empty. Sailor looked at the empty bottle noncommittally. I quickly got up and pulled a full one from my shelf, then twisted it open with my corkscrew. I held the bottle out over Sailor's glass, and she gave me a quick nod. This time I had her glass filled to the top before she made a cut-off gesture with her hand.

"So, Emily. Emily, Emily, Emily." Sailor said this while pulling long on her wine. I figured she was thinking about her and Slater's band again, but she surprised me. "Cole, what *about* you and Emily?"

"Me and—"

"Yeah, Emily." A shake of her hair. "You know, I'm just curious."

Sailor was looking at me almost cockeyed, and I wasn't sure how to respond or even what she was asking. I ran with: "Well, we've known each other almost since I moved here, we have lunch regularly, like I said, we're both in publishing, and—"

"Come on, Cole." The wine was in Sailor's eyes now, winking, provocative.

"I don't—"

"Oh, Cole, I've *seen* you around her." A deep nod, maybe more than a little tipsy. "And I *know* you adore her. You're like a ... like a puppy following Emily around." Sailor shook her shoulders side to side like a shambling animal.

"You think I'm ... I'm like a puppy?" My eyebrows went up in mock alarm, a silent comedian, mostly to buy time. "Hey, come on—"

"Cole?"

Good God, was I that obvious? I let out a sigh.

"So here's what I want to know, big boy." Again, saucy eyes. It looked as if Sailor was starting to have fun here, but I wasn't certain, and I didn't know why. "One question: What've you *done* about it?"

"What have I—" That was me, huh, a broken record just answering Sailor with the words she'd just used.

"You know."

How to answer this? What exactly was Sailor asking? Did she want to know if I'd told Emily how I felt about her? Confessed abiding love like out of some old movie? Or....

"I don't think there's anything *to do*."

"What do you mean?" Sailor leaned in, interested.

"Well, if ... if the way you say I feel about her is *that* obvious ... and I'm not saying it is, you know, but ... I mean, how could Emily not know, and—"

"Jesus, Cole, are you *that* clueless?" Sailor loud, direct. "Don't you understand women at all?" She fixed me with the most intense gaze. "You have to go *after* them! Sometimes you just have to get up and grab the girl!"

I took in a long breath. Of course you did. I knew that. But ... with Emily, it was just ... it wasn't going to happen. Unless it did. You don't grab the girl unless on some basic level you feel she *wants* to be grabbed. When that vibe came from Emily, I was sure I'd know. But I didn't know then. I'd never felt that. I had no blinkin' idea.

But how to say this to Sailor? There was no way. I hardly knew her. Sure, she could read me like the proverbial book—yeah, some children's book I'd never write, *Heartsick Cole*—but there was no way to actually talk further with her about *that*.

So I didn't. I changed the subject.

"You've, what, lost all interest in my song title?"

"Oh." Sailor kept the sharp look in her eyes. "Yeah, I almost forgot." She folded her arms over her breasts, leaned forward. "So, try me."

"*Savage Joy*," I said, quickly. "Just those two words, they're all I have, but—"

"They're brilliant!" she said before I could finish.

"You think?"

"Yeah, yeah. They capture the whole damn thing." She spoke with unexpected enthusiasm. "Savage ... joy. Right. Yes, that's it, that's just what we're after."

"So you—"

"I think it's gonna work perfectly, Cole."

Sailor sat beaming, and I felt terrific. Any writer loves his work, even two stinkin' words, to be appreciated; and even if a writer blushes and pooh-poohs, praise goes right to the heart, the same path that the best writing flows from.

I didn't say anything. But I was feeling things I didn't expect, feeling a lot of things. Sailor, that name I couldn't quite get my brain around, her tough-girl-pounding-the-drums persona, her early-movie-star hair, her job as a taxi driver, the way she'd blithely quoted James Joyce, how she was Slater's friend....

Yet *my* friend now. The way she'd torn into my pasta, and how she'd been thoughtful enough to buy two cannolis, the ones we both liked. The way kindness radiated off her. How when I mentioned Emily she jumped, surprised. Then the way she'd pushed me about Emily, as if she cared about me—my happiness.

Yes, I sat there, wine in my hand, and looked hard at Sailor (as she looked hard back at me), her tight burnished bob, perfectly drawn blood-red lips, and dimples ... look, Sailor had dimples, right up at the corner of her mouth, crinkling, adorable—

Loud knocking at my door. The metal door always rang kind of hollow, more of a thump than a rap, but it was steady and unavoidable. Somebody was there.

"Are you expecting anybody?" Sailor said, annoyed, as I got up to see who it was.

"No, no," I said back to her. "Not a soul."

I pulled the door open. It was Emily.

She looked in and said, "Oh, Cole, you've got com-pa-ny." A small wave. "Is that Sailor? Hey, Sailor."

"Hey, Emily."

"So what's up?" I leaned toward her, smelled her potent perfume, citrusy but musky, too, one I'd found on her a few times before; and as with the other times, the flagrant aroma went straight to my body. Emily's fine blonde hair, always like spun light, her easy, elegant way ... and now the heady scent swirling around her. Maybe I *was* a puppy, but I couldn't help myself. Just then I focused only on her.

"Oh, nothing." Emily shrugged her shoulders. "Just wanted to see if you were home and—"

"Because?" I did have some sense left and wanted to know.

Emily gave her head a blithe shake, tilted her beautiful head to the side.

"Just being neighborly."

Nobody said a word for a long moment, then Sailor came up beside me and said, "So, um, Cole, thanks for the spaghetti." She looked from Emily to me, then added, "And everything else."

The thing was, as soon as Sailor took off, Emily and her rampant perfume were gone, too.

# 14

*S*AVAGE JOY. I still didn't have a song, but the way it played out, the band had a name.

Slater loved Savage Joy, Emily loved it, and you know what Sailor thought. She lobbied for my two words, though when Slater decided to call the band Savage Joy, it immediately became *his* idea. He licked his lips, let out that curdled-sweet smile he had, and whispered hard: "What a perfect name we finally got. Pure inspiration." He kissed his fingers. "Savage Fuckin' Joy."

There it was, scribbled on the blackboard outside CBGBs a week later.

And there I was, too.

It was a Friday night, the band—O.K., Savage Joy—was moving up in the world. Not only a weekend night but a prime slot, 10:40. They were following a band called Talking Heads. Emily had heard of them and said they were great. An artsy deal from Rhode Island with a lot of amazing ideas. She was a little worried about following them.

"But you've been rehearsing," I said out on Bowery before we went in. Through the doors I could hear these Talking Heads: rhythmic funk with a high-pitched guy singing apparently senseless words.

Emily swatted at me but smiled. She looked nervous, though. The beat through the club doors was strong, and both our feet were tapping to it, our shoulders shaking.

"Where's Slater?" I said.

"Making me worried, that's what." Emily checked her watch, and I followed her gaze: 10:10.

"I'm sure there's plenty of time."

"Right." Emily started pacing, and I had to turn right, then left to keep up with her.

We were deep into September now, and I still had that odd feeling of not going back to school. I had liked school, at least college. Nothing to do but read books and be existentially lonely and miserable. Working at *The New Yorker* felt a lot like being in college, though better: The people you studied in school actually walked the halls of West 43rd Street ... and I got paid.

Anyway, Emily was still stomping back and forth, wearing this thin white-cotton skirt, as thin as a slip, that snapped when she spun. She had on heavy black engineer boots like Slater's, which couldn't have been less Emily.

I was looking away from her when I heard her blurt out, "Holy shit!"

I turned, expecting to see something like Slater limping up on crutches again. Instead I saw a tall, brown-haired guy in a pink polo shirt, a tiny dangling lamb as its chest insignia.

"What're *you* doing here?" Emily jutted her head forward, staring at this guy. He looked familiar. "Jesus Christ!"

Oh, right. Harper Hart, her rich Gramercy Park boyfriend.

"You're not returning my phone calls," Harper said.

"What're you talking about?" Emily said huffily. "What phone calls?"

"I keep leaving messages, and——

"Oh, didn't I tell you, my answering machine's on the blink." Emily shrugged. "But I don't know why you never got me. Didn't you call work?"

"You told me not to call you at the publishing house."

"And you *listened* to me?" Emily shot *me* a look, amused, disdainful, which I wasn't sure how to take. Then she walked right up to Harper. "That still doesn't explain what you're doing here? I mean, how did you know I'd even *be* here?"

Harper didn't answer, just looked angry, lips tight, sharp chin jutted out.

Emily stepped back, then looked up and down Bowery. "Where the fuck is Slater?"

"Emily—"

"Listen, I don't know what you want, Harper, but this is *not* the time for it. I have ... I'm going onstage in fifteen minutes."

"I know, but I've been worried."

"Worried?" Emily shot up an eyebrow. "Did I ever ask you to be worried about me?"

"Actually," Harper said, "you did. One night when you were over at my mother's and—"

Emily gave her blonde hair a quick shake, as if she were trying to toss away a bug landed on her head.

"Listen, Har-per, this is not the place or the time." She shot another glance up the street. "I ... I've got things to do."

"That doesn't make me any less wor—"

"Hey, babe." Emily and I both turned, and there was Slater. He was in his usual torn wife-beater, greasy black pants, and slapdash leather coat. His bowl of blond hair fell to his eyeballs. Where the holes in his T-shirt were too big, safety pins held them together. "You ready?"

"Let's kill it." Emily barked this out, then spun swiftly on her heels and followed Slater into the club.

Harper Hart stood there, mouth slack, eyes like hot coals. Emily and Slater were inside the club when Harper started after them.

"Harper," I said firmly, throwing my arm in front of him.

He stopped, looked hard at me as if trying to figure out who I was. Then a small light dawned.

"Oh, you're Cole." He nodded. "I guess I remember you. Emily's *friend*."

I heard the sneer in the word but chose to overlook it. The thing was, I felt sympathy for the rich guy, surprising to me. The way Emily had just eviscerated him, I could see the wounds all over him. Emily had never sliced me up like that, her cuts were the proverbial thousand small ones that came with just that: my being only her friend. I knew she could hurt, and I saw the hurt on this tall, patrician fellow standing next to me.

"I don't think there's anything you can do," I said to Hart. "Emily's pretty willful."

"Willful?" He snorted. "I'll say."

"So she's ducking you? Like really a-void-ing you?" Punching each syllable. My comment was pretty in his face. Though I felt some empathy, I still didn't like him.

Harper looked hard at me, then said, "Yeah." He gave me a privileged-guy lifted chin. "I don't know what's going on." His eyes narrowed. "Do you know, Collllle?"

He drew my name out as if it were something sticky on the bottom of his shoe.

"I haven't seen much of her either." I shrugged.

"It's this fucking band." Harper spit this out, then threw a look of contempt at the door of CBGBs. "It's ... it's polluting her."

I had nothing to say to that and was getting tired of him anyway, so I just gave him a head tip and went into the club.

The Talking Heads were wrapping up. They played a song with the words "psycho killer" over and over, with a strong *fa-fa-fa-fa* scat over it. A tall beanpole was at the front, jutting and jabbing his head into the mike; next to him stood a blonde bass player. She looked a little like Emily, just not as pretty, her hair shorter, chin blockier. Still, a chick in a band ... so Emily and Sailor weren't total anomalies in this dude-rich downtown rock world.

*Psycho Killer* ended the set, and then Savage Joy set up.

It was the same as before, Sailor behind her drums, all in black, her brass-red hair flaming, mysterious and witchy; Chet from Queens stolid on bass; Wendell Walter in his Eddie Haskell clothes and long Jesus belt, skinnier than I'd ever seen him, as if he hadn't eaten in a week; and finally Slater, fired-up, furious for no good reason, rat-intense moving up and almost chewing the mike.

"We're Savage Joy," he shouted into the mike, "and you the fuck ain't!" He spun, threw a finger at Sailor, and *wham! wham! wham!* the band was off.

They were tighter than before, and Emily ... well, she wasn't just the girl looking pretty and occasionally warbling into the mike. She had real presence now, standing shoulder to shoulder with Slater, and mimicking him scream for scream. Her mouth twisted thin and wicked, her eyes glowed with fire; it was all wildly a turn-on.

Savage Joy was louder than they'd been last time, and far more crazily audacious. Chet had a big boot stomp that fit his thudding bass playing. Wendell looked a little abstracted, almost a scholar of chords, yet when the music churned, he whipped his thin body in sync with Slater. And Slater! He prowled the stage, animal light on his feet, whirled his body, scrawed out wicked syllables, turned out his soul like a reversible coat. Savage Joy was a frenzy up there on the tiny wedged stage, and throughout it all, Emily tossed her head back, shook her corona of blondeness, stomped her heavy black boots, and spun along amidst the furious storm.

This was *not* the demure Farrar Straus girl who lunched with me at Mary Elizabeth's and traded stories about Susan Sontag. *This* was a woman I'd never before seen.

Savage Joy powered through the first song, words still pretty unintelligible, though the title seemed to be *Buzzer Buzzer*, at least those were the words that came hissing out of the stage frenzy.

For the next tune, Emily stepped up to Slater's mike to share it. His face, sleek and grave, warmed as she stood inches from him. It was hot in the club, and sweat poured down both their faces. As the bass and drums launched the song, Slater let out a slim, sly smile.

I heard words in my ear, turned and found Harper Hart. I

was startled, didn't think he'd dare go into CBGBs. But there he was.

"He's fucking her," he said. At least that's what I think he said. It was partly the sounds, partly reading his lips, partly the belligerent glare thrown at the stage. "I know that punk's goddamn fucking her."

His words sent a hot spar of dismay and jealousy down my spine.

But Harper wasn't there to talk to me. We were about fifteen feet from the stage, the howling music hitting us like a harsh wind, but Harper pushed through it. Fans were packed tight, but he just moved people aside and scrambled to the lip of the stage.

I couldn't hear what he was saying—more like shouting, head back, hands cupped around his mouth—but he was clearly aiming his words straight at Emily and Slater.

They paid him no mind, crying together into the one silver microphone.

As before, it was hard to make out lyrics, though this song had a chorus, or at least a repetition, of the words "The eyes of a killer." A lightning storm of a song, phrases like "he handled snakes" and "his hand in the small of my back" cracking through the room over Sailor's steady, ominous beat.

Then the song got quiet... eerily quiet. Just Sailor's rumble tumble, no other instruments, and Emily sang:

*I like to tease the edge*
*Set my senses bewildered*
*But that man I let into my bed*
*He looks at me ... with the eyes of a killer*

When she sang the final line, she looked right at Slater, then kissed him, full on the mouth.

Harper cried out, "You goddamn pussy!" straight at Slater.

Slater tried to stay in character, the guy this beautiful blonde chick was coming on to in the most lewd way, but when Harper went on with, "You're nothing but a goddamn loser. A freaking punk!" Slater's eyes sparked with fury.

A second later the singer threw himself off the stage right onto Harper.

Harper had nearly a foot on Slater, but Slater fell on him at an angle that pushed him to the ground, Slater on top of him. People close to the fight moved back a step; I could see through the angles of their bodies. There were Slater's fists, churning. That was the thing, my neighbor could go from zero to a hundred faster than anyone. He was at full speed now.

Harper didn't have a chance. Maybe he'd wrestled in prep school, played lacrosse in college, but the way Slater went at him, it was a junkyard dog bit through his chain and mouth-foaming out of control.

Over and over Slater slugged him, knuckles hard to Harper's face. I expected someone in the crowd to intervene but oddly no one did. I pushed bodies aside to get to the two of them, hoping I could help; but with the minute or so it took me, I found Harper curled into a ball on the floor of the club, his hands pulled over his head as Slater kept whaling on him.

Blood flowed from Harper's nose, sprinkled over his clean shirt. A cut to his forehead, another to his chin.

When I finally got to the two of them, a skinny guy was trying to pull Slater up. I joined in, grabbing his other arm; and though his attack never wavered, finally we were able to get Slater off Harper and pin back his fists.

My senses were all flung about, but I realized that even through the fight Sailor and the band had kept playing.

Emily was on the edge of the stage, her hair wet and matted, makeup streaking. She leaned down, pointed at Harper, and clearly said, "I never want to see you again, you shithead."

Slater was calmer in my and the other guy's grip. At Emily's words he turned to me and gave me his usual unruffled wink. Then he got up on the stage and went right back into *Eyes of a Killer*.

I was queasy. I really didn't want to be there. The violence had shaken me, I wasn't used to it, but everything else—what *was* going on with Emily and Slater?—kept churning inside me; so when the crowd turned back to watch Savage Joy, I bent down and offered Harper a hand.

"I'm gonna murder the asshole," he hissed at me, though with tired eyes and little conviction. It was bluster. Harper looked whipped.

"Come on," I said, half pushing him through the tight crowd and out of the club onto the Bowery.

"This is totally messed-up," Harper said as we stood on the sidewalk. He kept daubing at his nose and face but it looked as if the blood rush had stopped. His shirt, though, remained streaked, an unearthly copper-brown under the sodium streetlights.

There was quite a crowd milling about, waiting to get in. A quick thought: Had they been queuing to see Savage Joy? I looked at the chalkboard and saw that after Savage Joy was the Klitz ... right, that group from the first time I'd been at CBGBs, fronted by Slater's exotically dressed pal, Cherry. I had no idea which group was more popular, but somebody was sure bringing the people out. There was a lot going on here I didn't get at all.

"Come on," I said to Harper, "let's get coffee or something."

He looked at me with a flash of disdain, as if he didn't believe I'd actually suggested this, but then his shoulders sagged and he nodded in agreement.

We ended up at DeRobertis, the way-old Italian pastry shop around the corner from me on First Avenue. The tile floor buckled, the tin-plate white ceiling bowed. I loved the place, as close to *Godfather* New York as you could get. Plus the pastries were better than Veneiro's.

I got a cannoli and a tea, Harper just a cappuccino—"I'll probably be up all night anyway," he muttered—and when our order came, I asked him what was going on.

"He's balling her," he said, this time right at me, another lance to my chest. I swallowed the pain. I wanted to know what he knew about Emily.

"Slater?" I got out.

"Is that his name?" Harper tried to bare his teeth, but he was too well-bred and just looked toothy. I also couldn't take my eyes off his nose, swollen and turning blue. He grimaced now and then, but the old college lacrosse dude came out and he shook off any tremor of pain. "The little guttersnipe."

"They are in the band together."

"Yeah, and that's why she's spending all her time with him? And why she's turned on *me*?" He said the last sentence with a lift of effrontery: How could any girl deny Harper Hart?

"I don't know what's going on." I looked down at my cannoli, breaking the pastry tube with a nice crack. I didn't want Harper to hear anything too eager in my voice. "But Emily seems to be so differ—"

"It's like he's in her head." Harper scraped his teeth. "Got some power over her."

"Why do you say that?"

"Can't you see it, Cole?"

"I'm not sure," I said. "I know she dresses different, but that could be only for the band. You know, she used to be into music, she told me, though I guess Yale Glee wasn't this kind of deal." This sounded pretty stupid, didn't it? Harper shot me a look of contempt. "Still, maybe all this is just a harmless new thing she's gotten in—"

"No, no, it's deeper, like on a cellular level." His mouth formed an O beneath his bruised nose.

"And this isn't just because she's dumping you?"

Harper threw his head back as if I'd roundhoused him, this time when he wasn't looking. I felt a little bad but not much. He was such a dick, I figured he had it coming.

"I don't believe Emily is 'dumping me.'" He made air quotes. "I think she's under that punk's sway—"

"What, like he's Charles Manson?"

Harper didn't answer this, just glared.

"So what else?" I said. "What have you noticed?"

"She's just ... just distant."

"Because she's not into you?"

"Cole, will you stop that!"

"I just want to—"

"It's like she's changed, on a body level, but her spirit, too ... like she's another person. Doesn't focus the same, doesn't—"

"Hmnnn," I went. In truth I'd noticed that, too, like lately she was with you but also somewhere else.

"Yeah," he said, sipping his cappuccino.

"So what does it mean?"

"Your punk pal's bewitched her." Harper kept glaring at me, like it was my fault. "Clear as that."

I shook my head. Harper could think that all he wanted, but knowing Slater and Emily, I knew it was nonsense. Emily *was* willful. I didn't believe she did anything she wasn't into with all her body and soul.

I suddenly got very tired of Harper. I hadn't finished my cannoli but got up anyway, threw money on the table, and told him to take care with his nose.

Then I walked across First Avenue and climbed the five flights to my apartment.

I was still awake hours later, watching the late show, an old Preston Sturges flick, *Hail the Conquering Hero*, when I heard a knock at my door. It wasn't soft, it wasn't loud, just steady.

I didn't have a peep hole, so opening the door was always a gamble, though I don't recall ever not at least pulling it back a crack to find out who was there.

It was Emily, flushed, jubilant.

"What're you—"

"Oh, Cole, you won't believe this." She was bouncing on her toes, ballet-light. "It looks like ... well, we may be making a record!"

"*What?*"

"Oh, it's this insane thing. Sire Records—they're like the Farrar Straus of record labels—they were at CBs for that cool band before us, Talking Heads?" She said this with great enthusiasm. I nodded; they'd impressed me, too. "Anyway, the label guy stayed around for our ... for Savage Joy." She threw me a smile. "And, by the way, Cole at least *I* know it was your name." A wink.

"Anyway, the label guy liked us. Said we had a lot of raw energy—I like to think they meant more than Slater beating up that prick Harper." Emily threw back her head, let out a robust laugh. "They liked our sound, too."

"That's amazing!" It was. What, Slater and Emily with a record deal ... after only a handful of shows?

When I said that to her, though, she held up a hand.

"Well, it's not quite a ... record deal, it's—"

"What?"

"They're sending us on the road." She broke out in a huge smile. "Sire's dime, and they'll book the gigs. Want us to get more seasoned, see how well we do in different places."

"You're going to be on a *tour*?"

"That's it! Can you believe it? Slater and I slap Savage Joy together, and a few weeks later we're heading off into the wild blue!"

I couldn't believe it. My head spun with a thousand questions. I got one out.

"What about work?"

"Oh, work?" The thought fazed Emily for a moment, then she shook it off. "Well, I'll just have to talk to Roger on Monday."

"You think they'll—"

"I don't give a shit what they think!"

"So you're doing it?"

"Are you kidding, Cole? Emily Prosser in a punk band! With a near record deal!" She looked at me hard, then lowered her voice and said, "Do you think I should change my name?"

"Change your—"

I was shaking my head when she said, "I don't know." She looked genuinely puzzled. "Prosser—you know, people might find out that I...." She trailed off, swallowed whatever she was thinking. "I mean, Em-i-ly Pross-er, that's not very hardcore, is it?"

"But it's your name."

"You think?" Her eyes went very wide and round then, dilated. I wasn't sure what she was getting at. "I mean, whose name is it really?"

"Yours!" I'm not sure why I was so emphatic about this, but I was.

"Well, things are changing." She gave a deep nod. "I just wanted you to know, Cole. Like right away."

"When do you go?" Though I still had all those questions, the same ones Harper had raised, that was the only one I could get out.

"Soon as we can get it together, boyo. Gotta get a van, though Slater's already on that." Her eyes sparkled. "Probably find one over on the West Side Highway." She laughed. "Just kidding, right?" I looked at her; we both knew she might not be. "Anyway, midweek? Sounds like Sire can get us a show in Philly by then."

"Jesus!"

"You're thrilled, too, right?" Emily looked at me intensely. I wasn't sure why whatever I'd say would matter that much, but it felt like it did.

"I guess—"

*"Cole!"*

"No, it's crazy ... so quick. I don't really...." A wild shiver flew through me, my body nearly shaking. "But, yeah, it's amazing. Good luck. Really, Em, good, good luck."

# 15

EMILY STOPPED BY on Wednesday, dressed in a micro-mini pink skirt, black stockings, and a tight black satin blouse far racier than anything I'd seen her in before. I hadn't seen her since Friday night. Each time I walked past her apartment, it felt truly empty. Maybe she was out of town? Wherever she disappeared to all the time?

The thing was, I hadn't seen Slater or even Wendell either. We were probably just missing each other, but I worried that the band had taken off early. I didn't want to think it, that they'd leave without at least saying farewell. So I was relieved Emily was there in front of me.

"So we're off." She bounced that ballet lift on her toes. "Bags are all packed, we got a rented truck downstairs. Least that's what Slater's saying." She laughed. "No, but, this is for real. Sire's hired us a roadie, guy named Scrap, though Slater says I can drive some."

"You're leaving now?"

"This exact moment, Cole."

"Dressed like that?"

"Hey, I'm in a band, dude!" She let out a joyous laugh.

"What happened with your job?"

"What?" Emily looked puzzled for a moment. "Oh, that."

"Yeah, Farrar Straus and—"

"Roger won't let me take a leave, turns out—at least not for rock and roll—so I quit."

"You left FSG?"

"Sure, why not?"

"Because it's the best publishing house out there."

"Yeah, and they pay shit, and I live in a dump on East 11th—don't take it wrong, Cole—and I'm getting tired of all the pressure there to do something with nothing. You know, they make people bring back *soap* from business trips, they use them in the bathrooms at work."

"But Emily—"

"And I have a chance to make a record."

"But you're not even—"

"And who knows, FSG'll probably take me back if it comes to that. That's the thing with the place. They pay you crap but you're like family." She threw back her hair. "And, you know, Roger's never seen me in my new look!" She shimmied in front of me, her tiny skirt riding up her thighs. She let out a bright laugh. "That can't hurt, you know."

"This is for real?" That just kind of came out of me. Of course this was happening, but part of me had been hardcore denying it. Whatever was going on with Slater and Emily, well, they were going to be in a van and living out of hotel rooms for weeks. Of course, Sailor, Wendell, and Chet would be there, too, along with their roadie, I guess. But still.... "You're going now?"

"Yes, Cole, yes I am." Emily leaned in and kissed me, close to my mouth but really just on my cheek. "Wish me luck!"

I did, of course. When I shut the door, alone in my three-room apartment, I felt hugely emptied out, just hollow and unsure of myself. It wasn't that unusual a feeling, a deeper cousin of my general loneliness those early years in New York, but that didn't make it any the less overwhelming or depressing.

Looking back, I'm pretty sure I soon became classically depressed, if *depressed* means sleeping more than ten hours each night and hardly tasting food. The tenement building, without Emily or even Slater, felt empty. And work ... sure, I still worked at *The New Yorker*, still helped get out the best magazine in the nation each week, but all I was doing was typing letters and stupid Ved Mehta blather about his family, and I was sleepwalking through that.

Not that anybody noticed. I loved the typing pool, but no question it was a backwater at the magazine—hard to see how necessary it even was—and though I tried to keep writing my novel and my stories, my thoughts were desultory and unfocused. I'd find myself on the same page for a few days, then I'd throw it away.

It wasn't a good time, for sure. Just because I was missing Emily? Well, not just her, but Slater and Sailor, and even Wendell, too. I was surprised Savage Joy meant that much to me. I guess I really had fallen into another kind of life, and now it had vanished.

Messages and news from the band? Not for me. Nobody called, nobody wrote. Savage Joy and my friends were simply gone.

You live in a fifth-floor East Village walk-up, you can pretty much judge your mood by how you take the flights of stairs. You fly up 'em, you're in good spirits, soaring high. You trudge one step in front of the other and wonder how anybody can climb more than a story or two ... not so good. Except you have no choice: Your home, your bed, is up those five flights of cracked marble stairs, and any peace you hope for, if it's not there, where is it?

It was a Tuesday after work, I'd bought one more can of Progresso tomato basil soup from the Red Apple supermarket—soup was pretty much all I had the will to cook for myself—and was barely making it to the third floor, paper grocery sack in my hands, when I heard slow, huffy steps behind me.

I turned ... and blew my mind.

What I saw was a girl almost my height, with black hair pulled back in a bow, and a very white face, though I didn't see any makeup. She was wearing frayed jean shorts over black tights, a DISNEY WORLD T-shirt sprouting huge mouse ears, and sockless sneakers with sparkles on them. The girl was lugging two large, olive-green duffel bags, heavy ones, pulling one up a couple steps, then the other, then resting for a moment.

"Do you need any help?" I said.

She looked up at me and smiled.

"I think I do indeed." A lift of her pencil-thin eyebrows. "Do you mind?"

I went down to her and took a bag. It was heavy, but not too much, and I reached over for the other one.

"You can manage both of them?"

"Sure. How high are you going?"

"All the way to the top, I think." She had something written on her hand and she looked down at it. "Sixteen?"

That was my floor and Slater's apartment. I looked at her more closely, almost recognizing her but not quite. It was like I'd seen her before but wasn't quite cer—

"Hi, I'm Cherry."

"Oh!" I got out. Good God, this had to be that singer I'd seen at CBGBs, Cherry Kruntz of the Klitz. I hadn't recognized her, she was so, well, almost normal looking. No fierce cat's-eye makeup, no tight dress or ripped fishnet stockings.

"I'm staying at Slater's place for a while." She looked at me. "Are you Cole?"

"Um, yeah, that's me—"

"Slater said you'd be my neighbor, that I could ask you for an-y-thing." A flash of light in her eyes. "Looks like I don't even have to ask."

"No, ma'am," I got out. I sounded like an idiot kid in a movie, but I was so surprised to see Cherry here, especially looking so everyday.

"You're cute," she said, heading up the stairs. "Come on, let's get me settled."

Getting her settled turned out great. A little unpacking, a quick perusal of Slater's paltry pantry.... Hmnn, name for another band. Paltry Pantry? I mentioned it to Cherry, and she guffawed, a laugh spirited up from her knees all the way through her abundant chest.

But ... nothing in the pantry, and Cherry scribbled out a

list for me to take to the Korean greengrocer on First Ave. She was going to make me spaghetti alla puttanesca, her favorite—neighborly thanks for my help up the stairs. The dish was new to me. She laughed and said she was sure I'd like it. Did I like Fel-li-ni? Um, yeah, the movies of his I'd seen. Another laugh; she was a merry chick. Well, then I was sure to like this. She made it special. Just like Giulietta Masina....

I got the provisions she wanted, including anchovies (sweet deal) and capers, picked up a loaf of bread from the Italian bakery on Ninth Street, and a couple bottles of red wine for good measure.

By the time I got back, Cherry had two tapering candles lit and opera playing on Slater's stereo.

So how'd she do? Damn well. This was the best home-cooked meal I'd eaten in memory, and when we were done, and most of the two bottles of wine gone, I told her that.

"It's always good to have nice neighbors," she said. "You never know, you know."

"New York can be really—"

"You haven't been here long, have you?" Cherry was smoking long Parliament cigarettes, and she flicked an ash in one of Slater's crystal ashtrays.

"Little over a year," I said.

"College?"

"You mean, did I go to college?"

"Of course you *went* to college, Cole," she said, looking at me hard. "I mean, you didn't go in the East, did you? You're not part of a *Let's all move to New York City after Brandeis* thing?"

"Berkeley," I said. "And you're right, I didn't know anybody here. Just a wing and a prayer—"

"You're doing well, though, right? Your own apartment. Good job. Friends in a band that Sire Records is sponsoring."

I nodded.

"It's not easy, ever." Cherry took a long sip of the red wine, then lit up another Parliament. "Maybe for some people, but most of us—" She lowered her eyes, then let a long trail of smoke curl out of her mouth.

"Did you go to Brandeis?" I asked then in the deep silence, after it was becoming uncomfortable.

"Me?" Cherry shook her head in an upward twist. "Oh, no, no, that was just an example."

"O.K."

"You want to know where I went to college, don't you?" Her eyes were little more than slits. "Everyone always does."

"Not if you don't want to—" In truth, I didn't care all that much. This where-you-went-to-college thing was a big East Coast deal, and of course everyone had at least heard of Berkeley, but I always had the feeling my school was taken as a little exotic if not suspicious.

"Well, I have various stories that work damn well." She lifted her petite nose. "Which one do you want?"

"I'm good with the truth." I raised my glass of wine.

"Oh, the truth?" Cherry shook her head. "I don't think so."

"Really?"

"*Really?*" She said mimicking me. There was edge to how she said this, which I didn't get. What was so weird about wanting the truth?

Well, something was wrong, because Cherry didn't say anything more, just took in her wine. I sipped mine, silent. The thing was, Cherry was really pretty, with her delicate chin, thin but large mouth, and that midnight hair. This wasn't the first time since I'd bumped into her that I had a desire to sleep with her, just that at that moment my ardor was strongest.

She got up then to take the dishes to the sink, and I took her arm, turned her gently to me.

"Well, well," she said. She was standing, and I was sitting, and she had the Parliament burning in her mouth and her hands full of our dishes.

Still, somehow I managed it. The dishes went back on

the table, the cigarette solid in the ashtray, and Cherry on my lap.

"That was delicious," I said softly, "your spaghetti."

"I know."

Of course she knew. She also knew I was about to kiss her, and I'm sure she also knew exactly what she'd do when I did.

Which I did, and she did. Rock and roll? Is it too indiscreet to say she was even better at it here than at CBGBs?

The next morning I offered her the use of my bathroom, since it was actually in my apartment and more private; but Cherry declined, saying she was renting Slater's place and had to get used to the toilet in the hallway. She made it clear she'd seen much worse. And a lot better, too.

*****

MY MOTHER ONCE said to me, "Cole, I only have two promises I want from you growing up."

We were in the car, heading to Penney's for back-to-school clothes. This sounded serious, and I looked over at her as she drove. I was fourteen or fifteen.

"Just two things. That you graduate from college, and that you *never* get a tattoo."

Now that I look back on it, that doesn't seem like much. Not: We *insist* on law school or med school; if you earn less than half a million bucks you're a disappointment; how about at least six children?; oh, and make sure you can support me and your father in our old age. These were two expectations I was happy to live up to, and have.

The tattoos, though. I assume at the time that Mom voiced the expectation only sailors, carny layabouts, and degenerates had tats. Ink on your body? A one-way ticket to loserville.

What would Mom have thought about Cherry? She had tats everywhere, princesses and trolls, purple mountains and golden plains, and superheroes tucked in here and there: Wonder Woman, Spider-Man, Black Widow.

Ah, Cherry Kruntz, *my* Wonder Woman that early fall, my woman of wonders.

I only had two questions: Did I have a new girlfriend? And, did I even want a new girlfriend?

Either way, it didn't seem to matter. I didn't see that much of Cherry. She was out most evenings when I got home, and sometimes all night, well as I could tell. I knocked on her door a few times but got no answer, and after that I thought I should wait till I bumped into her.

Which I did five days later. I passed her in the hall on my way to the Koreans' for dinner provisions. Cherry brightened, asked if she could come over and watch the tube later.

"I'm missing it," she said, shrugging. "Slater doesn't own a TV."

"Too cool, I guess."

"Too something," Cherry said, giving me a pursed-lips look that I couldn't read.

I told her I'd be home all night and to come over whenever she wished. We watched *Barney Miller* on ABC, at least started to watch it. We didn't make it to the first commercial.

This time Cherry spent the night at my place. When she fell asleep I traced out the visible tattoos in the moonlight through my fifth-floor window. I imagined myself a drunken sailor on leave in Manila, a biker with downtime in the Mojave desert. I looked at Wonder Woman, stretched out down Cherry's left shoulder, and imagined bringing her home to my folks in California. I fell asleep embracing that dizzying, heartening, apple-cart-overturning notion.

In the morning Cherry used my in-the-apartment toilet, such luxury. She combed out her raven hair in the mirror above my sink.

"Can I—"

"Yes?" she said, turning. She wasn't wearing anything, and faced me with delightful naturalness, breasts high, inky tats abloom.

"I was just wondering how I can—"

"What, Cole, you want a *proper* date?"

I shook my head. That wasn't what I was about to ask, but no matter.

"Um, I ... yes," I said, "I'd love a real date."

"Flowers?" She brightened.

"Sure," I said right away. I had never been a flowers kind of guy, but in New York I was becoming a different man nearly every week. I sure as hell hadn't been a sleep-with-the–Tattooed Lady guy either.

"Sunday night? Pick me up at seven?"

"I like that, pick you up," I said. "Should I send up my chauffeur or is knocking on your door enough?"

"Ei-ther." A quick smile. "Either would be sweet." Her hair seemed to tangle easily, and she was really tugging at it with my hairbrush. "So, what should we do on our ... date?"

"I'll come up with something," I said quickly.

"A surprise?"

"Yep."

A long pause, then, "I used to *love* surprises. These days, well, I get a surprise, it's not usually all that good." She faced me, her steady breasts, her tightly curled dark pubic hair, the green-black ink slinking over her pale skin. "You'll make sure it'll be a *good* surprise, right, Cole?"

"Scout's honor," I said, then swallowed hard. Jesus, *Scout's honor*? Where did that come from?

But what I said made Cherry laugh ... nothing but gold.

\* \* \* \* \*

I WAS STILL missing my friends on the road bad. I wanted to talk to Emily, to Sailor, even to Slater to find out how things were going. All I knew was that they'd headed down to Philly; I didn't even have an itinerary for the rest of the tour and didn't know how to get one. Call up Sire Records and try to find somebody to ask? They might not even know. It was probably just the guy who'd seen them and his secretary, and how could I find them?

Was Savage Joy killing it? What was it like playing Lower Manhattan music in, say, Washington, D.C., Raleigh, Virginia, Pittsburgh, Pa., wherever they were being sent? Were they getting better each night, or worse? How was Wendell holding up on guitar? Any churches he could make it to to keep his faith going? Weeks on the road playing rock and roll, did he still *have* faith?

And what about Emily and Slater? Even with Cherry, that was a huge raw thing. I'd tried my best to throw Harper Hart's aspersions out of my head, but you can't do that, can you? Once you've heard something you can't *un*-hear it. And … long sigh … the more I thought about the two of them, the more angry and dispirited I became.

I threw myself into work. I started writing again. I was working on that first novel, *Negative Space*. Peter, my hero, wakes up in Los Angeles one day deciding the city is killing him and that he has to get out. Thirty-six bucks to his name, so he has to hitchhike … and that's what he does, till it turns out there is no way out of the city. Every ride curls back on itself, every apparent clear line away turns into a maze, every positive hope is inverted. *Negative Space* … where Peter learns minute by minute just how trapped he is.

The writing was slow going. I didn't know how to write a novel, and began to understand that the only way to learn how to write one was to do it, with all the mistakes, false directions, and mazelike traps included. So I plugged away, a page, half a page, maybe on a good day a couple, every morning at home before I had to race to the subway for my job.

At my desk at *The New Yorker*, as before, I worked on short stories and poems. They were pouring out again, maybe thanks to Cherry? I didn't worry that too much, just kept hitting the keys.

The thing with *The New Yorker* typing pool was that we

were just that, a little pond on the edge of the property where the fauna and flora could grow and be amusing and have very little to do with the big house of the actual magazine. We typed the magazine's letters and Our Daily Ved and the occasional Andy Logan column ... and each week somebody put together a new issue that landed on our desks. Who actually did the work? Well, it was probably everybody else on the 18$^{th}$, 19$^{th}$, and 20$^{th}$ floors ... just not us.

The essence of our job kept us pretty cut off from serious office business and politics, which made it all the more of a surprise when I found out there was a strong move afoot to form a union, that it had been brewing for a few years and was getting serious right around the time I started there.

I was making $90 a week when I got hired, which sounds like nothing (and was nothing), but since New York City was emptied out because of the financial crisis—yeah, that infamous headline: FORD TO CITY: DROP DEAD!—I was only paying $90 a month for my East Village railroad flat. I wasn't in too bad shape.

The way it seemed, *The New Yorker* had always been staffed mostly by trust-fund kids, so money wasn't much of an issue, but now it was. Maybe I wasn't the only one actually living not only on the honor of working at the Greatest Magazine in the World but actually paying rent from it; or maybe it was just a simple issue of fairness. Everything in New York was so new to me and I was trying to figure out this union business as it went along.

One thing for sure: The move to unionize an establishment as singular as *The New Yorker* was serious; for our editor, William Shawn, as serious as the proverbial heart attack (which, thank God, he didn't get stricken with during it all). Mr. Shawn, the Iron Mouse, who not only walked silently down the halls but projected a cone of silence affecting anyone within at least twenty-five feet.

"Hello, Mr. Shawn," I'd whisper, using his own voice; not purposefully, that's just how it came out.

"Hello, Mr. Whitman." Back at me in the same whisper, just fiercer.

And it wasn't only me, it was anyone anywhere near him. *Everybody* whispered around Mr. Shawn. His force field, a low electrical thrum, was surprisingly intense and immense.

Shawn controlled everything; contracts, deals, relationships were secret. Did he have favorites among the writers? My guess is he had nothing but favorites, and that each writer there probably felt he was the most favorite … at least at that moment, and till his or her contract was not renewed.

A crazy, hard-to-imagine idea: I'm a *New Yorker* staff writer but no longer want to be one! Did any of the writers ever feel that? I don't know. But if you did, well, the way you got paid was, you had what was called a drawing account, which meant that whether your pieces got published or not—whether you even deigned to write anything—you'd get a biweekly check to keep you going. Any work actually printed in the magazine would offset the drawing account.

Who was prolific enough *not* to owe the magazine a fortune? Maybe some of the regular columnists like Brendan Gill, Pauline Kael, Andy Logan. But your "of course I take five years to make my prose perfect enough for William Shawn" writer, well, that guy showed up at the company store every day wondering how deep in debt his body and soul remained.

This was pure control, subtle and ideal. Somehow it worked. Those were fat issues back then, accounts begging to advertise in *The New Yorker*. So everything, all power and discretion, every word in the magazine and the lives of those who worked for it, flowed from one man, William Shawn.

And now his staff wanted to form a union.

Did Shawn's heart pitch and reel, blood stammer to his throat? Hard to imagine it didn't.

What the hardworking staff saw as fair and reasonable (and essential toward buying food at Red Apple) was to William Shawn and others a threat to the magazine's very soul.

Still, everything stayed mostly quiet. I remember being surprised the day after Cherry spent the night to be invited to a meeting at a West Village apartment; I hadn't known any of the organizing was going on.

I was also deep, deep into my whole fairy-tale head where Cole Whitman from suburban Podunk L.A. was actually working at ... *The New Yorker* magazine.

So I was very appreciative when at the meeting Dusty, one of the fact-checkers, told me, "Cole, we know you've only been here a little while, don't worry. We hope you can help, but we're pretty far along, so just sit here and take it all in."

Was Mr. Shawn right? Would something as distant and codified as a formal union ruin his glorious tyranny? Deep breath. Robbie Robertson wrote on the Band's second album about being a union man all the way; in spirit, that was me, too. But still, this was *The New Yorker*. Even I had my worries.

As did, I'm sure, everyone who worked there, the others trying to live in New York City on $90 a week, or if you'd been there a while, maybe $130, before taxes. Concerns and uncertainties ... yet nonetheless the ever-stronger faith that we were all being exploited, that business was great and there was no good reason not to pay the staff—the drudges who each week put out the rag—a little more, that the whole enterprise teetering on one man's secrets and whims wasn't truly sound, was it?

Except that that's how the magazine had always been, at least since Shawn had become editor over twenty years earlier. Each week the covers radiated their hand-drawn charm, the column-after-column stories rippled along coffee tables all over the nation ... William Shawn had pulled it off once again.

I was so new—and, thanks to Dusty, exculpated—that

I mostly just watched the union process play out. Yet as it drew in more and more of my fellow workers, you couldn't say that the magazine—the whole dream of it—didn't look precarious.

Work was work, though, and I showed up every day at whatever time my leaving home when I was supposed to be there actually got me there; and every two weeks my pay was deposited into my bank account, and my personal checks never bounced. My own dream was going along just fine, thank you.

※ ※ ※ ※ ※

A REAL DATE! I'd picked up on Cherry's whimsy and decided to make an evening of it. Of course I only had *The New Yorker*'s pathetic pay in my pocket. (No trust fund back in California, though I did have a nice collection of First Day stamp issues from my uncle that everyone swore would pay for my old age someday—hah!) But of course we were, Cherry and I, East Village denizens, able to suck joy and delight out of beatdown apartments and mean streets, right?

Indian food! East Sixth Street, one inexpensive curry house after another. Entrées $2.50, samosas 35 cents, maybe a mango lassi for a buck to really kick things up. And sitar music and plush red-cloth drapings no doubt just as in a Bombay whorehouse. What wasn't to like?

"We're heading south," Cherry said when we turned right on First Avenue.

"Um, yeah."

"Where're we going?"

"Isn't it supposed to be a surprise?"

I had to say, Cherry surprised *me* when I knocked on Slater's door. I'd seen her, of course, in her Klitz costume at CBGBs, and in her shorts and T-shirt around the apartment, but the girl I picked up was ... well, as close to anyone I'd ever taken out, I'd call it an evening gown. It was sleek black taffeta, cut slim to her joyous curves, with spaghetti straps holding it up. The skirt was interestingly tiered, layers of fine cloth one longer than the other, elegantly flouncy. She had on a pair of way-high-heeled black shoes. Over the dress she wore a red light silk wrap. As I followed her down the five flights of stairs, she looked rich, classy, delectable—a lot like a movie star from the '50s.

"I thought we'd get some Indian on Sixth Street," I told her. "Have you been there? There's joint after joint of good places."

She shook her head.

"Not a problem," I said. "I've been to most of 'em, and Mitalis is the best."

Cherry didn't say anything. We made it two blocks down but stopped on the corner.

"Come on." I took her hand, but she didn't move.

"Um, Cole, on our ... well, our dream date." A quick laugh; was she joking or what? "I was hoping for something a little more—" Cherry tugged on my hand. "Hey, I have the per-fect idea."

Before I could say anything, Cherry turned right on 9th Street and led us west to Fifth Avenue. She stopped outside an apartment named the Brevoort.

"Do you know what's special about this place?"

I shook my head.

"Buddy Holly lived here." A deep, respectful nod. "Apartment 4-H. With his wife, right before he died on that horrible day."

Cherry's eyes were bright. I knew of Buddy Holly, of course, but his stardom was before my time ... an oldies artist when the Beatles and Dylan came along. But Cherry, in her Kim Novak outfit, was radiant.

"I was in his apartment once, a friend knows his widow, Maria Elena. She served us an aperitif." A quiet, deep smile, clearly a profound moment.

We headed down a block, then across the street to a restaurant called One Fifth, and pushed in.

"Do you know this joint?" Cherry said over her shoulder. It was loud, clamorous, elbow-to-elbow. I shook my head.

"You'll love it!" she cried over the din. "It's totally happening." Then she took my hand again and pulled me into the farthest room.

There was a long table there, and it was surrounded by people, chairs chock-a-block, another row of guests leaning over the diners, talking and picking food off plates. The whole room felt in motion. Men wore slim, well-cut suits, though almost none with ties, and many with shirts unbuttoned halfway down their chests. The women were in highly tailored short skirts and tight blouses, or flowing satinlike onesies. It was a far more chic deal than anything at *The New Yorker* or the book parties I went to. *Glam* was the word, and this was glam.

It turned out David Bowie was there. I wasn't into Bowie that much, couldn't make the leap from being a fan of Dylan and The Band, and I didn't even recognize him. Later, Cherry was astonished that I hadn't, though by then that was the least of my concerns.

Everybody there knew Cherry. She went around the whole table, her elegant black dress swaying just so, and each person she talked to kissed her cheeks, whispered into her ear. As everyone cooed at her, she lit up just like a junior high girl asked for a dance ... or so it seemed to me. Turned out, I was the wallflower. She didn't once bother to introduce me to anyone. Of course, it was so noisy it wasn't easy to hear anyone anyway, and I understood that nothing formal was going on ... it was just that I kept imagining leaning across a starched, dark-green tablecloth filled with samosas and pakoras and finding out more about who the Kewpie girl punk rocker I'd already slept with really was.

No such luck. There was nowhere to sit in this back room at One Fifth, but that didn't seem to be the point. Cherry wanted to make the scene, and that's exactly what she did.

Finally she introduced me to a wiry guy, thick black hair combed back from his perma-tan face.

"Paul, this is Cole." She pointed from him to me ostentatiously. "Paul's a writer. Cole is too, and he works at *The New Yorker*."

Paul looked to be my age, maybe a few years older; and it was interesting, I saw a eye-slit flash at the news that I was a writer, then a total change when my job was mentioned.

"Really," this guy Paul said. He leaned in toward me. "*The New Yorker*? What do you do there?"

"I'm in editorial."

"You're an editor?" Paul's eyes got hungry. "Fiction or nonfiction?"

"Um, neither really." A shrug. Why play games? "I'm in the typing pool."

"The—"

"It's where we type things."

"Oh." Paul shot Cherry a look, and she giggled.

"You writers!" she said. "Jeez, so com-pet-i-tive."

Is that what we were? Was I missing something? What exactly *was* I missing?

No matter. This Paul guy without another word took his shiny silk shirt and tight Italian pants and out-of-season suntan to the other side of the room.

I was getting hungry. Samosas and pakoras kept dancing before my eyes, not simply as symbols of private, impoverished-artist soul divulging but actually as nice hot, puffy doughy things you could pop into your mouth. *Hmn-nnn-hmmn*.

"Are we going to eat?"

"What, get a table?" Cherry shouted into my ear.

"I guess." I looked around. Getting a table would mean leaving the sleek back room.

"Can you afford it?"

Could I.... I didn't know, hadn't looked at a menu. Though I felt sure I wouldn't be laying down a tenner for both of us and smiling at how great a tipper I'd become in the big city.

Eating here would probably eat up half my weekly paycheck, but truth was, right then I didn't want to be at One Fifth at all. I just wanted to go home.

"Cherry," I told her a few minutes later, after she'd left me alone and drifted over to the far side of the room, talking to a woman in a purple jumpsuit open to her navel. "I'm going to take off, get a sandwich or some—"

"Cole?" Her luminous eyes looked confused.

"I just ... it's not my scene, you know. I'm glad you're having a good time. And ... well, we can do something again sometime."

"If you're leaving, I should go—" Cherry was looking straight at me, the same eyes I'd fallen into when I'd fallen into bed with her. I felt a moment's tug but not enough.

"No, no, you're having a fine time, I can tell." I nodded, actually sincerely. "I mean it. Really. We're only a few blocks from home." I started backing up. "I'll catch you later. It's all good."

Now I *never* use a phrase as lame as "It's all good," but I said it then.

Cherry's eyes darkened, unknowable thoughts beating around her head, but she didn't come after me. I slipped and slid through the crowded back room, then exited the place as quickly as I could. As I stood in the nicely cool night on the corner of Fifth and Eighth Street, my head lightened even as my stomach swirled.

This life in the big city. Could be complicated, couldn't it?

# 16

WHEN I TRUDGED UP the stairs after my "date" with Cherry—just a bit of a disaster, right; and, oh, God, next time I saw her, she'd be right down the hall—I saw the light blinking on my Radio Shack answering machine. I rewound the tape and heard this:

"Hey, Cole, it's Sailor. Just wanted to check in with you, let you know we're all still alive. At the moment we're in ... hey, Slater, where the hell are we?" Gritty tape-spinning pause. "Oh, it's Columbus ... Columbus, Ohio. Hey, Chet, do you remember heading into Ohio? I thought it was still PA.

"Anyway, Cole, that's where we are, I guess. Another totally crappy motel, this one's worse than last night—we're finding them on our own, no help from the record folk, and Slater ... he *loves* a roach motel. I try and, well, there's nothing any of the rest of us can do, and it's not like we have the moolah to make a difference. It's just that, the worse the joint is, cracked floors, broken doors, mattresses spouting foam, pee smells floating off the walls, the more that boy wants it. It's like he's got some weird thing for degradation. Ugh!"

A pause. I could see Sailor shudder, then shake her pretty red head.

"At least we've been playing most every night. A lot of steeltown bars, where, believe it or not, the crowd's into us. Yeah, they are. Sire's not wasting their bloody dime on venues, but it doesn't matter. And the great thing is, we keep getting better!

"I mean, like, *really* better. Emily and Slater, it's almost one voice on some of the songs—slower songs, and we got a few—but the energy ... you gotta believe me, whatever you saw at CBs, well, we're blowin' *that* lame-o band off the stage!

"Oh, and your name for us is *perfect*. Savage Joy. What can I say, Cole? We keep growin' into it." A big laugh, I imagined Sailor throwing back her sleek head and letting fly. "I'll tell you more when I see you—if I *ever* see you. I'm not seeing any end to this gigging, but, hey, that's what we're here for, right?"

There was a pause, then Sailor called out, "Hey, keep it down!" A pause, and I imagined her waving the phone at a full room. "Jeez, Cole, everybody's whuppin' it up. We got a night off ... in Columbus. I mean, what the fuck're we going to do, you know? Lots of ideas floating around. Come on, quiet, I'm on the friggin' phone!

"I really wanted to just let you know all's fine, Cole. I'm outside the motel office at this pay phone, and the guys are all jumping around and ... here, let me whisper a little, I hope you can hear me O.K."

Her sweet voice dropped. If I pressed the receiver tight to my ear, I could make out most of what she was saying.

"So, Cole, listen, there're a lot of things in play here. I ... I guess you want to know—or should know, or something.

"Anyway, nothing much with me, if you know what I mean. I mean, steelworkers aren't really my—" A long pause, which I wasn't sure how to take. "But, listen, with everybody else, well, there's *a lot* of drama."

A pause, and I imagined Sailor nodding to herself, carefully picking her words. That's the way it sounded. Then she was back.

"I've been in a lot of bands, Cole, a lot of bands. You know, if I've learned anything, drama's not always the best thing. Maybe you get a good record out of it, like Fleetwood Mac, but ... well, there's a toll. You don't always know it at the time, but later—

"So what am I saying? Jesus, I can't say too much now, even whispering. Just that it's not all what you think. No, Cole, not at all what you think."

Another pause. What was I thinking? What did she think I was thinking? At the moment I was just listening, happy to hear Sailor's voice, not sure how good I was with whatever she was implying ... and I didn't have a clue what that was.

Sailor's voice dropped even lower.

"I don't know how much I should leave on your answering machine, but, well, let me start with the easy stuff. Chet, you remember, the bass guy, he's ... I'm not sure he's all there. Doesn't matter much, he plays fine, just that there's not a whole lot of him in the van. Kinda like a stump." She laughed guiltily. "Wendell Walter ... he's reading his Bible all the time. Least that's what he makes it look like. We got a little close to Kentucky, he got spooked. Guess that's where he's from. Some backwoods hollow, he was mumbling something about snakes one night, you know, like that tat on his arm. But, really, Cole: snakes?

"Anyway, then there's your pal Emily. You know, Cole, I'm not sure *what* to make of her. She sure wasn't raised like I was, like any of us were. Nope, we're never gonna be peas in the same pod, but ... I mean, given all that's going on—Cole, don't get me started!—well, Emily and I are getting along fine. Still there's this whole ... oh, shit, there she is. Hey, Em, I'll be off the phone in a few, all right?"

A pause, and I half heard Emily in the background, couldn't make out what she said.

"Well, I'll tell you more about Emily next time. Looks like, Cole, we're heading off somewhere, I gotta go in a minute, but the thing I'm getting to is Slater ... what's really going down is mostly coming from Sla-ter." I heard a long, low breath. "Whew! That boy, he's playing it loose, you know." A short, unjoyful chuckle. "I mean, really, really loose. Am I surprised? That's Slater's way, he's the lead singer and all, but his deal ... man, his deal is rolling and tumbling all over the damn place." Sailor's voice rose. "I mean, *all over*! I know he's handsome as shit, least if you like that short kind of dude, and no-bo-dy can resist him ... except me—hah! He's also a friggin' prima donna, that ain't gonna change. But, Jesus, we're on the bloody road, all of us in one van, sleeping [words I couldn't make out] you'd think he'd have some [more garble] I mean, the way he's carrying on with—"

The tape ran out. Click, the spindle on my answering machine stopped cold. That was it. Damn. My tape had run out.

I sat there staring at the machine, willing it to play more. Then I stared at my black telephone, willing it to ring. A night off in Ohio. What was there to do there but eat pizza and drink beer? Maybe Sailor would call later.

But she didn't. I undressed, went to bed, tried to read. Instead I kept going over and over what she'd said. Slater was playing it loose? Of course he was. As Sailor had said, he was the lead singer; I'd never known him not to play it loose, whatever that meant.

So what did it mean? Was it Slater and Emily? I had my suspicions, her old boyfriend Harper Hart had more than that. I'd kind of swallowed and kept down anything with the two of them. I mean, Emily wasn't my girlfriend, and—

But Slater and Emily hooking up on the road, was the same as Slater's "deal rolling and tumbling all over the place"? What did Sailor mean by that? What was his *deal*?

I had no idea. Crazy thoughts crashed my brain, but I was able to shake them off. It wasn't like Sailor had said things were a disaster, so maybe everything I was thinking was way overblown. And, anyway, what business was it of mine?

Out of sight, out of mind. Yeah, that was the ticket. I put my eyes back to my book, a reread of Nathanael West's *Day of the Locust*—an inspiration for my own L.A. novel—but they wouldn't focus. Out of sight, out of ... I kept trying, I did. It just wouldn't work.

And then there was tonight with Cherry.

Remember, my bed was right next to the hallway door. I could hear everything that went on out there, people trudging up the stairs, opening their own doors, going to the toilet in the hallway.

I kept listening for Cherry to come home. I was sure I'd hear her, turning her key in the door or using the facilities.

I tried to read to stay awake but still couldn't focus. Did I doze off? I guess I must have because I remember waking with a start about 3 a.m., ears ablaze.

But I heard nothing. Had Cherry come home at all? I didn't know ... I just didn't know.

Did I sleep the rest of the night? The way I felt at work the next day, I was pretty sure I hadn't. But I also didn't hear anything. No door opening, no toilet flushing, nothing.

✳ ✳ ✳ ✳ ✳

THAT NEXT DAY didn't start off a good one. No, just all that confusion in my head. Jumpy, very jumpy. I went out to lunch, solo sushi again, then for no reason started worrying that the fish had gone bad and I'd be wrenched over a toilet the rest of the day ... and when I got back to my desk, there were two self-addressed-stamped manila envelopes.

Yep, a two-envelope day. Two stories rejected. *The Atlantic* and *The Paris Review*. I sat there kind of numb the rest of the afternoon. At least my stomach didn't blow up.

Then, right before five o'clock, the poetry editor, Howard Moss, called me down to his office.

"Cole," he said, standing and shaking my hand. "Good news. We're going to publish a poem—that one you sent along last week."

My hand went to my forehead. I'm sure I rocked on my heels. "You're—"

"Yes, the one you call 'Memory.' It's going into the bank. I can't promise when it'll run, but since it's fairly short, it shouldn't be too long."

"That's ... that's great," I got out.

"Well, congratulations." Howard was the sweetest guy, short, bald, always cheerful. He shook my hand again. "Now you better get back to work, right?"

I spun about, wobbled down the hall, didn't feel ready

to tell anybody, just let it all sink in. I was ... going to be ... published in ... *The New Yorker*.

It took a while. The poem came out on my twenty-eighth birthday, as I said—yes, on my actual birthday.

The key thing is that in my secret thoughts I'd been telling myself I could play at being a writer until I was twenty-eight, then I might have to consider some kind of real career, like law or something. I'd been waiting for a sign.

A poem in *The New Yorker*: a distinct sign. Right on the money.

I've just now gotten off the phone with the magazine, three buildings on from the old West 43rd Street offices, making sure I could reprint my poem. They said that was fine. I'd written it while filling in at the 20th-floor reception desk. Part of the job was to take phone messages and scribble them on yellow notepaper, then hand them to writers coming back from lunch. I can remember the exact shade of yellow-gold paper, though I barely remember writing the poem. Looking it over, it's all right, it's just that ... well, I have a surfeit of emotions about all of this. Let's just leave it at that and reprint the thing. Here it is:

**MEMORY**
*When the door opens*
*And you go out and in,*
*A message on yellow paper*
*Sometimes appears.*
*And if you remember, you call;*
*It's as easy as that.*

*Sometimes it's responsibility;*
*Sometimes it's avoidance;*
*Sometimes it's the capricious*
*Turn of a gold-scaled fish*
*Taunting the hook.*

# 17

How long do you float on top of the world after selling your first poem to *The New Yorker*?

Ten days. Ten glorious, lighter-than-air, next thing you know you'll be in the *Norton Anthology of English Literature* days. Having a poem published in *The New Yorker* hadn't ever crossed my mind, though of course once it happened, turned out I'd had that dream all along.

Did it help work on my novel? Actually, the opposite. I kept typing, but I was a bit full of myself, and it all came too easily. Writing a novel is rolling a boulder *up* a hill. You ever think you've crested and now all you gotta do is let the book speed along on its own ... well, no good writing happens like that. It's put your shoulders and back to it and fight for every inch.

I wasn't fighting, I was floating. A poem in the friggin' *New Yorker*! (So what, I worked there; they'd turned down everything else I'd sent down the hall as a submission.) Yep, everything was going great, finally, finally going my way ... for ten days.

Then I heard a new noise outside my door. I was in bed, seeking sleep. I'd heard Cherry a few times, late at night, while I was tossing and turning, her soft feet in the hall, the faint creak of the bathroom door, and her padding back to Slater's apartment. Should I have bounced out there in my underwear to find out what was going on? I wasn't *that* crazy.

It was 1:30 by my illuminated alarm clock. The steps in the hall were way heavier than any I'd heard since Slater left, the liquid plash into the toilet loud and long; then there was a distinct male grunt as whoever it was clomped back to the rear right apartment.

Shit. For the last two weeks I'd kept Cherry pretty much

out of mind. When I thought of her, I remembered the misbegotten dinner date, not the tumbling bed play; and since I almost never heard her—she simply wasn't around but those couple times—it was easy to tell myself to give it time, bump into her casually, check out the vibe, take it from there.

Now there was a guy in her apartment, and my brain was whirling like mad.

Was Cherry there? Maybe it was just an old friend whom she'd lent the place to. Had I heard her come home earlier? I couldn't recall. Maybe it was a cousin, even a brother, just off the bus at Port Authority and needing a place to....

I lay there quiet and still, head pounding, willing sleep but not even getting close. No further noises. Maybe, just maybe I had no reason to be jeal—

A light shuffle in the hallway, Cherry's silk sleeping dress rustling her legs, a tiny cough that could only be hers....

I didn't sleep the rest of the night.

I saw the guy the next morning as I headed groggily to work. About my height, five-ten, with short-cropped dirty blond hair, an eighth of an inch long. A tight chin, firm nose, thin mouth. He looked a little like the actor Steve McQueen, stolid, handsome. Oh, and he was built, too. He had on a well-washed olive-green T-shirt stretched tight across his chest, muscles popping the short sleeves.

All of which surprised me. I kept flashing on Cherry and the crowd I'd seen at One Fifth: elegant, fiercely stylish, epicene. In my head I'd written Cherry off to *that* world. So what to make of this solid middle-American dude in the hall?

I nodded to him, he did a slight flick of his fingers salute back to me, and that was that.

O.K., a one-night stand. Cherry sure didn't owe me anything, so what could I say? Besides, a hunky guy like that, I was sure he wouldn't be around again.

He was walking to the toilet as I was heading to work the next day.

"Hey, buddy," he said. Flashed me a lopsided white-tooth grin.

"Hey."

"Toilet in the hall, kind of a drag, eh? You use it, too?"

I shook my head.

"You got your own?"

"The front ones—the de-luxe suites," I said.

"Sweet indeed." He was only a foot or two from me, just a little pressing. "You know, I'd whiz in the sink, it was just me. But I got the chick there."

"Cherry."

"Um, yeah." A slight pause, as if he were double-checking that that was her name.

"You staying with her?"

"It's tight, man, tight. But till my brother gets back, well, that seems to be the deal." He looked at me hard. "You think she'd ever know if I pissed in the sink? I mean, I could run water—"

"Your brother?"

"Oh, shit, you gotta be Cole. Slater's told me about you, the fancy writer in the front." He stuck out his hand. "I'm Dale—Dale Smith."

"Smith?" I was shaking his hand, mine getting crushed.

"Slater's my half-brother. Same Mom, different scumbag father, you know what I mean."

"So you're—" My eyebrows must've arched up in a telling way.

"Oh, you think I'm banging Cherry? I mean … popping her?" Dale laughed big. "What, you got a thing for her?"

I quick shook my head.

"Cole, Cole, it's written all over your face. You always so transparent, bro? You want to join me in a poker game sometime?"

Dale laughed, and it was such a rich, hearty one that I felt myself liking him a lot, even if he was making fun of me. Maybe *because* he was making fun of me. He sure wasn't talking to me like I was somebody who had just sold a poem to the most prestigious mag in the land.

"But, no, Cherry don't need me for *that*." Dale snuffed, tellingly. "We're just coexisting. So far, it's been fine."

"Cherry's a sweet girl."

"I think more tart, man, than sweet, you know." A wink. "But at least she hasn't thrown a knife at me."

"You get much of that," I said, leaning into Dale, my own press into his space.

"Much of what?"

"Chicks throwing knives at you?"

There was a pause, a growing pause, as he tried to figure out how to take that, I guess. But he'd decided we were already going to be friends, so he laughed it off.

"Knives are nothing, you see the forearm go back, you got plenty of time to duck. Other things ... not so easy."

"But you're still here."

"Yes, my friend, Dale Smith is still all the way the fuck here."

I hustled off to work but not before asking Dale if he wanted to get a burger sometime, and he said he was free that night. Indeed, he was free every night. He didn't really know anybody in New York except Slater, who was who-knows-where right then. (I hadn't gotten any further calls from Sailor or anybody in the band, so I had no answer for Dale.)

At work I found out that a friend of mine down the hall, Nancy, had just sold her first Talk of the Town piece to the magazine. She was jubilant ... as I'd been those ten days earlier. And another friend, Vicki, Howard Moss's assistant, had also sold a new poem of hers. Looks like *The New Yorker* was on a junior-employee buying spree. Happy as I was for both of them, my ten days of literary grace were definitely over.

Which meant the tall beer Dale had ordered for me when I met him at a dive on St. Marks truly hit the spot.

"You are the writer, right?" he said after I'd gulped down half the glass. "I hear all writers are drinkers." A smile.

"In truth," I said, wiping the foam off my upper lip, "I'm pretty much an aspiring writer—a pretty grim thing in this town—and I really don't drink that much."

"Yet?"

I laughed. "You never know."

"And you came up with the name of my brother's band?"

"Unless they've changed it," I said. Dale nodded at that. "What have you heard?"

"Well, there're lots of things Slater don't tell me, you know." Dale ran a hand back over his near crew cut.

"And things he does?" I leaned in with a crooked smile. Sitting here with Slater's brother, I was struck with new curiosity about my neighbor. It wasn't like I'd ever gotten much out of Slater.

"Not much, man, not much. Slater's a private dude." Dale chuckled, not warmly. "Mom wanted us to share a room once, the little fuck refused. Went out and slept in the garage instead." Dale nodded to himself. "That went on for five fuckin' years."

"Wow."

"He's always been, well, following his own drummer, as we said in the Army."

Ah, the olive-green shirt, the cut muscles. I looked at Dale longer, didn't see any tattoos. Since being down here in the East Village I was swimming in tattooed dudes and ladies, this struck me as curious and interesting.

"How long were you in?"

"Six long fuckin' years." A slow nod. "Slater was probably still sleeping in some friggin' garage then, too."

"Were you in—"

"Nam?" Dale nodded. "Yeah, mostly Nam, till we turned tail and ran a couple years back. Rattled around Hood and Leavenworth for a while till there didn't seem to be any point to it anymore."

"So you're out?"

Dale looked at his heavy aluminum watch. "Twelve days so far."

"Got it."

We were silent for a while, then I felt my hands tighten. I said, "Can I ask you one thing?"

"Sure, anything."

"Did you like it ... I mean, the war?" Apart from one friend who'd gotten drafted and now wouldn't talk about Vietnam, I didn't know anyone who'd been over there; and certainly nobody who'd chosen the military as their career. That just wasn't my world, for better or worse. But I wondered about it.

The look I got from Dale—wary, ears up, eyes tight—it could've been like I'd taken a shot at him. He held those fierce, scary eyes for a moment, then relaxed. I guess he realized it was only me, the writer down the hall.

"What can I say?" He spread out his hands. "You're the scribbler, Cole, what would you say?"

The way he was looking at me now, it was odd, but I had the true sense that he wanted me to step into his character and explain the whole thing. Even odder, right then I thought maybe I could. My fiction-writing energy was flaring.

"Once I got past the horror of it," I told him, trying to move in on his persona, "I have to admit I kinda dug the intensity, the sense that anything could happen at any minute. I ... I *like* to live my life that way, on an edge, wits always kicking, every moment life and death." I fixed him with my gaze. Was I getting close? I ended with: "Who wouldn't?"

Dale took a minute, then gave me a nod.

"Not bad, señor, not bad at all." He raised his chin. "How you know this?"

A long sigh. Could I tell him? He'd probably get mad at me, but there was an answer within me, and it really wanted to come out.

"Don't laugh, but although all I really do is sit before my Selectric and stare out the window, when I write ... when I'm right there, *writing*, it's the same deal."

Dale hooked me with a dubious eye.

"I mean it, man, don't laugh," I said. "I'm really *there*. The same kind of all-or-nothing intensity, every word life or death, every moment anything can happen ... way out there, wits end, throwing every fuckin' thing I have—" I pulled up then, hearing myself. This guy had been in friggin' Nam. What was I thinking? I looked down at the table.

"Of course, nobody ever *shoots* at me," I went on, shrugging. "So I guess I'm a total asshole."

"No, man, you're not," Dale said quickly. His eyes were tight flares. "I can tell you mean it, it's not bullshit. Right?"

"I don't—"

"Own it, Cole. There're a lot of *safe* things out there, yes there are, but there are also a lot of ways to hang out your ass for anybody to take a crack at. Writing, I don't know shit about writing, but I'm guessing it ain't easy and safe. Neither is what my fuckin' brother's up to, either. Right? Playing shows, pushing the music, doing fuck-all crazy shit." Dale rolled his eyes.

"Yeah, there's a lot of ways to be real, man," he went on. "Nam ... Nam was fuckin' real, but the Army now, without a real war, it's just a bunch of pussy lieutenants getting their rocks off pushin' punks around. Just a lot of fuckin' paper— and not the good kind, ya know.

"So that's what *I* gotta do, Cole. I gotta come up with something new and real, something that keeps my ass hangin' out there ... for the rest of my goddamn life." He fixed me with a sudden illuminated stare. "Hey, you think *I* should be a writer?"

I took a deep breath. Was he serious? I didn't know Dale at all, yet in a gut way I felt I knew him really well. I couldn't explain it. But I knew his question to me was serious; and that he was a deadly serious man asking it.

"It's nothing I'd wish on anyone, writing, but if you can get your energy and passion down on the page—if you can tell it like it really was over there—I sure as hell think you should give it a shot."

It took a minute, then he nodded.

"A shot, right?"

I hadn't intended a pun but took it with a smile.

"Don't pay for shit, *amigo*?"

"Probably not." I laughed. I was told I was getting $75 for my *New Yorker* poem, not even a week's pay as a flunky typist.

"Well, I'm up for anything." And Dale's whole face shown so bright it was like a bulb had been flicked on. "Bring it all the fuck on!"

There was nothing to say to that, so we ordered burgers, talked small talk, then I said, "You know, this girl I know, a good friend, she's the one in the band with your brother, and—"

"Sailor?"

Huh? I shook my head. "No, Emily. She's making a career change probably wilder than your becoming a writer. She's up there singing with Slater and—"

"Not only singing, from what I hear."

"Oh." That was going to be my question, of course. This Dale was good, wasn't he? Looked like he could see things coming.

"It's a pretty small van, what I hear." Dale winked. "More I think about it, maybe what my brother's doing ain't that different from being in a Humvee, heading out to the jungle—"

"So you know for certain that they're—"

"Doing it?" Dale nodded. "Least if my brother's to be believed."

"He told you that?" My voice rose as a sear of heat hit my stomach. Not just the jealousy but the idea of how cavalierly Slater was treating it.

"Hey, you got a thing for her, too?" Dale said. "This Emily chick?"

"I—" I didn't know what to say.

"I hadn't heard about *that*." Dale leaned forward. "You keep secrets well, Cole."

"I ... I don't know how much of a secret it is," I blabbed out. "More like nobody notices or cares."

"How long this been going on?"

"Since I moved to New York last year, since I met her."

"You do anything about it?"

"Like what?" A long inhalation.

"I don't know, like fuckin' grab her."

"I don't—" I halted. Shades of Sailor ... and certainly the last thing I wanted to talk about. "There was never a—"

"Shit, Cole, is *that* your style?

I went silent.

"What about letting it all hang out there, throwin' every fuckin' thing you have at it?" Dale shook his head. "You just sat there, bro?"

I stayed silent.

"Oh, man, oh, man." Dale put his burger down, stared at me. I felt his gaze scrape down my face like the edge of a razor. "You haven't learned by now you gotta just go the fuck after what you want?" Sharper shaded eyes. "I bet as a writer you fuckin' do everything you can to get published, people to read your shit. Right?"

He barked that at me, and I nodded. I did, didn't I? Send a story out again as soon as it came back rejected. Chat up everyone I met at literary parties. Hell, I would do anything—*anything*—I could to get my work out there.

"Listen, I got one question for you, bro." Dale pulled his head back. "Did you ever really want that chick Emily? I mean, *really*?"

What? This was coming out of nowhere. Didn't I *dream* about Emily Prosser? Her cool blonde hair, thin lips, sly eyes. Her being an editor at FSG, junior literary royalty. And didn't my heart jump a little whenever she called me up?

"Maybe that's part of being a writer, dude," Dale went on, "you get lost in your own head. But my experience, sure, I can get way lost in *my* head, but when something's the fuck real, I'm right there. Don't have to be in Nam with the Cong shooting at you or mines blowing up to feel *that*." He leaned back, put his hands behind his buzz-cut head. "I don't think you're that into her at all."

"What do you mean?" His words had come fast, and my head was spinning.

"I think that you *think* you want Emily, but maybe you don't really, Cole. I don't know if Slater wants her or not, but I do know that he was there, and she was there, and well, somebody didn't just sit around waiting for something not the fuck to happen. *Comprende*?"

I half nodded.

"So now they're on the road together. And your precious Emily's singing rock and roll."

"So?"

"So either you're a total pussy, Cole, or that chick's not really for you." Up went his sharp chin again. "So which is it?"

There was no answer, at least not right then over beers and burgers at this joint on St. Marks. So I kept quiet. Dale did, too, as if he realized maybe he'd gone too far—or maybe he just didn't care.

He'd gotten to me, though, and I was mad at him. I was going to pick up the check, then I thought, Fuck it, not this asshole ... but then I grabbed it anyway. I don't know, maybe even that quick I was realizing this new guy down the hall was on *my* side, had a real chance of doing me good.

It was only ten bucks anyway. When we left the place, I really wanted to be alone, but, well, we were both living in the same building, so we walked the three blocks north together.

"Just suck it up," Dale said to me as we pushed through the front door at 340 East 11th. "That's Army wisdom, bro, but I don't know no better anyway. Just suck it the fuck up."

Even if I didn't feel it then, Dale was right. Suck it the fuck up. Yes, yes, of course he was.

When I realized later that night I'd never asked Dale a word about him and Cherry, well, maybe I didn't care for her the way I thought I did either.

# 18

THE BAND WAS BACK. I was sleeping, then jolted by a loud banging in the hallway, blinking awake, the clock 4:15 a.m., more ungodly clatter, followed by a loud pounding, then an aroused voice. Was that Slater? I hadn't heard his voice in over a month, but that was my first thought.

I pulled on a robe and opened the door.

There he was banging away. Had he lost his keys? He was looking pretty much the same as I'd last seen him, the thick bowl of blond hair down to his eyebrows, and the same clothes, the dirty jeans, engineer boots, torn T-shirt, now with a short, tight silver-lamé sport coat over it. As usual he looked both sweet and menacing. I felt a cheerful lift of friendly memories.

"Hey, Slater, you all right?"

"I can't get into my bloody apartment." He kept throwing his palms against the metal door.

"Don't you have a key?"

He looked at me like I was crazy, then banged his bare fists again.

"I know you're fuckin' in there, Dale. Open the fuck up!"

I hadn't seen Cherry in a couple days, but I had seen Dale bringing home takeout Chinese just a few hours back.

"I saw your brother earlier, but maybe he's gone out."

"Naw, not at 4:30." Slater seemed sure about that.

"Is he a heavy sleeper?"

"Yeah, he is." Pound, pound, pound. "You got something I could use, a bat or anything?"

I did have a softball bat in a closet but didn't think it would be a good idea to have Slater swinging it at his door this late, so I shook my head.

"Is Emily back, too?"

"Should be. Why?"

"I mean, maybe you could crash with her for tonight." I tried to say this casually, but even I heard the edge in my voice, all those weeks of brooding, I guess, over what I'd heard too many times from too many places about the two of them.

Slater hooked me a severe look.

"I want my own home, man."

"Worst case," I said, "you can pull out the futon on my floor. Just for a few hours. I mean it is after four in the—"

Slater's door jerked opened, Dale's sleepy head popped out.

"Jesus, man, what the fuck?" he said.

"Hey, bro, I'm home." Slater flashed a big, glad-hander fake smile. "Let me the fuck in."

And that was all I saw of either of them for a couple of days.

When I did see Slater next, I found out his coming home basically set off a round of musical chairs. Cherry was gone—nobody knew where—and Dale was out, too.

"Do you know where your brother is?" I missed him already. We had had dinner a few more times, always intense and interesting. He pulled me out of myself, and I truly enjoyed that.

"He'll turn up, I'm sure." Slater laughed. We were in the hallway, I was coming home, he was heading out. "That boy always does."

"You did tell him he could stay at your place with Cherry, right?"

"Sure." He lifted his thick shoulders. "I was gone, why not?"

"But you don't want him—"

"Man, you know how small it is. Barely enough room for me." A hard look. "Hey, what'd you mean the other night about me and Emily?"

"Just that, you know, it looked like you might need a place to crash. You are in the band together and—"

"We were in the band."

"*Were?*"

"Cole, a whole lotta shit went down on the road. It's amazing we didn't all fuckin' kill each other."

"Wendell and Sailor, too."

"You're lucky you're a writer, bro. Only gotta travel around in your own head, the characters you make up, right? Try actually runnin' the country in a tiny van with those freaks, see where *you* end up."

An intriguing point, and I had no answer.

"So the whole band's, what, finished—"

"Nope, Savage Joy, we made it. We're friggin' signed … to … Sire." His thick helmet of hair bobbed, eyes danced. "It all worked out, gonna start on an LP next week. Just that, well, not Emily."

"Really?"

"I said it, man, didn't I?"

"Can you tell me—"

"Better ask her. She's your friend, dude." A shrug, and Slater took off down the stairs, boots clattering as always.

Emily *was* my friend, and it was strange I hadn't bumped into her in the halls. I'd even knocked on her door a few times but got no answer.

Turned out she left Manhattan the day after the band got back, though I didn't know where. When she got back a week later, the first thing she did was come up to my apartment.

"*You're* a sight for sore eyes!" Emily let out as I let her in.

"Really, sore eyes?" I smiled. It was great to see her. She looked different, though. Her hair was spiked with silver, and I saw a large tattoo—couldn't make it out—at the top of her arm. "So, how sore *are* those eyes? Achy? Eye flu? Or maybe just an end-of-summer eye drizzle?"

Emily looked at me curiously, as if she'd stumbled into a foreign world. But then she lit up.

"Hold on, Cole, is that *wordplay*?"

"Um, I think so." I was goofing on her, and it felt good.

"Oh, my God, I am *so* not used to that." She reached out and put her hands on my shoulders. "You mean, here we are, both of us literate souls, and we're having fun playing ... with ... words?" She shook her head, not wholly in mock disbelief. "I gotta say, Cole, rock and roll, there ain't a whole lot of true wit there. It's a huge deal if you can get your drive-thru McDonalds order right the first time. 'Yes, please, make that a really big Big Mac!'" Emily shot her gaze to the side, acting out. "'And, Slater, I am *not* talking about your damn cock!'"

"Hey, it's good to see you, too," I said, though I took a step back. It was a touch odd to have Emily just standing there with her hands on my shoulders. Not to mention what she'd just said about Slater.

"And, Jesus, I can't believe I used such a cliché as 'sight for sore eyes.'" Emily shook her head. "Hey, maybe my eyes aren't hurtin'" She rubbed them then, elaborately. "Nope, don't seem too painful at all." A cheerful shrug. "Guess I was wrong."

"Then does that mean you're *not* happy to see me?" I said this deadpan. We were still playing, right? But Emily stepped back, looked me up and down, taking me in scarily serious.

A moment later she flew into my arms. She was dressed in one of her wrap-around sheath dresses, a copper-and-turquoise Native American pattern, and the fabric was very thin.

"God, I am soooooo happy to see you," she sighed, right into my ear. I hadn't held her like this since that first night at CBGBs, and as I did, through the thin dress I really did hold *all* of her, and it felt good: her shoulders, narrow and steady; her strong back muscles flexing against my curious fingers; her lovely breasts tight against me, soft, tractable, so close ...

and her scent, faint citrusy perfume along with her generous Ivory soap smell, a fever cloud surrounding me. It all kind of went to my head. Oh, yes, it did.

"Cole, Cole, Cole," she whispered, then pulled her head back just far enough to hold my gaze. "God, I missed you out there, I really did."

Maybe it was her surrounding scent or just the startlement of Emily Prosser—this woman I'd imagined embracing time after time in my lonely bed—actually deep in my arms, but I never thought to ask her why, if she'd missed me so, she hadn't once called, or even asked Sailor to put her on that one time that she had phoned me. Of course it would've been crazy to stop then and say, *Emily, what exactly do you mean when you say you missed me?...*

Because she wasn't going anywhere. She stayed locked in my arms, tight to me.

Did I hear Dale in my inner ear? Or did I reach around and grab her all on my own?

We fell onto my bed. Emily was with me all the way; in some ways ahead of me. She looked at me tight, light dancing in her eyes, then licked her lips so they shone bright under my overhead lamp ... till I reached over and flicked it off.

Then it was all shadow and touch, clothes dropping away, secret places appearing, fingers stroking, sighs and gasps, hands fluttering, backs arching, legs tangling, eyes rolling back, more gasps and pants bursting out, and—oh, we were *so* literary—*Yes*, Emily cried, *yes, I will, yes, yes, yes....*

Later, we talked.

"It wasn't for me," Emily told me, sitting up and facing each other, the sheet over her upper body. "I thought it would be an adventure, and I guess it was, but it turned out not to be mine."

"Really?" What I'd heard from the road was that Emily was totally into it.

"You doubt me, Cole?" She fixed me with her sharp blue eyes.

"Of course not," I said quickly, "but from what I heard—"

"That there were six smelly people in a van? Driving around God-knows-where America? Guys like the bass guy who didn't say a word—Jesus, I can never even remember his name—and crazy creeps like Wendell Walter. Only one other chick, Sailor, who at least made it tolerable—"

"What about—" I held up, not ready, I guess, to ask about Slater.

"Taking turns driving!" Emily harrumphed. "I'm a shitty driver, girls who know Pushkin and Thomas Mann backward and forward do ... not ... drive!"

"But you had to?"

"We were eating miles, Cole. Even with Sire's minder, when the next gig is in some skankhole in St. Louis and you're in Memphis, that's gobbling down miles."

"I always wanted to go to Memphis," I said.

"Yeah, it's a sweet city, Beale Street, rundown but with some great blues." Emily brightened. "We did have a couple days there."

"So it wasn't all bad?"

"I don't know." She let out a half smile.

"How about onstage? The singing. The sharing the mike with—"

"Slater?" Her eyes clouded. "You want to know about *that* asshole?"

"I heard that—" But no, not then, not right after I'd slept with Emily—finally was in bed with her—could I ask about him.

"What did you hear, Cole?" She shifted and the top of the sheet lowered. I could see the lifting curves of her breasts, the sweet light flesh my fingers had traced, then held on to for dear life.

I wanted her again, right that moment, just like this.

"Were people talking about *me*?" Emily arched her eyebrows. "People in the biz. Tell me, what were they saying?

Lots of rumors, I bet. Rumors and more rumors. Oh, I know book types, they pooh-pooh but love nothing more than good gossip." She leaned toward me, hungry. "Come on, what *were* they saying about me? Was it about me and—"

I shut her up with a kiss. A hard one. She pecked me back, slowly, tentatively. There was a long moment when I wasn't sure what would happen next. She pulled back an inch, thinking hard; but I leaned in again and kept kissing her, my tongue flicking the top of her lips, her tongue ... and finally something clicked. She joined me then, faster, harder.

The sheet fell away. It wasn't quite like before, more distracted, not as energized, yet ending with more than one explosion....

After, I was dozy, almost asleep, Emily's head on my shoulder, easeful breathing in my ear—slow susurrations, gentle puffs of air—when I heard steps in the hallway, the toilet door creak open, and the splash of pee (I assumed it was Slater, I hadn't seen Wendell around) into the bowl.

Emily stirred.

"I think I need the bathroom, Cole," she said and got up.

Now my bed was only a few feet from the hallway door, and Slater's toilet was only a yard or so left of that. On my wall were hooks with a few jackets and my bathrobe.

Emily slipped on the bathrobe, and the moment before that registered and I was about to tell her she really didn't need it, that my toilet was in the next room, right off the kitchen, she slipped out the front door.

"What the fuck!" Slater's voice, sharp and loud. "Emily, what're you do—"

"Oh, Jesus!" she cried. "Slater, you startled me."

"Is that Cole's bathrobe?"

Silence, though I imagined Emily wrapping it tighter around her. It was light seersucker, with a full cord.

"What the hell are you—" A pause. "Wait, are you in there *fucking him*?"

More silence. Try as I wanted, I couldn't imagine Emily's expression. Was she scared? Was she proud? Was she—

"You *are* a goddamn slut, aren't you?"

"Me?" Ah, now she spoke up. One word, with spirit and alarm.

"Yeah, you, you friggin' slut."

"You're one to talk, you fuckin' pig."

"Who're you calling a pig?" I could just see Slater's balled fists. I got up, quickly pulling on jeans and a T-shirt. I had to get out there. But Emily beat me to it.

"I have nothing to say to you!" She brayed this at him, then tugged open my door and stormed back in.

I was sitting on my mattress, my feet going into my pants. She looked dazzled, shining.

"Are you all right—" I started to get out.

She didn't say anything, went right to my toilet and closed the door tight. She was in there for a long time. All the while I didn't hear a thing.

When she was back, she looked even brighter.

"Well, *that* was awkward," she said straight at me, smirking.

"What were you ... didn't you *know* my toilet is right over there? Isn't it the same way in your place? I don't really get this at—"

I was saying all this sincerely, of course, hot and disturbed, but I needn't have bothered. Emily was already out of my robe, a long flash of her pale skin luminous in the moonlight through my window, and, *whifff!*, back into her clingy sheath dress.

Emily didn't answer me or say or do anything as she was leaving. No kiss, no loving words, no explanation. Nothing. She was simply gone.

# 19

Turned out, a week later I just missed meeting J.D. Salinger. Word was he was visiting the magazine to have lunch with Mr. Shawn, and while I was out getting a sandwich, this tall, gray-haired man in an old-fashioned tweed suit had been hanging around the 19th-floor lobby. Then he and Mr. Shawn went out to the Algonquin together.

That would've been something, seeing J.D. Salinger. Like every other kid, I'd loved *Catcher in the Rye*, at least at the right age—I think I was fifteen, in public school in L.A., with no idea of what going to a Back East prep school was like, but it didn't matter—and I was thinking now about the part of the book when Holden talks about how he'd love it, after finishing a book, if he could just call up the author and talk to him or her. Just think, if I'd been back from my tuna fish ten or fifteen minutes earlier, I would've met the author of *Catcher in the Rye*. Would I have said anything to Salinger? Probably not. Probably wouldn't have recognized him.

But had I talked to Salinger, been able to call him up on the phone, what would I have asked him? I didn't remember *Catcher in the Rye* enough then to ask about that. Probably I'd just ask him what the hell I was supposed to do with my life, with Emily a couple floors under me, who I wasn't talking to, and Slater—whom she still seemed obsessed about—right down the hall. What would Holden Caulfield's creator have to say about *that*?

There were no ideas of what I should do around the halls of *The New Yorker*. Lately, work had been awfully predictable, even tedious. I was in the typing pool, for God's sake. And that's what we'd been doing a lot lately, typing. Somebody's book project, and every day there were another twenty-plus pages for each of us to type over. The subject? I can't recall, probably not as deadly as Shawn's mid-'80s debacle, still rolling eyeballs: E.J. Kahn's infamous five-part series on grains (the first one, on corn, ran for 40 pages); but what I was pecking away at on my Selectric wasn't much better.

Nothing to go home to at night, either.

My worst self wanted to knock and ask Emily to come up to my place. The thing was, I couldn't shake the way she'd said, "Oops, *that* was awkward," after setting it up to bump into Slater that night after she'd just slept with me; and every time I tried to figure out what she was really up to, my head hurt.

So I was ignoring Emily, even if she didn't know that, or care. Ignoring Slater, too, who I was sure could care less. He was probably off working with Savage Joy, getting ready to make their record. I'd heard they were going into the studio in a month.

Meanwhile, I kept getting all my latest stories and poems turned down. I had another two-rejection day, those SASEs whispering on my desk after lunch: *You're a failure! Sure you have a poem coming out soon in the best magazine in the country, but guess what: That was weeks ago. You'll never sell anything again! Nobody cares!*

On Mondays I heard about Saturday-night *New Yorker* parties—somebody often had something brewing on weekends—but either I hadn't been invited or didn't feel like going. In truth, I didn't feel like doing much of anything. I just headed home after work, whipped up a little dinner, read books by authors far better and more successful than I'd ever be, then fell asleep early ... and did it all over again the next day.

I guess I was depressed again. Did I know it? I don't think so, certainly not enough to do anything about it. Everything felt gray, shapeless, merely endurable. I told myself that this wasn't good, I was just plodding along, going nowhere ... but I didn't see any way to make it different, so I just kept on doing what it seemed I was supposed to do every day.

But my heart and soul weren't into any of it, no way.

That was my mood, gray, sodden, grim, when I was heading home on a Thursday evening and heard loud singing and tambourine banging pouring out of the next-door Church of Jesus Christo. I was never particularly moved by ecclesiastical exuberance, but something about the noise that night sounded lively, and without particularly thinking about it, I stepped in.

Mr. Strump was up at the lectern. There were eight or so people in the pews. I recognized his ever-shawl-covered wife and two of their grandchildren. Wendell Walter was playing his Gibson, and a teenage girl with acne was hitting a large tambourine.

Mr. Strump saw me, sincerely smiled his toothless grin, and beckoned me to a seat.

Was I going to stay? Why had I even walked in? I wasn't sure why I was there at all, but Mr. Strump kept grinning in his slightly lunatic way and pointing to an open chair, and finally I took it.

The song ended with a loud *whoop!* Louder than you'd think from so few people.

"We're here to praise the Lord," Mr. Stump said. The room was so small he didn't even need a microphone. "We're gathered at vespers time to raise our voices and declare ourselves ready for the night, the Lord as our Shepherd. All praise!"

Cheers and cries of "All praise the Lord" rose up around me, surprisingly rousing, though I stayed silent.

"I want to tell you," Mr. Strump went on, taking a step forward. "Listen to me closely."

People leaned forward.

"We all know these words, they're from *Acts 2: 1-47*, and they're the reason we are here. 'When the day of Pentecost arrived, they were all together in one place,'" Mr. Stump intoned, no Bible before him. "'And suddenly there came from heaven a sound like a mighty rushing wind, and it filled the entire house where they were sitting. And divided tongues as of fire appeared to them and rested on each one of them. And they were all filled with the Holy Spirit and began to speak in other tongues as the Spirit gave them utterance.'

"I want you to feel it now, the Holy Spirit." The old man lifted his hands, lifted the room, which seemed to rise with him. A curious, lifting wind. Mr. Stump's orotund voice, fierce certainty. And it was crazy, but I felt it ... I felt something in that room.

"That's the Spirit!" he cried. His silver hair shook. "It's in you, it's always inside you, and it is ... in ... you now!"

Everyone there began to chatter, half under their breaths, not fully intelligible, but clearly enunciated syllables. I strained to make out the words, though quickly realized they hardly mattered. All around me was everything missing from my life: lively noise, fellowship, exuberance, joy.

That moment, me in my forsaken state, sitting in this storefront church, certainly a little needy ... young and unexpectedly curious ... well, there was a mood upon me that made me feel right then there might be something here I needed to know. I can't explain it, it wasn't like I was suddenly seeing a vision or hearing any kind of clarion call; no, it was just an unexpected urgency, and a shifting, a lifting, as if under the rumbling glossolalia lay a power that could move me—*would* move me.

I leaned forward.

"'His eyes are like a flame of fire,'" Mr. Strump went on, voice surprisingly vibrant, "'and on his head are many diadems; and he has a name inscribed which no one knows but himself. He is clad in a robe dipped in blood, and the name by which he is called is The Word of God.'"

As Mr. Stump called these words out, the wild thing was that I could almost *see* it: those tongues of fire and eyes aflame ... the robe, dripping....

"'Then I saw a new heaven and a new earth; for the first heaven and the first earth had passed away....'"

A new heaven? Was that what I needed? This old, rough, crumbling world weighing me down, every footstep a drudgery, pointless, soul-withering ... and yet all I would need was the courage to step into this new heaven aborning?

I was never much of a churchgoer. I'd been raised a Congregationalist, taken in a spiffy suit with my parents and sister to church every Sunday; and yet early on I'd realized I was not a soul for any of that, the very act of sitting in a pew was literally stifling, smothering. Up there in the pews my chest grew tight, my palms sweaty, my eyes darting desperately toward the exits—yet no way I could push past all those crisply suited grown-ups. So I sat there for years of Sundays, almost dying, till I finally got old enough to ditch having to go with my parents to church, hiding out under the sun a block from our home till it was so late they had to leave ... and they would, leaving me free in my rebellion, literally grasping freedom, clutching the light—

What freedom, what light did I have in my life now?

And yet this *was* a church, even if only a storefront a few doors from my own place; and even though I was curiously moved, a moment later I was also gasping for breath just as I'd been high up in the balcony of Mount Hollywood Congregational Church, my throat tightening, chest heaving ... like that, up I stood and stumbled out onto East 11$^{th}$ Street.

A moment later Wendell Walter was out there with me, guitar in hand.

"It's a lot, isn't it?" he said. He was right in front of me, moving a little, back and forth. I smelled the must of his worn clothes.

"What is?"

"Cole?" He raised his eyebrows. He was swaying now, slithery, snakelike, as if something around him was moving him. His guitar brushed his leg and played a discordant set of notes, muffled quickly. "I *saw* you in there."

"I just stopped in for—" I halted.

"For what?" Wendell twisted closer.

I had no answer. I hadn't been able to finish my own sentence, and I couldn't answer Wendell Walter.

"We'll take it slow, Cole. We're not going anywhere." Bright shiny eyes cast back at the metal sign above the cracked doorway: CHURCH OF JESUS CHRISTO. "The Lord *is not* going anywhere. The Holy Ghost *is not* going anywhere."

"No, no," I said. "That's not at all what——"

"Slow, Cole, whatever you need, brother." Wendell was rolling his narrow shoulders over and over, a creepy thing. I saw the curling red and green snake up his arm. His smile was wan yet beguiling, a near simper. "Very, very patient. We have all the time in the world, profess—"

"I'm sorry," I said, interrupting him. The tightness was still there, right in my chest. "Whatever you're thinking, Wendell, that won't happen. This is … this has just been a … a mistake."

"Sure," Wendell said, shoulders rolling, torso slipping, slithering. "No problem, professor. I understand. And we have all the time in the.…"

His words trailed off, yet Wendell kept standing there, smiling his thin but haunted smile. A heavy dose of the willies rushed up my spine, making me forget my tight chest.

*Well*, I thought as I climbed the five flights to my apartment, *that sure was odd*. I kept asking myself what stopping into the Church of Jesus Christo meant and whether I'd go back; and I was shaking my head, telling myself no way.

Yet that night I felt different, lighter, with glimmers of hope. Undirected, for sure; insubstantial, definitely … yet true hope.

I can't explain it, don't want to explain it, it was simply enough that I felt so much better. Way more than enough.

## 20

WENDELL WALTER came by early Saturday morning, knocking on my door. I was eating eggs and bacon.

"Hey," he said at the door. "Can I come in?"

"What's up?" I said, though I knew.

"I just want to talk to you, Cole." He looked slighter than he had on the street, more himself.

"About the other night?"

"If you want to." That simple simper on his face.

I shook my head. I hadn't wavered since Thursday, knew I wasn't going to. Whatever happened was just ... curious.

"Well, then," he said, taking the other chair at my small table, "anything on *your* mind. Anything at all."

I don't remember Wendell's being in my place before. He wasn't the sort of person you invited over. The funny thing: Even being in Slater's band, that month-plus on the road, hadn't changed him much. He still looked like the just-a-little-off kid in high school, the waist on his pants too high, that crazy long belt dangling down his thigh, pant cuffs showing white sweat socks under black loafers. His pale hair was a little more downtown than before—short on the sides, a long flap of it on the top—but it was surely still home-clipped. I imagined him before his mirror, scissors in hand, the Lord and Slater in his eyes, jabbing away.

Of course he had that curling green and red snake, fangs bared, on his upper arm. Don't recall any of my Studio City, Calif., classmates with that.

"You know, professor, it was a surprise to see you the other night at services." Wendell leaned forward. "I saw it, the way your eyes lit up. You know, there's an awful lot of room in Jesus's heart." Now a goofy, loose-toothed smile. "Plenty of room enough for you, Cole, plenty of—"

"I'm glad you're here, Wendell, I really am."

"Of course you are." The smile beamed. It was pretty creepy.

"I've been wanting to ask you since you've been back about what really happened out on your tour." I smiled at him, as his lips went straight. "Especially what happened with Emily."

"That's not what I'm here for, Cole."

"But *you're* here, Wendell." I gave him two quick nods. "And I really want to know what went on. Can't get a thing out of Emily or Slater."

"We just played music."

"Is it ever odd to you to play that music with Slater and also be in your church?"

"Why should it be?" Wendell tight, defensive.

"The music is pretty, well, unrestrained."

"It's joyous!"

"I know, but it's savage, too, Wendell. Savage Joy, my name for you guys."

"Your—"

"I came up with it, Savage Joy, didn't you know that? Sailor asked me to. I was going to write a song, but Sailor heard the two words and ... well, that was that."

"I thought it was Slater's—" Wendell's eyes widening.

"All me." I smiled, thin and sharp. "You could almost say I'm the band's sixth ... well, now, fifth member." I leaned forward again. "So what did happen with Emily and Slater? Why is she out?"

"She, um, I ... well, uh, she ... she didn't really *fit*." It took Wendell almost a minute to get this out. I watched the second hand *tick*, *tick*, *tick*.

"She sure seemed to," I said. "I was there at CBGBs both times, looked like she took right to it."

"No, no, I don't think she ever really be-longed." Wendell shaking his head. He looked either sad or angry. "She's not like us, she's—"

"But Slater wanted her, right? He was *fucking* her, wasn't he?"

Wendell flinched at the word. He barely got out, "I don't know."

"You were in the damn van all that time. Come on, Wendell, what happened?"

"Emily ... she was different. Not really a musician and—"

"So that was it, she's out because she's not a musician? For your three-chord crap music?"

"That was a lot of—" Wendell's gaze kept slipping mine.

"No!" My voice rang out. I'd given up on Emily, at least for now, yet was still pissed as hell at her. I deserved to know what was going on.

"Why are you yelling at me?" Wendell's soft, shaky voice.

"You all went off together. The shows must've gone well because you're making a record now. Right?"

No answer.

"But Emily's *not* part of it. I want to know what happened."

"There were ... conflicts."

"Conflicts?" I barked this out.

Wendell stood up.

"That's all I'm going to say, Cole." He swallowed, his heavy Adam's apple bobbing.

"*Wendell.*" I heard the edge to my voice.

"This is what it's like when you've forsaken the Lord." Wendell crossed himself, his snake and Bible verse tattoos flexing. "I thought I could *save* you!" His voice, high, plaintive.

"Did you try to save Emily?" I threw this at him, mostly because I was still angry and frustrated. The question stopped him cold.

"It wasn't possible."

"What do you mean?"

"She's a confused soul, Cole. And she confuses *everything* around her. Every last—"

"What are you getting at?"

Wendell blanched, then shook his head. There was a lot in him that wasn't coming out, I could sense it. The way he was blinking fast. The way his hands frittered and danced loose by his side. His body was rigid, though, nothing snake-like now.

"She ... she doesn't, not always, does she, well, feel good about what ... what she *wants*." Wendell was shivering as he stammered this out. "What she ... she truly *wants*."

"She wanted to play in Savage Joy, right? And she wanted Slater, too." I bore down on him. "Didn't she?"

"It wasn't possible." Wendell crossed himself again. "It was all too confused and—"

"Why?" I shouted.

Wendell shut down. Whatever he was saying to me—and whatever he *wasn't* saying—I could see it all blow up in his callow face. His lips, his eyes moved every which way; then they stopped moving at all.

"I'm going to go now, Cole." Wendell's forehead shining. "But I want you to know the Lord has *not* forsaken you. *You're* always welcome under his tent." He gave me a big, vapid smile that quickly curdled. I wasn't sure what was going on, but his voice changed, as if he were no longer speaking to me. "Yes, everyone is *always* welcome under His tent, even when ... when they're not sure they belong." His eyes folded back, then with a force of will he looked straight at me again. "He *is* forgiving, He is, He is!"

"Wendell, what is it?" I took a step toward him. "What's going on?"

He didn't answer. He stayed there rigid, terrified.

"Wendell?"

Finally he got out a few soft, trembling words: "I'll be

praying for you, Cole, yes, I will, I will"; then he slipped out my door.

\* \* \* \* \*

LATER THAT DAY I heard another knock on my door. It couldn't be Wendell. I was sure whatever he was hiding was too deep to come out, at least this soon. For a moment I thought it was Emily, coming to apologize or something. I steeled myself for her radiant blonde smile, her lovely face. I was still furious at her, and I took three deep breaths before I pulled open my door.

It wasn't Emily, it was Sailor.

"This is a surprise." I stepped back to let her in. Was I happy to see her? I was, yes. This was the first time since the band took off; first time for any contact since that abrupt phone call from the middle of nowhere.

"It's great your building has no lock on the door downstairs," she said, laughing. "Anyone can just walk right in—how democratic." Her eyes lightened. "And, Cole, you *never* ask who's at your door?"

"I'm pretty democratic myself." I smiled. "And always up for a surprise."

"Always?" She laughed again, light and airy and immediately making me feel better.

I didn't answer that, just stood there taking her in. The thing with Sailor was, though she was Slater's friend and the drummer in his downtown band, with all that implied, she always looked very clean, even well-groomed to me, even with her dyed bright red-orange hair. It was something in her cheeks, naturally peachy, and her white, well-shaped teeth. Emily had perfect teeth, of course, Connecticut teeth, but Slater and Wendell and the rest of Savage Joy had teeth of shame. But not Sailor.

"Good." Sailor sailed past me, straight to my refrigerator. "Got a beer?"

"Probably something." I gave my head a half-shake. I

didn't drink much beer at home, but who knew what was in my fridge. "If you find something, help yourself."

She was already in there, of course, and I was a little taken aback by her boldness, though of course that was Sailor's way.

She emerged with a Beck's in its shiny green bottle.

"So why am I here?" Sailor said, falling into my foam couch, the one with the seat folded back and ready to spring out with just a touch. This probably isn't the time to mention it, but a year after I bought my tan fold-out foam sofa, I saw a Bloomingdale's ad for the same piece of furniture, calling it "A Conversation Extender." Hadn't extended enough conversations on it myself, but hope was eternal.

"O.K., why are you here?"

"You're a writer, right?"

"Yeah," I said. The true answer, of course, was *I hope to be a writer someday*, but I had just had that poem taken by *The New Yorker*. Maybe I *could* say I was a writer now? But even as the affirmative came out, I doubted it. Did doctors and lawyers feel this way? Probably not. They were credentialed, for what that was worth, and also made real money. Poets and story writers? Hmmmph!

"And you gave us our name—at least *I* know you came up with it!" A bright laugh. "You know, I'm digging it more and more. Gonna look great on the LP cover. SAVAGE JOY. Just, I keep trying to figure out what it means." Sailor pursed her brow, looked at me with firm inquiry.

"You're asking me?" I shrugged as she nodded. "The two words just popped into my head. They sounded good. I was going to write a poem called that and—"

"Have you written it?"

"Not yet." I shook my head.

"That's why I'm here, Cole. That phrase, the two words fight themselves—at least they do for me. I can't get my head around the contradiction. Is it *joy* that's *savage*, I mean, wild and fierce? Is that what you were thinking? Like a tiger in the forest?"

"Burning bright?"

"Yeah, William Blake." Sailor's eyes lit up. "Fearful symmetries and all."

"I wasn't thinking of Blake," I said, surprised that Sailor got the reference that even I hadn't, though fortunately I was too quick to let her know I was surprised. "But Blake's the guy I did my senior seminar on in college."

"So maybe there's something there." Sailor nodded, mostly to herself. I have to say, I was more and more impressed—a few words, and she nailed a source for my scribbles I hadn't even thought of. I remembered that James Joyce reference when I first met her. Scribbledehobble, indeed. Did she really know a lot more than I thought the drummer of a raucous downtown band fronted by Slater Martin possibly could?

I was turning over this idea of Sailor when she said, "The thing is, I can't get it out of my head ... and the idea came to me, we *need* that song."

"What song?"

"*Savage Joy*—the song of our band."

"Are you saying that I—"

"Cole, our songs, the lyrics *suck*. They suck big time. Slater, he's one complicated dude, and he holds down the front like—well, he makes the band, don't get me wrong. And he can write music ... well, three, four chords that slam along. But the lyrics? They're really kinda banal."

"And—"

"Let's start with *Savage Joy*. You got the title, we got Blake in our corner now, and—"

"You're saying what?"

"We write ourselves some songs, dude." Sailor lifted her beer bottle in bright salute. "Push those contradictions. Let the tiger lay down with the lamb."

"Have you written much be—"

"I've been writing verse since I was eight," Sailor said. "I use the word *verse* consciously, not sure I ever made it close to actual poetry—by the way, congrats on getting that thing taken by *The New Yorker*. Can't wait till I see your name in the Table of Contents—"

"That's right, you told me you read *The New York*—"

"Of course I do." Sailor laughed, as if my utterance was too dumb to answer. "Listen, I have some song ideas, and I'm sure *you* have ideas. And I know we damn well need something."

"O.K." This just popped out, not really considered. I had no idea if I could write actual lyrics, though for a band as loud as Savage Joy, probably nobody would hear them anyway.

"You mean it?"

"We can try." I heard hesitation in my voice. My name would be on them, right? Did I want that? Mr. Just Sold a Poem to *The New Yorker* now writing punk lyrics? And what if Sire printed them inside the LP?

"Don't go prissy on me, Cole."

"Don't go—"

"I can see it, dude. You're thinking about your fancy career. Mr. Big-Shot Poet. Wanting to be John Ashbery."

"I don't want to be—" Wait, Sailor knew who Ashbery was?

"Listen, you know anything about Patti Smith?"

"Um, didn't you mention her before?"

"Right, I did." I saw Sailor recall the first time she talked about my writing the band lyrics. "But have you read her?"

I shook my head.

"Oh, Cole, Cole." Sailor half-shook her head. "Patti's a real poet, man, has books of po-e-try up on the wall at your blessed Gotham Book Mart. The genuine deal. Thing is, she fronts her own band—that's her true calling—and her band's really good. Got an album out on Arista. I'll have to bring it over, give you something to think about."

"Um, sure," I got out, "I guess I really should." My head

was spinning. It always surprised me the way Sailor was able to get me going.

"Yeah, you'll learn something, I promise. Hell, *I'll* learn something ... and maybe we'll make something great."

"Simple as that."

"Don't mock me, kiddo."

"Oh, I'm not, I'm not—"

"Good." Sailor pulled down the rest of the Beck's, wiped her mouth with the back of her hand, and got up from the Conversation Extender.

"You're leaving?"

"Got a rehearsal up on 30th Street, yeah. Busy busy these days. We got to get everything ready, hitting the studio in a few weeks."

"I—I was hoping you could tell me more about what happened when you guys were on tour and—"

"You want to know about Slater and Emily?"

I went silent, didn't want to admit to that.

"Oh, you and your girls. Jesus, Cole."

I stayed silent, had no idea how to respond to that. *My girls?* Good God, did Sailor know about Cherry, too?

"Listen, there're some real good road stories there. Way good ones." A sly smile. "But they're pretty friggin' long, and, well—" She threw back her head and chortled. "Let's write that first song, Cole—get *Savage Joy* down on paper—and that'll be the reward." A huge smile, those ideal teeth. "For both of us. Me, telling the wild, depraved saga of *Savage Joy in America* ... and you hearing it." She stuck out her hand. "Deal?"

I shook her hand, no hesitation. It was still cold from the beer. And wet.

When Sailor was gone, not right away, but ... well, I finally pulled a towel off the rack behind my kitchen tub and daubed my hand dry.

# 21

THERE WAS A LOT about working at *The New Yorker* that was like being back in the 1940s and '50s, and not just lunching at the Mary Elizabeth Tea Room. In James Thurber's old office on the 19th floor, ink doodles of his on the wall—yes, *The New Yorker* was a place that if you were a genius, you could draw on the walls—were dutifully painted around, pale yellow paint shining under the current light, bright tangerine. Old guys who'd hit their prime in the '30s and '40s still shuffled about, like Rogers Whitaker, a red-nosed Santa Claus who still wrote Talk pieces under his nom de train, E.M. Frimbo, and the always delightful Philip Hamburger, who was actually friendly to us typing-poolers.

The most mysterious denizen of the 20th floor was the great essayist of New York City, Joseph Mitchell. As I already mentioned, Mr. Mitchell would come in every day about noon, usually wearing a 1940s fedora and a tan Burberry's raincoat. I wanted one, wanted to be a real writer in the Bogart mode; just couldn't afford it on my $90 a week—and silently went into his office and shut the door. Mr. Mitchell hadn't published a piece in the magazine since 1965 but sat in his closed-door office dutifully till five, when he'd say goodbye to the receptionist (sometimes me, sitting in) and leave till the next day.

*The New Yorker* was that kind of place.

Except that the movement toward a union was heating up. The word was Mr. Shawn was too upset to speak, though his subalterns were negotiating. Even I could feel the silent, rampant fear that the ill-paid whippersnapper underlings could destroy the magazine's special magic.

There *was* a special magic, no question. I've never not said it was an honor and a privilege daily to be buzzed through the 20th-floor door. And with my $90-a-month East Village apartment I was getting by.

Part of me loved the old-time quality of the place and my life there. We had read E.B. White in elementary school, when our teacher would pass out order forms for Scholastic Books, and consulting with Mom I'd get to pick out half a dozen or so; I remember few days more exciting than when the teacher opened class with, "Children, your books have arrived!" E.B. White (with *Charlotte's Web*) was one of the gods of mid-1950s Scholastic Book orders.

And there E.B. White was, walking the office floors, in his own fedora and raincoat, stopping off on his way from Maine to Florida for the winter.

"Can I help you, Mr. White?" I asked him once. He was standing silently in the main lobby, looking distinctly bemused in a suit and tie, as if though the offices looked the same, they were not his *New Yorker* ... and who was this twentysomething kid in an untucked sport shirt and jeans doing here anyway?

"No, I'm fine," Mr. White answered softly, not wholly convincingly. "Thank you, though, for asking."

To me most of the time, from my boring San Fernando Valley suburban upbringing, working at *The New Yorker*, just hanging in its offices, was like being in an extraordinary theme park—an intellectual's Disneyland. And there E.B. White was, a historical equivalent of Walt, walking the old halls, recalling all the dark careers and booze-hardened souls that had gone into making the place ... creating what was mostly dreamy history to all of us ill-paid '70s kids now.

I loved that dreamy history, which was one of the reasons I didn't rush to CBGBs and clubs like that when I first hit New York. But there was another reason. I'd actually seen protopunk local bands like Love and the Seeds (at the Valley Teen Center, of all places, me trying to pick up girls in high school, those venerated '60s combos grabbing a couple hundred bucks for playing a Valley rec center), and I'd listened to a lot of the rest of the inspiration for punk (Knickerbockers, Electric Prunes, the Leaves) on AM radio all through high school. All that down-the-street CBGB music blasting away the creepy mid-'70s radio goop (ELO, Foreigner, Yes) was not that new or radical to me. The Cramps and the Ramones learned a lot of what they knew from Lenny Kaye's *Nuggets* LP from '72; and on that double LP were the bands I grew up with.

Maybe I'm making excuses, but the true fascination for me, the most radical change from where I came from, was right here in NewYorkerLand, hoping to chat up E.B. White, taking in the Thurber sketches, helping in my small way to put out the perfectly mannered columns of Adobe Caslon type that streamed through each week's rich pages.

I loved *The New Yorker*, still do. Yet a few more bucks in my pocket wouldn't have hurt. To that end the union thing kept rolling. There was talk of an upcoming vote, portrayed by Shawn as a radical stake through the heart of everything we all loved, and by my cohorts as simple justice.

As before, I was still too fresh (and lowly) to help in the negotiations. I just got news and rumors ... and remained a bit ambivalent, too.

*****

I BUMPED INTO Slater a couple days after that Saturday when both Wendell and Sailor showed up. I was hurtling down the stairs to work, and he was trudging up them, blue takeout coffee cup in hand.

"Hey," I said. "What's up?"

It was my usual ten in the morning dash to the subway. I didn't think Slater was ever up before noon.

"Huh?" Slater looked pretty beat, rings under his eyes, a kind of dull slant to his usually expressive mouth.

"You're up early."

He looked at me for a moment as if I made no sense, then finally said, "Just coming home."

"Ahhh."

"Yeah, a rehearsal. Motherfuckin' long rehearsal."

"How's it going?"

"What?" He looked way distracted, which was unusual. The thing with Slater, he always beamed in on whoever or whatever was in front of him. It's one reason he made such a good front man for Savage Joy. "Oh, it's going."

"Meaning?"

"Meaning, I'm friggin' beat, Cole." He shrugged his thick shoulders, ripped arms, then pushed past me. "Do you mind?"

"Nope, I gotta get to work anyway." I shrugged off his rudeness. "I'll catch you later."

That look he gave me, a wan smile, a vaguely genial lift of his blue eyes. This was unexpected, Slater trying to be pleasant. It didn't work. The man I saw looked whipped, shaken.

What could it be? Something with the band? With the music? Or something else altogether....

By this point Slater was opening his door and I was heading down the stairs. I made a note to ask Sailor about it the next time I saw her. I realized then that I wasn't sure when that might be. If Slater was just coming home from an all-night rehearsal, Sailor would be, too. Was she feeling that beat also? I hoped I'd hear from her soon, that we'd find time to start writing our song. The recording date was still weeks away, but it couldn't hurt to get going.

\* \* \* \* \*

I WAS AT MY *New Yorker* desk, no work at the moment, just playing around with a few lines from a poem of mine that might work for Savage Joy, when I got an unexpected call.

"Cole?" A man's voice I couldn't quite place. My first thought was Slater, wanting some help or something, but it didn't sound like him. Of course, Slater hadn't been himself this morning anyway.

"Um, yes."

"Hey, it's Harper."

"Harper Hart?"

"One and the same, sport."

"What's up?" I had no idea what Harper could want, not even sure how he'd found me ... except that he knew I worked here and probably just asked the switchboard operator to put him through.

"You free for lunch today?"

"Um, today—" I didn't have any plans but wasn't sure I wanted to go out with Harper.

"My treat. I need to talk to you." Harper sounded a little desperate, not at all like him. What could he want to talk to me about, unless it was—

"I haven't seen her in weeks."

That caught him. I could hear Harper pull in a long breath.

"Well, *I* haven't seen Emily since she took off with that ... that ridiculous music thing." Harper quickly recovered. "So you know more what's going on than I do."

I was right, it was about Emily. Did I want to talk to Harper Hart, of all people, about her? Not really.

"I don't think I know anything that will do you any good."

"Hey, Cole, let *me* be the judge of that." I felt him leaning into the phone, that I-was-born-to-move-the-world way he had. "'Sides, there could be a few things about Emily that *you* might wish to know." I could feel his tongue trace his lips. "We on?"

In truth I was curious, if for nothing else to know how bad a case of Emily Prosser he still had, so I ended up agreeing to meet Harper at the Yale club a couple blocks away, on Vanderbilt near Grand Central, at 1:30.

I had simply to mention Harper's name and a tuxedoed maître d' showed me to a white-linen-clothed table festooned with fresh flowers, fancy silver, and gilded THE YALE CLUB OF NEW YORK CITY embossed plates. Sunlight streamed in from tall windows overlooking Vanderbilt.

Harper was natty: midnight-blue suit, French-cuffed shirt, red-and-gold bow tie.

"You ever been here, Cole?"

I shook my head. Emily never proposed it, I don't think she was a member. And I might've gone to Cal, but there sure was no wood-paneled UC Berkeley club in New York City. I'd once been taken for a beer at the Harvard Club right across 44th Street from *The New Yorker*, so I'd had a taste of wood-paneled Ivy League club glory, but that was it. We ordered right away, me a burger, Harper some poached fish thing.

"Well, make yourself at home." And he snickered.

So that was the game. Still, I wasn't here to be chums with Harper, I was here to find out what I could about Emily. Right?

Only one thing to do: take the offensive.

"So what do you know?" I said. "About our mutual friend."

"What do you mean?"

"You said you had things about Emily to tell me." My own thin smile, chin lifted in a gesture Harper would understand. "Here I am."

"I want to know what she's doing with that creep."

"You'll have to ask her."

Harper flinched. "She's not talking to me."

"And I'm not talking to her," I said right at him. Our food had come by now, but we kept talking as we ate. The burger was actually not bad.

"Really?" Harper looked surprised by this. "Why not?

"So what do you really want to know, Harper?" I said, ignoring his question. "And why? Really, why when it's so—?"

"Because I'm crazy about her." He said this flat, almost deadpan, but I had no reason to doubt him. "And I can't get over her."

"I was starting to say, *When it's so hopeless*—"

"*Nothing's* hopeless."

"That's what the Harts are taught, eh? Wearing your little bow tie at your grandpa's knee—"

"Fuck you!"

I smiled. Guess I deserved that.

"I don't get it myself," I said to him, a sweeter voice. "Why she just ran off with Slater. That ... that's not the Emily I know."

"But you don't really know her, do you, Cole?"

Ah, the battle—pointless as it was—was still on.

"What *don't* I know about her, Harper?"

"Like how rich she is."

"I always assumed she was—" I started to say, then half-shook my head. "How rich?"

"Old money. Way old money." A quick, up-tilted chin nod. "*Prosser* money."

"She's from Connecticut, right?"

"Old Connecticut. Avon, in the center. Went to Miss Porter's—"

I shook my head.

"Miss Porter's School? Most exclusive girl's finishing school in the country?" Harper lifted a thick eyebrow, as if he couldn't believe what a rube he was lunching with. "Jackie Ken-ne-dy? Gloria Van-der-bilt? A lot of Rockefellers—"

"And that's why you're crazy about her, Harper? She's big money?"

He let that go by.

"The thing is," he went on, "Emily was, well, forced to go there, and from what her friends have told me, she rebelled a lot."

"She does have her own spirit."

"Yeah, like, Why not take everything special in *my* world and wreck it?" This came out sharper, more bitter than Harper seemed to want. He looked as if he'd surprised himself.

"What has she wrecked?" I said.

"Well, me, for one." Harper lifted his fine chin, trying to show strength. That's the way he was. "And her family. She's hurt them a lot."

"Because she won't play along?" I didn't understand really rich people, had some prejudice; I guess it was coming out.

"At bottom, they're just people, you know, Cole." The way he said my name was ripe with disdain. "The wealthy can get hurt, too."

"What has her family done? Have they cut Emily off?"

"They do what they can," Harper said sniffily, "but it's never enough."

"And all because of Slat-er Mar-tin?" I felt my friend's name was a spear, and I threw it at Harper as sharply as I could.

Harper shook his head. "That ass is just the latest. Emily dropped out of Miss Porter's—*nobody* drops out of Miss Porter's School—and took off around the country."

"Wasn't it the late '60s?" I said. "A lot of people 'took off around the country.'"

"Yes, but ... a Prosser?" Harper rolled his eyes as if he couldn't believe what Emily had done even now. Then he went on.

"Emily has this ... well, this impulse to just tear everything down. All that she was given, all that she has." He leaned forward, his voice dropped. "There was this boy, she was tutoring him in East Hartford, and—"

"What, she took off with a poor person?" I interrupted with mock alarm. "How '60s was that!"

"There was a lot more to it."

"Like what?"

Harper looked as if he were going to speak but didn't. He held his head tight, then gave it a jerky little swing back and forth.

"Just that, Cole." He gave me a fake sage nod, more annoying than anything else. "Things got very com-pli-cat-ed. There was a *lot* more to it."

"Meaning you're not going to tell me."

"Meaning that once Emily gets going—she just up and left her publishing job, right?—there's no telling where she will stop ... *if* she stops."

"And this is your business because...."

"Because I love her." The way Harper said that, he pushed it in my face. "Because she's ... well, she's said certain things." A deep, whistling breath. "But most of all because I'm *good* for—"

"That's not for Emily to decide?" I said, interrupting him.

I put this to Harper that firmly, with all the feeling I still had for Emily. Of course it was up to her whom she loved. Even if it wasn't me. It was *her* life.

That rattled Harper. There was a long string of seconds there, quiet, inward looking, as if he were truly asking himself whether I might be right. Or maybe I'd misread his face, taken for true self-examination simply a sudden flash of confusion.

Finally, he shook his head slowly, side to side.

"Not if you look at the evidence." A slow, contemptuous smile. "And what her family wants."

"Ahhh, you believe the Prossers want *you*." A look of disdain. "Harper Hart ... your name sure *sounds* rich. Are you?"

"We do all right."

"Way better than the likes of me, I bet." Harper stayed silent. "And sure as hell better than Slater Martin ... though you know he just got a record deal?"

"For that unbearable noise?"

"It's with a real company, Sire. They're with Warner Bros. and—"

Harper wrinkled his nose, muttered something that sounded like "parking lots." I ignored him.

"Sire's signing lots of new bands." I thought about that Talking Heads I'd seen at CBGBs. "Really good ones."

Harper kept pursing his lips, not impressed. He looked wrapped up tight in his Harper Hart–ness, his Yale club surroundings, all that separated him from me. A quick thought:

"So what am *I* doing here, Harper? You can't imagine I'm going to help you win over Emily—is that really what you think I'll do?"

Harper didn't answer that, just ate more of his pale white fish.

"I don't even know what I can tell you," I went on. "As I said, I haven't seen Emily in weeks."

"And that ... that loser kid?"

"Slater's around but busy with his record."

"And Emily's with him." Harper said this so matter-of-factly it didn't register right away. It took me a minute to realize he was that far out of the loop.

"You don't know?"

"Know what?"

"Emily left the band, Savage Joy. Something happened on the road, and when they all got back, she was out."

"She's out of the band?" Harper dropped his fork. It clinked against the heavy china. A couple at the next table looked over.

"Yeah."

"What was it?"

"I don't know." I shook my head. "Nobody will tell me."

"Then where is she?" Harper said, agitated. He'd quickly picked up his fork, which he was twitching against the white tablecloth, of course here in the Yale Club totally muffled.

"I'm not talking to her, remember? I have no idea."

"Have you seen her in your building?"

I shook my head.

"That could be coincidence but I doubt it," I told him. "I think she's away." I felt light flow into my eyes. "Maybe she's gone home to A-von, Con-nec-ti-cut." I pronounced every syllable, the way everyone around me seemed to do all the time. "Maybe her no doubt loving family knows ex-act-ly where she is."

Harper let that go by, too. I could see the unexpected news rattling around his head.

"So she's not with Slater?"

A long pause. I thought about that night she'd spent with me, not that long ago.

"I don't know that."

"You don't know—"

"I think she's still into him." I was speaking more to myself than Harper. Digging into my own wounds. "I think she could be more into him than ever."

"Then where is she?"

"Truly, Harper, I have no idea. Maybe she's at her apartment right now. Or maybe she's actually shacked up with Slater. Maybe she's using some of her mon-ey? You know, treating Slater in a way he—" I shrugged, calmly jerking my right shoulder at him.

Was that gratuitous? Probably. But just because we both loved the same woman, who evidently didn't love either of us, that didn't mean I had to like Harper Hart. This was not some quirky buddy comedy.

And was it possible I was right? Emily off with Slater right now? I hoped it wasn't true, but all I really knew was that Emily had left my bed, wearing only my robe, to intentionally bump into Slater in the hallway. Who knew where that had led?

"The little fuck!"

"Harper, words like that ... in the Yale Club?"

He ignored that. Instead he stared hard at me, that patrician, I'm-above-you-but-maybe-you-can-do-me-some-good look Harper Hart was so good at. I'd seen it before, and it didn't faze me.

The only difference this time was that the answer Harper came up with was so patently clear: *Nope, this loser I just bought lunch for has no further utility to me.*

With that Harper thanked me for coming, got up, signed a chit for the meal, and simply walked away.

## 22

A WEEK LATER Slater stopped me in the hall as I was coming back from a late Saturday-night cannoli, said, "Hey, Cole, I keep missing you, bro. You want to go on a run with me?"

"A run?"

"Yeah."

I recalled that day in the subway, that odd trip up to East Harlem, then all around town, ending up flashing the nuns. I couldn't suppress my giggle. I'd missed Slater's crazy energy; missed, also, that innocence of only those few months back.

"Sure, when?"

"Right now, buddy-o." Slater peered at me. I'd pretty much resigned myself to just going home and falling asleep—it was almost midnight—but with no hesitation I told him I was totally up for it.

"Great." He looked me up and down. "You're dressed just right." He smiled.

"What do you mean?" I was in jeans and a wrinkled blue dress shirt under a burgundy crewneck sweater.

"Nothing, man, nothing." Slater threw back his head and laughed. "Listen, get a coat—old one. Might get chilly out there."

"Where're we going?"

"You'll see."

"Can't you give me something?"

"Nope. You're in my hands now, Cole, baby." He tossed his bowl of hair back and cackled.

First we hopped the subways as before, heading north.

"I can't sleep, bro," Slater said when we took seats. The 6 train was only a quarter full. It was about 12:15.

"What's going on?" I was still surprised to be with him, but thought if nothing else, I could catch up on the latest.

"What do you mean?"

"What're we out here for?"

"Why not?" A shrug, but not so light. It felt like something was weighing on Slater.

"No, really, man, what's going on?" I pushed my question at him hard. I'd pretty much decided he wasn't doing anything with Emily, who wasn't back. Still, I was thinking about seeing him early that morning a few days ago trudging up the stairs.

He bit his lip, looked away, then said half under his breath. "This record thing, it's, you know, getting close. Way close."

"I thought the session was starting in—"

"Nah, they moved it up."

"When?"

"Next fuckin' week." Slater spit this out.

"That soon?" I was thinking that Sailor and I hadn't gotten anything written yet, and how much she wanted better songs for the LP.

"Sire says, 'Studio's free. Gotta go!'" Slater clapped his hands, echoey in the almost empty subway car. "Like we're not artists, just performing monkeys."

"But you're ready?"

"Of course." Slater threw this out, but it rang a little false. I searched for his eyes, but he'd turned away from me, looking up and down the subway car, distracted. Then he spun back on me. "But this—this here tonight is good, just what I fuckin' need." He shot me one of his wide, charming smiles. "Thanks for coming, bro."

"Sure." I rolled my shoulders. "So, this helps? Just run the subway when you can't crash out?"

"Man, I got all kinds of things that help, you know." Slater winked. "But we're not just runnin' aimless, just got some time to kill."

"For what?"

"Party, dude!" He nodded to himself, then brightened noticeably. "Righteous party."

"Which hasn't started yet? Like way after twelve?"

"Just stick with me, Cole, it'll be worth it." Slater nodding, like that, back to himself. "Just stick with me."

I was ready, of course. I'd actually been really jumpy this evening, flitting between my black-and-white TV and a book, and kind of crawling with that deep New York Saturday night loneliness where you just know everyone's out having a great time except for you, you stupid loser. In truth it was a godsend that Slater had swooped me up.

Then I met Zog.

We ran the 6 train uptown, switching at Hunts Point in the Bronx, then back downtown, no purpose I could see, just riding. We switched to the F to Brooklyn. At Essex Street a tall, stringy guy got in the car, went up to Slater, and said, "Man, you're a damn genius. I really didn't believe you'd make it work, man."

Slater just smiled his cat grin.

"Hey, I'm Zog," the skinny guy said, sticking out his hand. I shook it, his palms sweaty, his fingers twitching in my grip.

"Slater and I go way back, man," Zog started saying. "We've been in this crazy city forever, and you know what our bro did, he told me to be on the third car from the front of the F train at 12:45, and there I was, man, and I'd only been waitin' there five minutes when you guys pull in." He threw his palm back, slapped his forehead. "Ain't nobody knows this city like Slater, you're the king, man, the friggin' king!"

All the while Zog was snapping his fingers. Compulsive, just *snap snap snap*. He sat on the seat next to Slater. He had silver taps on his cowboy boots, and as he sat there, his black boots kept jumping about, clattering heel and toe against the floor, the edge of the seat. He radiated so much crazy late-night energy he almost sparked.

I mean, really sparked, and not just his boots. Zog had this long, straight blond hair, brushed shiny past his shoulders, and it glowed. It was straw blond, like what you'd see on a model on a Clairol box, and shimmery under the subway car lights. I immediately thought of the girls I grew up with, watching *Shindig* and *I Spy* and brushing their hair through the whole hourlong shows. Zog's hair was the only truly clean thing about him, the rest was greasy jeans, a scuffed leather jacket with star-studded epaulets, dirty fingernails, and wisps of pale hair on his chin.

"So what's with this party, brother, it gonna be hoppin'? I'm feelin' it—" finger snap, finger snap "—I'm ready, steady, spaghetti ... ravioli, macaroni—" snap, snap "—cannaloni, cannastroni...." A jut of his dirty hand, wiping his mouth. "Feelin' parched, starched, Fredric Marched—" All this in a rat-tat-tat of words I could barely keep up with, barked and scatted, snapping, snapping, winding Zog up, making him more frenetic like he'd never—

Slater shot out his right hand and slapped him.

Zog took the palm to his cheek, eyes popping, a slight lurch, then he looked to start up again ... and Slater slugged him again.

That got to Zog, slowing him, diverting him.

"When's the last time you slept?" Slater leaned in.

"What?" Zog's eyes bulged.

"I said, Zog," Slater went on, each word enunciated molasses slow, "when's the last time your fuckin' head hit a pillow?"

Zog's eyes blanked. He shook his head.

"I can't recall, brother."

Slater nodded to himself, then reached into his own heavy leather jacket and pulled out a small packet of crumpled aluminum foil.

"You're gonna make me fuckin' nuts," he said, unwrapping the foil. "Here, take some of this."

There was a light brown powder there, a few teaspoonfuls.

"Now?" Zog said.

"Right this fuckin' second or I throw you off the fuckin' train."

Zog swallowed hard, then nodded.

Slater daubed a finger into the powder, then held it under Zog's nose. He quickly snorted it up. What was left on his finger Slater licked off. Then he dried his finger on his shirt and stuck it back in the powder, then to Zog's other nostril and back to his own tongue. They kept doing this, the crumpled foil glittering under the lights. There were ten or so other people on the train but nobody paid us any mind.

After a half-dozen doses of the powder, Slater said, "Zog, go sit over there till it hits, probably by the time we get to Fourth Avenue."

"Why?" Zog got out.

Slater just shot him a look. Zog shuffled across the roaring subway car, sitting across from us. He looked forsaken for a moment, then started snapping his fingers again wildly.

"Jesus fucking Christ," Slater muttered. "Fuckin' speed freaks."

I didn't say anything.

"Hey, Cole, you want some?" Slater turned to me and held out the foil pouch.

I wasn't sure what it was, but I had my ideas. I was hardly an innocent when it came to drugs, at least the growing-up-in-the-'60s variety, but once I got old enough to know my own ways, I realized I never liked them much. I think I smoked my last joint in 1971, six years back. I'd tried cocaine a time or two, but it had always made me so wildly paranoid I thought I was losing my mind.

Was this coke? I forgot what color cocaine was, not always white, right? Could've been, but I don't think coke would've slowed Zog down that much. Maybe it was some kind of downer Slater poured out of pills and carried around in foil. It could've been that.

Anyway, I shook my head.

"You sure? This shit's guaranteed to put a righteous smile on your face." Slater pointed across the subway car. "Keep your eyes on Zog. Ten minutes from now that boy's gonna be smiling like he's standin' at the gates of heaven."

"Nah, sorry," I said.

Slater turned to me, "You're a bit of a pussy, ain't you, Cole?" he said, drawling out my name. "A bit of a leetle chicken—"

"Fuck you, Slater."

Slater's head flicked back, like he'd just been scratched. His eyes went cold and hard, and I tensed; but it was only for a second, then he relaxed and laughed heartily.

"One way or another, you're gonna have a good night tonight, son." That thin, spooky Slater smile. Then he lifted his chin, jutting it at Zog. "Oh, look, that boy's just made it to seventh heaven."

He had, too, a big, moony, beatific smile draping Zog's long face, as bright as his Clairol blond hair.

We all got up a minute later to leave the car, and as we did, Slater moved between Zog and me, reaching up and putting an arm around each of our shoulders.

"Thing is, boys, *I* don't stop at seventh heaven. Don't pay seventh no mind. The heaven I'm after, that sucker's waaay down the line. Ninth, tenth … maybe a hundred?" Slater winked. "Hundredth heaven! Any of you boys got balls enough to head to hundredth heaven with me?"

※ ※ ※ ※ ※

WHEN WE GOT OUT of the subway the streets were empty. There were stacks of discarded tires, cracked asphalt, darkened buildings. It was also eerily silent.

"Where are we?" I said to Slater.

"Gowanus Canal."

I'd heard of that, a part of Brooklyn you just didn't go to.

"Are we safe?" came out of me, though I felt like a fool once the words were there.

"You're *never* safe," Slater said, laughing. It was his full-burst cackle, echoing off the empty buildings. "Not ever safe, nowhere in this life, right, bro?"

There was no answer to that and I let it go. Finally we turned into the darkest and emptiest of buildings. Down a corridor lit only by a wire-caged yellow light, down another with only the faint reflection of the sickly yellow light to guide us.

Slater led us into the largest elevator I'd ever been in, at least twenty feet across, wood floors, rusted iron gate that clanked closed once we were inside. You could watch the floors go past as we rose, each one painted with slapped-on white paint: 1, 2, 3 ... 6, 7.... That last number caught me.

We got off at nine.

The noise seemed to sweep into the elevator, swirl about like a strong wind, then pull us all out the door.

Turned out we were in an unused manufacturing loft still full of large metal contraptions I later found out were knitting machines. It was a big, big room, but it was packed; had to be a couple hundred people there, all in their twenties, most dressed rough and ready, at first glance like the crowd at CBGBs. Hmnn, whatever that Bowery club thing was, it looked to be spreading.

Slater led us up to a tall pyramid of beer cans, evidently for display, since beneath it was a row of large, plastic-lined trash barrels full of ice and more beer. Slater pulled out five Schaefers, one for me, one for Zog, three for himself.

Music, all slamming fuzz guitar and wall-shaking bass, came through a line of speakers. Close to the source it was too loud to talk. There was also a cloud of smoke everywhere; everyone seemed to be puffing away on something.

"What's the deal?" I yelled at Slater as he downed half his beer in one pull.

"Whattaya mean?"

"Whose party is it?"

"Nobody's."

"Nobod—"

"It just happens. An art commune squats here, people come and go, most Saturday nights there's a scene."

"Open to anybody?"

"Are *you* anybody?"

"What do you mean?" I was still yelling, though we'd moved across the room, standing next to a large metal loom twelve or so feet high.

"Whether you're somebody or not, bro, isn't that up to you?"

"I don't know." What was Slater talking about? "I guess."

"Well, if you *are* somebody, then you're here." His eyes shone. "Got it?"

I shrugged, took a pull of my own beer. I didn't like Schaefer all that much, it was an East Coast thing I hadn't gotten the taste for yet, but it definitely fit the scene here, so I drank it down.

Slater had killed his first one, like that. He was on to his second. I looked around for Zog. He was talking to a girl with curled midnight-black hair and an attractive, exotic face … blink, blink, but she wasn't Cherry Kruntz. Nope, nobody at first glance looked familiar.

"Anybody here I know?" I said to Slater.

He started to answer, then just gave me a deep smile. "I think that all depends, Cole, on *who* you know—or who you *get* to know." A wink, then he clapped me on the shoulder and took off into the crowd.

I started walking around. Even if this was an art commune, I didn't see evidence of anyone living here, no beds, no kitchen; didn't look like much of anything other than the old, tired machinery. Maybe there was another floor? I wondered if the party was in any way official or just people who'd found the space. Probably the latter. As I've said, this was still New York City in bankruptcy time, and there were empty buildings and squatters and who knew what all over the place. Especially out here in deep Brooklyn.

Where did all these people come from? They sure weren't the type I'd meet at book parties. They were like that Bowery crowd, but in some ways rougher. I saw guys in jeans and work shirts who could've just come from doing time, chicks with fluffy bouffant hairdos who might've stepped out of a '50s JD flick. And they were the most normal looking. A host of guys had almost completely shaved heads, though they'd left various insignia behind: short tufts of hair cut as arrows or swastikas or hammer-and-sickles. There was a group of folk in black leather, head to toe, with high collars and skin-tight pants. They all seemed to be wearing makeup, a lot of kohl around their eyes. And almost all of them were dudes.

A *lot* of makeup... on the girls at the party, too, though it was hard to see many of the chicks' eyes, a lot of them had on big sunglasses, black curvy shades that nearly swallowed their faces. Some of them looked wealthy, shoes from Saks that had to brave the cobblestones out here in Gowanus; but a whole lot more of the partiers sure looked, well, poor. Thrift shop clothes, baggy pants, ugly-as-sin green suede shoes, tight shirts with yellow blushes under their armpits, stringy, half-inch-wide ties loose around necks. A lot of people were keeping whatever they had on going at all costs. I saw pants held together with silver duct tape, shirts with wide holes narrowed by safety pins, wool jackets sporting Girl Scout patches barely covering moth holes, shift dresses that actually once had been some dude's well-worn XXL shirt....

The funny thing: None of this *looked* like poverty, or like Wendell Walters' cluelessness.

It simply looked like style.

There was also an artier bunch, paint drippings streaking down ripped T-shirts, short-clipped hair that looked highly contrived. There were girls in black tights and slight T's with glitter on them spelling out phrases like LICK ME, DADA

NOT PAPA, and TEENAGE LOBOTOMY. All of them, the leather boys, the shaved-head dudes, the art chicks, the Salvation Army half-off-sale kids, they all seemed to be making some kind of statement.

A statement. That was a way of thinking about it, that most of the folk at Slater's party were making statements, though what all they were saying I really didn't get. Hey, those book parties I was so jazzed to go to weren't like *this*. Here in Brooklyn, not a square inch of tweed in sight!

I perambulated through the loft, the loud pounding buzz-saw music, some kids dancing frenetically, most in groups shouting and laughing and swilling the cheap beer, and I just didn't see any way in. At the book parties there'd usually be somebody from work, who'd introduce me to other bookish folk, or somebody I'd met before whom I could go up to and ask how it was going; as well as the occasional famous face: Look, there's Allen Ginsberg!

Quick aside: I remember meeting Ginsberg at a very high-class party on Fifth Avenue, at some consulate. I edged into his circle, spoke to him a bit about something, and all the time wondered what Allen Ginsberg was doing at such a uniformed-waiters-passing-out-crystal-flutes-of-champagne affair. Turned out Ginsberg lived around the corner from me on East 12$^{th}$ Street; he was probably at the party for the same reason I was, a little glitter and sparkling conversation, maybe new connections ... and free food.

At Slater's party of punks and artistes, the longer I moved about, the less I felt I could relate to anyone. I can get oddly lost to myself at a party, more alone than when actually alone—one reason I ended up a writer?—and that's what I was getting here. I did end up standing next to a guy with a Keith Richards shag cut, hanging by him long enough that it didn't seem strange to try to make a connection. He was also alone, and I shouted over the searing music, "Hey, how're you doing?"

Not clever, I know, and worse when the guy turned, his leather jacket flapped open, and I saw that it wasn't a boy at all but a girl, with small but distinct breasts under a V-neck white T-shirt. She had wide violet eyes and was almost pretty in a gaminelike way. Not exactly my type but she had something about her.

I was dropping a winsome smile on her when she looked me up and down, checking out my Levis and crewneck sweater, shook her head, then called out across the room and moved off to somebody else.

Smooth move, Cole.

Where was Slater? I looked for him but couldn't see him anywhere. How about that weird guy Zog? (What kind of name was *that*?) But even Zog was nowhere to be seen.

More and more people kept crowding in, if anything, the assaulting music got even louder, and I was pushing myself between people just to move about, apologizing to their indifferent backs, not catching anybody's eye—feeling invisible and lost.

Over in a corner two tense guys were facing off, like a fight was going to break out. One had inky tats up and down his arms and a tall Mohawk, black hair sprouting high in a line down the middle of his head; the other guy's head was shaved, gleaming pale skin, with iron crosses dangling from his ears and a T-shirt full of safety pins. I heard yelling over the music. Didn't see any weapons, just fists, bared and held out.

I had no interest in seeing a fight, so I kept wandering through the thick smoke—worse than any smog day growing up in L.A.—picked up another Schaefers, then found an open window and stood there catching some fresh air. Next to me was another huge open window, at least ten feet high, and this one people were climbing out of ... oh, it was the fire escape.

There was actually a line to get out the window, and I queued up. I liked the idea of midnight air and figured I wasn't getting anywhere inside anyway.

A cute redhead in a pixie cut stood in front of me.

"Hi, I'm Cole," I said, tapping her on the shoulder. This close to the window I didn't have to yell so loud. "I don't know anybody here."

"I'm Zooey." She brightened. "And I know ev-er-y-one."

"Really?"

"Ev-er-y-one," she repeated.

"And who is ev-er-y-one?" I bounced each syllable just as she had.

"Hey, who are you?" She was eyeballing me top to bottom. When Slater told me to get a coat, I'd grabbed the first thing hanging on my wall, a gray tweed sport coat, and she seemed fixated on that. "Are you realllllllly Mr. Rogers?"

*"Touché."*

No response to that. Then she was through the open window. I heard more shouts and alarums behind me, as if the fight had started, but nobody around me seemed to care. A moment later there was room outside, and I climbed through the window. Zooey was nowhere to be seen, not that it mattered. It looked as if I could either go up or down. I went up.

I had to pick my way carefully over partygoers spread out on the black-iron fire escape. Up a flight, then one more, and I was on the roof...

... my head thrown back, stunned.

The view was back toward Manhattan. There was the low sweep of Brooklyn, a slice of the Brooklyn Bridge, and then the lower flank of my island: a row of all-lit-up buildings, glowing, light oozing up into the sky. I loved it here in New York, but the thing was, I was usually just going about my business, subways, work, walking the streets, maybe a basement bar, a streetside restaurant, a second-floor Gotham Book Mart party... it wasn't that often I comprehended the whole blooming thing.

But that's what I saw this night: Brooklyn, Manhattan... this enormous, enthralling city I'd chosen over boring L.A.

Boy, was I lucky! What fortune to find my cheap railroad flat, that Mrs. Walden had taken an interest in me at *The New Yorker*—that I'd been able to get a solid perch in this amazing town.

As I turned away from the city glow and my eyes grew accustomed to the dark, I saw there were a lot of people on the roof; and over there, with his stringy bowl of hair, was my buildingmate.

Slater wasn't alone. To my surprise, that girl I'd tried to talk to waiting to get outside, Zooey, was with him.

"Hey, Cole, how's it hangin', bro?"

"Mind if I join you?"

Slater looked to Zooey, who didn't look that into it, focused on anywhere other than me. Slater shrugged, then said, "Sure. There's a spot right here."

They were on a small ledge around thick metal mesh covering a huge fan, some kind of exhaust for the lofts, turned off now. There were faint greenish-yellow safety lights at the corners, which cast up an unearthly glow. Slater had pointed to a place next to Zooey, but instead I dropped onto the roof right across from him.

Slater had two empty Schaefers at his feet, a full one in his hand, and a dozen more lined up on the ledge. He offered me one, and I took it gladly. Zooey was drinking one, too.

"So, what do you think?" Slater said.

"About what?"

"The party, man. Your cuppa?"

I took a deep breath. In truth, I guessed I'd rather be at this party than at home—the view up here certainly was great, the whole scene intriguing in its way, and there was always the whisper of *something* happening—but overall....

"You gotta make the most of it, man. Gotta make the most of ev-er-y fuckin' thing." He turned to the girl next to him. "Right, Dix?"

It took Zooey a minute, but she nodded. She looked more spaced than when I'd met her getting out here, a logy, droopy smile on her face. Then I saw, thanks to the bilious safety lights, between Slater and the girl, a chunk of folded-up aluminum foil.

"Zooey here knows how to make the most of ... ev-er-y-thing." Slater winked at me, then leaned over and kissed her, hard on the mouth. A quick lunge, the long plant ... for a moment I thought of him and Emily. My stomach jumped.

But Zooey wasn't Emily, just a party girl—a fan of Savage Joy, it turned out, who lifted her head enough to show mild interest when Slater told her that I'd "kinda helped" come up with the band's name. I nodded, surprised at the recognition.

"O.K., *not* Mr. Rogers," she said, eyebrows fluttery. "How about ... 'bout T.S. Eliot? In the old guy's banker days?"

Slater shot her a look, and both of them cracked up.

I was thinking about Emily. Just that one flash and she was back in my head. You remember, I'd tried to find out what had happened between her and Slater, with her and the band, from asking her and asking Wendell ... but I hadn't asked Slater himself.

"What about Emily?" I said to him then.

"I'm thinking more ol' Bob Lowell," Slater said to Zooey, who thought about it way more deeply than made sense, her brow thoroughly pursed, before finally nodding.

"You guys know Robert Lowell?" I said.

"Cole, Cole, baby, don't *ever* un-der-es-ti-mate me." Slater fixed me with his intense glare, the one that shot out of him at the most unexpected moments; a sudden machine-gun strafing right at me. "Now what were you saying?"

"Emily." I looked back at him as fiercely as I could. Slater like this was scary, but he didn't scare me. "You remember Emily, right? A little like Syl-vi-a Plath—"

Slater glared at me a long moment, then he came around.

"So what's the question, Cole?" he said, smiling.

"Slater, listen, nobody will tell me what happened.

To the band. On the road. Why Emily left it. Why—"

"How 'bout this, Cole?" A sharp but scattered light in his eyes. Playing me or—

"Yeah?"

"That woman just wasn't *savage*." Slater tipped back his sharp chin, laughed loud at the black sky. "She wasn't even *joyful*."

"What kind of shit is—"

"Oh, Cole, come on, come on. I'm just funnin' with you." A wink at Zooey, who wasn't paying attention. "Listen, bro, I really can't go into it ... not now." Another tilt of his head toward Zooey. "But the thing is, Emily just didn't see things the right way."

"The right—?"

"Yeah. A band ... a band's gotta *all* be on the same page, bro. You gotta move as one. Somebody says *jump*—well, *I* say jump—everybody gotta the fuck jump."

"And Emily didn't—"

"Jump." Slater chuckled. He lit a cigarette, one of his hand-rolled ones out of his rusty Sucrets case.

"Yeah, but what does that *mean*? Slater, I know you were sleep—"

A quick tilt of Slater's head toward Zooey, clearly meaning: Don't say too much, eh? I nodded back: I got it.

"But you gotta know, Slater, that made me fuckin' crazy. You have no friggin' idea—"

"You're right," he said through his slit smile, interrupting me. "I really have no friggin' idea—" He snickered again.

"And you don't *care*?"

"I can't be—" Slater started to say, then pulled up. He took a minute, thinking. Meanwhile he emptied his beer, took a pull off his cigarette, grabbed another can, popped the top with his teeth, and threw it back.

"Hey, Cole, you drunk?" he asked me out of the blue.

"Yeah," I said after a second, checking myself. I hadn't

had that many beers, but it never took many. "A little. How about you?"

"Naw." Slater shook his head.

"But you've been drinking all night—all day. And that ... whatever is in your packet of foil down—"

"I don't *get* drunk." Slater said this strong, throwing his finger at me. "I don't get high, man. I *am* high." A slow burning interior turning that put a goofy smile on his face. "And *that's* what was wrong with Emily, pal."

I shook my head. I didn't get this, what he was saying. Drunk was drunk, right? High was high, and....

"She seems pretty spirited to me." I turned over that word, *spirited*; yes, I'd stick with that. *Spirited* was one of the reasons I'd loved Emily, along with *beautiful, fierce, smart, always surprising*....

"You're not hearing me, Cole."

"What aren't I hearing, *Slater*?" I punched out his name.

"I like you, man. You're a good, what ... counter to me? An opposite? Something like that." Slater nodded.

"Oh, that's what I am?" Again, I wasn't quite tracking what he was saying, just felt it was derogatory. "What, I'm here to balance you out? That doesn't make any sense at—"

"It *all* makes sense, man." Slater reached down and lifted up the aluminum foil, unfolded it. With his other hand he took a twenty-dollar bill from his pocket and rolled it up. "Hey, babe, you want some more?"

Zooey nodded, and Slater passed her the twirled bill, then held out the foil. She snorted a pinch of the brown powder—actually, more black up here under the yellow safety glow and the starlight—then passed it back to Slater, who snuffed up most of what was left.

"Still got a little, Cole?"

"What is it?"

"What *is* it?" Slater chuckled. "If you gotta ask, then you *really* the fuck need it." He thrust out the rolled-up bill.

I looked at it hard. This was a strange night, this rooftop, all these curiouser and curiouser people, and it was true I was in many ways sick of my life—at least the lonely life that had me at home on a Saturday night watching the goddamn *Mary Tyler Moore Show* and going to bed early—and I was, I realized, truly thankful to Slater for dragging me out to Brooklyn on this adventure. Did that mean I was ready to put something up my nose I only had a suspicion of what it was? A deep breath. Nope. Not me. Didn't do that. Not tonight. Probably never.

Slater saw my decision in my eyes, thankfully took the powder back.

"You know, Cole, we are *so* different." Humor in Slater's eyes. "Not that I'm putting you down or nothing."

Another dig, right? But this time I just didn't care.

"Same with Emily. I dug her, too, man, but she couldn't do it." A nod. "She just could ... not ... do it.

"Do what?"

"Do what she needed to do."

"Jesus, Slater," I burst out, "stop talking in fuckin' riddles!"

Slater just laughed.

"O.K., one more time," I said, cooling a notch. "What did Emily *need* to do?"

"I already told you."

"Slater!"

"Man, all I'm saying is that she could not go as far as she had to."

"Go as far as she had to?" I took a breath. "Was it the drugs?"

Slater took a moment, then shook his head.

"Meaning?" I said.

"Not part of it, bro."

"So what was it?"

Another long pause, then Slater said, "You'll have to ask Emily."

"Like it's private?" I hit the last word hard.

More notions banging around in his head, then finally Slater said, "Why do you care, Cole?"

"Because I fuckin' do."

"Well, then, yeah, I guess that's the deal, man." Slater nodded, though again I wasn't sure what exactly he meant. "Talk to Emily."

"But *you* could do it?" I leaned forward, heard the edge in my voice. Yeah, right, talk to Emily. I didn't even know where she was. So I went at Slater. "That's what you're saying, that *you* could do it—whatever the fuck we're talking about?"

"Of course." His self-amused eyes, bright.

"Because *you're* so friggin' liberated?"

"Because—" now Slater leaned forward "—because I understand how things work, bro."

"Oh, yeah," I said. I was getting worked up, probably because of Emily, maybe because I was pretty loaded. "And how is that, Mr. Slater Martin?"

"Cole, I think you *are* drunk." He said this to me deadpan, but I brushed him aside.

"You're one to talk."

"But that's it, man. You don't get it. I just explained it to you, and you ... do ... not ... get it."

"That you're high? What's so great about—"

"No, you idiot!"

"Then what?"

"It's not about *getting* high. It's just about the way you—"

"Yeah, fuckin' high!"

"Come on, Cole, Jesus!" Slater snapped "Listen, we don't even talk about that. You just ... you get to the right place, man, and you don't even have to talk about *that*."

"Ooooh-woooooo." I went spooky voice on him, like we used to do when I was a kid and somebody was babbling LSD talk. "Ooooh-woooooo-woooooo."

Slater ignored me, as usual.

"It's kind of like, You have to ask, bro, you'll never know."

"Ooooh-woooooo-woooooo-wooooo-woooooo."
Now Slater laughed.

"All I'm saying is, I thought Emily *could* do it, I did." He fixed me with his razor eyes again. "I never thought you could, Cole, so it never came up. But Emily, yeah, I thought she could."

"And what is *it*?" I nearly yelled at him. I really didn't know what he was talking about if it wasn't drugs—whatever was in the aluminum packet. I didn't think I was clueless. I just think he wasn't saying anything.

"We're going in circles," Slater said.

"Exactly!"

He shook his head dismissively. Part of me wanted to give up on this nonsense, too, but since it was about Emily ... well, I said, "We may be going in circles, but if I knew what the fuck you were saying, I wouldn't keep asking."

Slater was silent a moment. Next to him Zooey let her head fall onto his shoulder. He didn't acknowledge it. Finally, he spoke.

"You put it into words, it doesn't—"

"*Everything* can be put into words," I blurted out, Mr. Writer all the way.

"You don't mean that, do you, Cole?"

Even as I'd said it, I knew I didn't, at least not with such utter conviction. Words—what I was giving my life to—the whole point of words was to use them as accurately and thoroughly as possible, to push them as far as you could toward what could not ... ever ... be expressed. Because the truth with writing, with literature, was that even in the most glorious of hands, there were worlds that could at best only be hinted at, poked, with good fortune closed in upon ... but never seized. At least not with only words. Even *I* knew that.

"You're talking about the ineffable?" I said softly.

"Heff-a-lump to you, bro." Slater's eyes sparked.

"I mean, Mr. Rimbaud, that I *know* what you're saying

about words." I was falling into my serious, we're-talking-'bout-heavy-ontological-shit voice, as if I were with some of my *New Yorker* pals at the Cedar Tavern on University at 3 a.m., the shades of Jasper Johns and Robert Rauschenberg in the corner. "Words can't capture all of experience, there's a whole ... a whole knowable but ... but in-ef-fable world out there that—"

"And that's where *I* am, man." Slater gave me a serious nod, almost like he was across the wood table at that bar, almost as if Jasper Johns's spirit were passed out in a corner. "In-ef-fa-ble." He laughed. "Or at least that's where I gotta be ... *always* be."

"What's that mean in real life, like, what, anything goes?"

"I guess." Slater shrugged. "That's one way of putting—"

"Anything and everything ... whatever, it's all fine for you."

"Not fine, bro." Slater's eyes burning. "Ex-pect-ed. Every breath I take in, every thought I—"

"So you're saying, for you, *anything* goes?" I was still trying to get my head around what he was getting at, not sure I was.

"Cole."

"What, like murdering somebody?" Thinking of all this, and Dostoevsky popped into my head.

Slater gave me a long, hangdog look.

"This ain't a philosophy discussion at your top-tier college, Cole. Of course not mur-der." A slight shrug. "Unless, of course, it has to be done." Slater laughed, but it wasn't clear how funny he was being.

"So what are you—"

"I wish you'd just listen to me, man." Slater leaned toward me. Zooey, still leaning up against him, shifted. He put out a hand to keep her from falling away.

"I am, I *am*!" And I realized if there was any time to actually listen to Slater, this was it. He'd been a hard nut to crack since I met him, and now—tingled and looped on this Brooklyn roof—finally, Slater Martin seemed to be speaking from the heart. "Just keep going."

Odd, it was like he was waiting for my encouragement; Slater wanting *that* from me.

"Here's the deal," he said. "You see, we got these walls, no, this ... this *thing* pressing against us." He waved his hands about, pushing and pulling an invisible cloud. "We all feel it. All of us. This tight, cottony, smoth-er-y thing. It's, like, everything we're sposed to be and everything we're sposed to do." He hit those *supposed to*'s hard. "You know it, right?"

"Like what, the law?" I said, still not quite—

"Don't be a dick, Cole." Slater jerked out his hand, a rough gesture. "I'm getting ex-is-ten-tial here. You can dig me getting existential, right?"

"Don't mock me."

Slater's eyes lifted, went back a moment, then stared hard at me.

"I'm ... Cole, if I've ever *not* mocked you, this is it, bro."

"O.K., fancy big words. I get it. You've been reading again, right?" This was snobby of me. I hadn't earned that at all, and as soon as I said this, I regretted it.

"Yeah, of course I've been reading."

"Emily?"

"What about her?" Slater looked perplexed.

"On the bus, maybe. She was helping you—"

"Fuck you." Slater glared at me. "You're so fuckin' lost, bro."

"What do you—"

"First off, I *can* read." Slater started making a moronic stupid-face, mugging, but with an edge. "I know you think I'm some barbarian, but—" He kept glaring, then swallowed whatever he was about to say. "But actually it was Sailor. In the bus, Sailor was reading to me, O.K.? Like while I drove."

Of course, Sailor. Why hadn't I thought of her, the *Tyger* poem and all.

"But I've been reading all along. You've seen me."

I nodded, had to admit that.

"And Sailor, she wasn't telling me anything I didn't friggin' *know*, bro. And what I know is we all got this ... this shit around us, smothering us, choking us, holding us down.

"But me ... for me, there's just one purpose, to kick it away—to kick the fuckin' shit out of the shit." Slater sped up now, seized by a passion not always apparent through his cool demeanor.

"That's why we got the band, the fuckin' record deal—" He pulled up then, flashed anxious a moment, then kicked past it. "The deal with the band, it's *not* to make records and make money, it's to ... to lead the friggin' charge. For freedom, man. Pure fuckin' freedom. And ec-sta-sy. An ecstatic life!"

I was here with Slater, right, and it was well past three in the morning on a roof in a part of Brooklyn I'd never been to, so I was hardly innocent. Freedom and ecstasy? Hey, I'd studied William Blake at Cal—I'd *chosen* to study Blake. Of course, my class met in the rare book room of the library so we could pass around high-class repros of Blake's illuminated works. So it was school, and it was in my head—it wasn't being at a freak party in darkest Brooklyn way after midnight with a possible lunatic. It wasn't watching him toot up God knows what. It was enough beers to make my head spin ... and know I'd wake up with a hangover, but basically sober, tomorrow. It was not *my* life. Not at all....

"And Savage Joy," Slater went on, interrupting my tumbling thoughts. "You know, Cole, I'm gonna start givin' you credit. Yeah, I know the words're yours—I'm not a total dickwad." He let out a towering laugh. "Thing is, I really can't believe *you* came up with Savage Joy, it's too fuckin' perfect. Man, that's just what we're after: Savage Fuckin' Joy. *That* kind of contradiction. Weird jux-ta-po-si-tion—yeah, I know *that* dollar-fifty word, too. I been workin' it. Bing-bang!

"And I got me some more of 'em. Yeah, your words got my ol' brain roaring. What do you think about Brutal Grace? Like maybe we change the band's name each show we do? Harsh Ecstasy. Maybe Ragged Radiance." Slater winked at me. "I'd love to fuck with our fans, keep 'em guessing. Fuck with Sire Records, too, that corporate fuckface. And there're a lot of possibilities, don't you think? You like any of them? Brash Ecstasy? Jagged Radiance?"

In truth, his word spritz impressed me. He'd caught my antonymic compression and was playing it out. Had Emily—or Sailor—helped him? I thought to ask but didn't.

"So, yeah, that's the point—the whole friggin' point, Cole. Savage Joy. Harsh Ecstasy." He swallowed, this was taking all his energy. "And I'm getting close. Burnin' close. The band ... the *band's* getting close. But it's not just being in a band, it has to be a life: *my life*. The only friggin' thing *in* my life." Slater was almost shouting now, rousing Zooey next to him. "Do you understand?" He shouted at me as if right then my understanding him was all that truly mattered. *"Do you?"*

I took a minute, then I half-nodded. I think I pretty much got what he was saying. It was Blake, but up to the moment. Blake not dancing naked in his Lambeth backyard but stumbling around a Brooklyn roof in a ripped T-shirt and a leather coat, crying to the heavens. But still William Blake. You embrace all desire. Don't think, act. Don't stand still, move. Never philosophize, materialize. And never accept, simply charge on through....

Slater held out a fresh beer, shook it vigorously, then popped the top. Foam burst out of it, showering into the air, falling on all of us. Slater, whooped up on something, waved the can around like Slim Pickens at the end of *Dr. Strangelove*, whirligigging even more beer on us.

"So let's get you good and fucked up!" Slater laughed, passing me the can, which I took. "All this ... this phil-os-o-phiz-ing, my friggin' head hurts. Come on, bro, really good and wasted!"

The wet beer was all over my hair, my face. I took off my jacket, wiped it down, then took off my sweater and wiped the brew off as best as I could with my shirttails. Slater had sent the beer flying all over him and Zooey, too, though neither of them seemed to care.

Slater kept laughing, and it was jolly enough, and what the fuck did I care, I pulled down the Schaefer. I got drunker. So what the cold night air was biting at me. Slater was ... well, whatever Slater was. Zooey, she was whatever she was.

O.K., I did bundle up again best I could. And we kept talking, though for the life of me I can't remember anything else we said. I went back down to the party to take a piss and better wash off the sticky beer, and I ended up chatting up some artists, I think. Smart guys. Interesting women. I think.

I made it back up on the roof with Slater and Zooey. They were making out, haphazardly, off and on, but kissing and feeling each other up while I just sat there, staring into the distance, drunk and blank.

Dawn broke, J.M.W. Turner swirling pale and yellow and orange and blue. I almost never was up to see the sunrise and took it in joyously. Sure, my head was pounding a little, and I was still wet and cold, but this was a beautiful fall morning ... and I took it all in, with a swelling of abundant freedom and ecstasy. It had been that kind of night.

We left not long after that. Slater and Zog, who materialized out of who knows where, and Zooey, too. Stumbling through the cobblestoned streets back to the F train. Silent, my head in my hands, to the Second Avenue stop; then somehow up Second to 11th. I was in Veneiros getting a cannoli to fill my rattling stomach when I heard shouts in the street. Clearly Slater's voice ... and another I half-recognized, too.

I ran back out there, yelling for Slater and Zog to stop, but it was too late.

# 23

THE OTHER VOICE was Harper Hart's, his lacrosse yell, snarling and angry. I saw him take a swing at Slater, his long arms missing his head but clipping his shoulder.

Slater wriggled away. Meanwhile Zog moved behind Harper, shadowing him.

"You're a fuckin' dead man, you little shit," Harper cried.

He went at Slater again. I was surprised, Slater was on the balls of his feet, moving with as much grace as I'd seen onstage, almost as if he'd studied boxing. (Later I learned he had.) He wasn't punching at Harper, though, just avoiding him.

It was an astonishing dance, this fight—this violence—right outside my front door; and I stopped outside the pastry shop, watching it.

Harper charged at Slater, who, tight-lipped, slipped around him like a bullfighter. Zog, running the perimeter, followed Harper, moving up right behind him.

That's when Slater made his move. It was elegant and yet weirdly elementary-school-playground, too. Zog went down on his hands and knees, and with the lightest of touches Slater jabbed Harper in the chest and sent him over Zog, Harper's back hitting the sidewalk, his head following with a muffled crack.

Then they were on him. As Harper lay sprawled on the sidewalk, Slater came in from one side, Zog from the other, heavy boots flying, kicking him all over. Kicking him hard, chest, arms, head.

My heart seized up. Harper looked bad, dazed, his fierce voice now way softer, whimpering.

"Stop it!" I cried, running up to them. They were right in front of 340, right in front of our home.

Harper had curled up into a ball as Slater's and Zog's boot heels rained down on him.

I waved my hands, shouted again for them to stop.

They weren't going to, though. There was something wild and feral yet crisp and contained, at least from Slater. Zog's kicks to Harper were mostly intermittent stomps, his cowboy boots clattering on the sidewalk, then lifting up to his victim's arms and legs.

Slater was different. He moved with that Ali butterfly-bee thing, his fists still balled, his feet shuffling and dancing, and then ... strike. A kick to Harper's ear. More slipping and dancing. Then a blow to his solar plexus.

Harper's cries and whimpers sounded like a wolf in a trap, furious yet wounded, caught and crying for release.

At least Harper was still making noise. I had no experience with violence like this. I had no idea how it could end.

Fearing the worst, I went up and grasped at Slater's shoulders, fingers feeling his tight muscles, his tense back.

Slowly he turned and gave me the most terrifying look I've ever seen.

"Get away from me, Cole, get the fuck away." A low hiss, then he turned back to Harper.

I looked around, frantic. There was Zooey, with her head in her hands, still out of it as far as I could tell. This early, there were only two other people on 11th Street. One looked like a postman, off to work, the other possibly a homeless guy. Both stood far away from the fight, in disbelief though perhaps relish at the violent scene. Either way, I didn't see any help.

But somebody must've heard Harper's initial cries and called the police. Eleventh Street was one way going west, but west is the direction two blue-and-white cop cars rushed in from, sirens going, cherry tops spinning.

Even as Zog stood there transfixed, Slater took off. I saw

him run down 11th Street toward First Avenue, then head north up past the elementary school.

The first cop car kept going, whirling up First. The tailing one stopped in front of 340. One cop grabbed Zog and handcuffed him. The other went right to Harper.

One look and the cop barked into his walkie-talkie. An ambulance got there four minutes later. Two attendants put Harper onto a white gurney and wheeled him into the back, then sped away.

A few minutes later the first cop car was back, this time moving slowly, the correct direction down 11th Street.

In the backseat, behind black steel mesh, Slater's pale face shone out.

# 24

On Tuesday I saw Emily outside her door as I climbed the stairs to my apartment.

"Cole, Jesus, have you heard?" Her eyes were wide, startled.

"About Slater?"

"Yeah."

"I was there," I told her. "It was ... well, it was the morning, a few days back. We were coming home from a party—"

"And Harper attacked him?"

"Yep."

"That's so crazy!" Emily looked flushed, perhaps from climbing the stairs. But she seemed definitely disturbed.

"Harper was waiting for them, but then Slater and this strange friend of his, Zog, really went to town on him. Harper was down on the ground and—" I felt myself wince. The brutality was still shaking me. I'd pretty much turned away from the whole thing, going to *The New Yorker* on Monday—basically, escaping to work—and then staying out of it. I don't know what I'd expected when I got home, but nothing was going on. No Slater, no further news, nothing.

"Last night I went to Harper in the hospital." Emily spoke in clipped words. "I mean, I felt I had to, you know, and—"

"How is he?" I recalled him crumpled up on the ground, Slater's and Zog's boots flying at him. Those whimpers slipping out of him....

"He's going to make it," Emily said after a moment. "But Slater and his friend almost friggin' killed him."

"Slater was arrested, you know." As I said this, I couldn't tell if she already knew. "Last I saw of him, he was in the back of a police car. That was two days ago."

"I just got back from—" Emily clipped her tongue, looked down. "Have you heard anything since then?"

I shook my head.

"You didn't follow up, Cole?" Emily's voice rose with clear accusation.

"Um, work and, well, you know, Slater and I—"

"Shit!" she let out, interrupting my pathetic rationalizing. "Jesus, I feel ... I feel friggin' responsible for this." She stomped down her foot. "Goddamnit!"

"Emily, I don't—" As I looked at her, she grew more and more flustered.

"No, no, I have to deal with it. Shit! This is all the fuck I need."

"What're you going to—"

"Listen, Cole, if I need you, I'll let you know." Her eyes flamed up. "Jesus fuckin' shit, I can't believe there's this on top of everything else."

She went into her apartment, pulling her door shut.

I felt lousy that night. Was Slater my friend, I mean, so much that I should be doing something? I'd assumed that from jail he'd call his brother Dale, that he'd take care of him. I thought maybe the charges would've been dropped—Slater had been attacked by Harper—or that at the least he'd be out on bond by now. I was a little surprised I hadn't seen him in the halls but figured he could easily be staying with Dale or something.

Emily had been seriously alarmed, though, and now I felt I should've done more. I still wasn't sure what that could've been, but I should have done something. Gone to the jail? Made sure that Dale was on the case? Something.

I made my usual Chinese food and ate it watching the Walter Cronkite news. There was a lot of horrible stuff going on out there, but none of it registered. Even my food didn't have much taste.

After I washed up, I knew what I had to do. I threw on a

coat, double-locked my door, and headed down to Emily's apartment.

The first thing she said when she pulled it open was, "Slater's still in jail."

"What?"

"He wants to stay there."

"He wants to—" I shook my head. "What do you mean?"

"I mean, I talked to the asshole, and he says he wants to stay at the jail. Behind bars."

"That doesn't—"

"Cole, what're you doing here?" Emily stood there, her hands planted on her hips, staring at me.

"I want to help."

"How?" She said this sharply.

"Anything." I swallowed. "I mean, maybe I should've—"

"I don't know what good you'll do, but, O.K., you can come with me if you want to. I'm meeting Slater's brother and my lawyer at the Tombs."

"That's down by Chinatown?" I'd heard of the Tombs, it was the main detention hall in Manhattan.

"Yeah, that's where Slater is—where he wants *to stay*." Emily shook her head in disbelief.

"But why's he still there?" I looked at Emily hard, trying to read her. "I was sure he'd be out by now, I mean, wasn't it just basically a fight and—"

"Oh, Cole!" she cried. "They got him on possession. He had a chunk of smack in his pocket."

"You mean, hero—"

"Yeah, Slater had fuckin' heroin in his pocket. Not just a little. It's aggravated assault and possession to sell." Emily shook her head. "That idiot. He's so friggin' screwed."

"Jesus." I thought back to Zog on the train, Zooey and Slater on the rooftop. I really didn't think it was heroin they'd been blowing up their noses, but now that I knew, well, I guess I wasn't surprised.

"You can say that again."

"So you really think I should—"

"Keep me company?" Emily snorted. "Yeah, I don't see how it can hurt to have you along, Cole. At the least you can help try to keep me sane." She laughed, dark, gallowslike. "You've always been good at that."

She must have seen that I wasn't sure if she was being sarcastic or not, especially with her stunt the last time I'd seen her, because she immediately added, "I mean it. I think you'll help." Another nod. "For Slater. Come on, you ready to go?"

I nodded. My jacket on my shoulders, my apartment locked.

"Good," she said fast, "we can share a cab."

※ ※ ※ ※ ※

It wasn't official visiting hours, but Emily's lawyer—Richard Finnegan, in a fine-cut charcoal suit and an eye-blinking neon-blue tie—must have had sway, because twenty minutes after we got there Slater was brought down to a well-guarded room on the third floor. Slater's brother Dale was already there. I saw a mutual glance of greeting between him and Emily, and wondered how they'd gotten to know each other. That wasn't the only question the night would raise.

"So bail's set at $40,000, which we can handle, right, Miss Prosser?" Finnegan said. We were all sitting at a scarred wood table, Slater in a blue jumpsuit with a number in black across the front, Emily, Dale, the lawyer, and me circling him.

"That will be no problem," Emily said.

"So, Mr. Martin, are you ready for your freedom?" Finnegan's voice lifted in a curious way. I guessed he'd heard about Slater's intransigence.

Slater just sat there.

"If it makes you feel better, I don't think the authorities

have that great a case, first impressions aside," Finnegan went on. "You were attacked by Mr. Hart, right?"

Slater's look didn't change much, but he did finally nod.

"And Mr. Whitman." Finnegan turned to me. "You were there, right?"

I felt a quick heat go through me, the surprise of being singled out legally. Yet I, too, nodded.

"And you can testify to that?"

"That Harper was waiting for Slater?" I said softly. The lawyer gave me a curt nod. "And that Harper went at him first?"

"Yes on both counts." Finnegan looked like he wanted something more from me, I wasn't sure what.

"That's all I'll have to say?"

"If I can make it that Mr. Hart's assault is all that's pertinent, yes."

"And the drugs?" Emily leaned forward.

"That could be a problem, but it's a first offense, and I got some tricks." Finnegan shrugged. "I think we have a fighting chance."

His confidence filled the table, and we sat there not saying anything. Slowly we all looked at Slater. I was thinking of what Emily had said, that he didn't want to leave the jail, and I still couldn't understand what that meant.

Turned out it meant just what it sounded like.

"You don't need to do anything," Slater said softly, almost as if he were speaking only to himself. We all looked at him. A slow shake of his head. "Nothing."

"Slater, that doesn't make any *sense*," Emily said, her voice rising. She'd been through this with him before, right? Her eyelids beat up and down. Then she looked to Dale, sitting next to her.

"Bro, you're in goddamn jail," Dale said. "What the fuck is going on with you?"

Slater went silent. Hard, truculent silence.

"Mr. Martin, you're in the Tombs." Finnegan folded his hands together. "You'll stay in the Tombs until you accept bail. If you *don't* accept bail, you'll go to Rikers in a few days. Rikers makes this place look like Disneyworld. And you'll stay in Rikers till you go to trial." Finnegan was folding his fingers in and out of themselves. He was an unflappable soul but this looked flappable. "Trial, if you're lucky, might be in three months, six months, even a year."

Slater still silent.

"And if you don't accept bail, should we infer that you might not actually *go* to trial—that you would simply plead guilty?"

A long silence from Slater, then a faint nod.

"Seriously, bro, what the fuck are you thinking?" Dale's mouth twisted in deep confusion.

"It's in my blood," he said softly, as if he were only talking to himself.

"It's in your—" Dale went.

"How can being in jail be that ... that thing?" Emily said. "Like, what, Slater, your true calling?"

"It isn't," Slater whispered.

"Then let us help get you out," Finnegan said.

Slater held fire.

"There's nothing here, bro," Dale said. "I know you like tight spaces, know you like things about to trap you. All those games we played as kids, your hiding—I remember all that." He shook his head twice, hard. "This ain't that. Nobody's gonna come looking for you." He hit his hand on the table, a dull but loud *whap*. "This is not the fuck *that*."

"I know," Slater said softly again.

"You know fuckin' what?"

Silence from Slater at his brother's outburst.

"So you really are going to stay here, right?" Emily said.

Slater nodded quick.

"You have, what? New things to find out? More boundaries to push." Emily sighed, an odd whistling sound from her.

"You always have 'boundaries to push,' right, Slater?" She flicked quote marks over that part of her sentence.

Slater simply stared at her.

"This is fuckin' real, bro!" Dale got up and walked around behind his brother, reached out his long hands. "I want to friggin' strangle you!"

It took a long moment, creases on his forehead, crinkles in his cheeks, but finally Slater laughed. It was loud, cackling, disruptive.

Finnegan looked at Emily.

"You're willing to keep paying me for this?" Dismay in the lawyer's voice.

"Rich, come on."

Finnegan settled back in his chair, looked up at the ceiling.

"I know you think I'm crazy," Slater said, softly as ever. "But there's a music here. There's a ... a song I hear. From my blood, but not just that—"

"Bro, you're sounding way craz—"

"But I'm *not*, Dale." Slater slow shook his head. "I'm the same as always.

Dale let that go by with a dubious look, then said:

"You're the fuck in jail—and you want to stay there."

"For now."

That caught us. Finnegan was all over it.

"That's not the way it works, pardner," the lawyer said. "It's *not* in your hands."

Slater didn't look as if he'd even heard.

"This music," Emily said, "what's it like?"

"An open sound," Slater said quickly. He was looking straight at Emily, truly interested in her question. "A sound like home—like an endless wind whistling over the prairies."

"In jail, bro?" Dale, a harsh whisper.

"And this is, what, more free—more liberating—than anything on the outside?" Emily went on. "More than our— well, Savage Joy?"

"The music needed something." Slater looked hard at Emily. "I just couldn't find it. I tried. I tried all the fuckin' night long." Hard glare. "*You* know that."

"I know that you couldn't be trusted, that's what *I* know." Emily's eyes burned. "I know your favorite word, *freedom*, can contain every goddamn sin there is."

"Ahhhh," Slater went, eyes alight. "Then *you* understand *why* I have to be *here*." Those hard, unreadable stressed words.

What? This was a leap I couldn't follow. I looked around the table. Finnegan was starting to look bored. Dale, knotting his hands together, was clearly consumed with fury at his brother's intransigence. Only Emily seemed to be really listening, caring.

"But I *don't*, Slater," she whispered, light as a drifting feather. "I really don't."

"You didn't understand before, remember."

"Of course I remember."

"Then that's why we're here." Slater leaned back, folded his hands together, a picture of satisfaction, even triumph.

"No, we're here because you're selfish," Emily said, loud and angry again. "Because you can't recognize something wonderful when it's right the fuck in front of you."

Slater, silent again.

"Why did you do it?" Emily said, almost a whisper.

More silence.

"Slater, I asked you, why did you betray me like that?"

"I never be—"

"The fuck you didn't!" From a whisper to a scream, as the saying goes. Emily sputtered on. "And with that ... that Jesus-crazed nothing!"

Slater was silent for a moment, then said as soft as dust, "Why ... why, dear heart ... why couldn't you come along?" A slow, enticing murmur, as if only the two of them were at the table.

"You know why."

"But that was never—" Slater's eyes had warmed, a sudden surprise. It was the way he and Emily had first looked at each other onstage at CBGBs. "I truly never believed that was enough."

"It was for me."

"Because of—"

"Yes, because of Sally." Emily said this softly, with a chastened tone.

Sally? Was I confused? Of course. So who was Sally? And if "Jesus-crazed nothing" pointed to Wendell Walter, what could that possibly mean?

This was a private talk. I felt awkward being there, I think we all did, yet I hung on every word. I kept trying to get what they were saying to make sense. It had to be at the heart of what happened with the band on the road, what I'd been dying to know; and yet as they lofted their words back and forth, nothing came clear. I had a quick impulse to interrupt, ask them what was going on, but I killed it. This had to play out on its own, right? I could work to make sense of it later. I could always just ask Emily, too.

"That's exactly *why* I'll be *free* in here, babe." Slater stood up then, walked over behind Emily, who turned to face him. "'The killers on the wall wrap themselves in dawn.' Don't you *see*?"

Even with the crazy talk, I could feel a genuine, vivid tenderness between them. A flash of jealousy, quickly dampened. They were talking about Slater's choosing to remain in prison.

"No, I don't." Emily still looked as puzzled as I felt. "Is it because of the damn record? Something to do with—"

"No!" A quick bark. Slater's eyes burned. "You're not listening to me!"

"Then what—"

"My *blood*. 'Sweat, sperm, and blood.'" Slater gritted his teeth. "My goddamn singing, stinging blood!"

His rhyming outburst silenced everyone, even Emily. I could see how hard she was trying to get this. Working her brow, drawing quick breaths. She truly cared for Slater. I guess I'd always known that, and it was clear now. She wanted to understand him *for* him. To do what she could. To help, to....

"Slater, I'm trying—I'm really try—"

"Then you'll know I gotta do this, babe." The way Slater spoke, his best singing voice, the words rang with finality. "This is for real. I understand that—I totally get it. But my blood, my ... oh, Em, I *need* this. I really, really need this."

I looked around the table. We were all silent, half-stunned. No one had a word to say back.

Finally, the lawyer, Finnegan, spoke.

"If you change your mind, Mr. Martin, let Emily know. I'm on the clock. And I'm an excellent attorney. You'll be outside kneeling and kissing the sidewalk soon as you wish."

Slater smiled wide at that image, then nodded.

"I got it," he said. "And thanks."

It was still clear none of us truly understood Slater, but just as obvious there was nothing more to say. So we left.

"Should we take a cab home?" I said to Emily.

She looked surprised, then dug into her purse. She held out ten dollars.

"Um, I'm going to go with Dale here," she told me. "We have so many things to talk about. But here's cab fare." She waved the bill at me, but I wouldn't take it. "Come on, Cole."

"No, that's fine. I'll just take the subway."

"I don't know if that's safe this time of—"

"Safe enough for me." I was feeling pissed, and not just for the obvious reason.

"You'll be O.K., promise?" She looked truly concerned.

"Yes, I promise."

"Good." Emily smiled, that lovely, devastating smile I'd fallen for a year before. "We'll catch up soon, I promise that. And ... and *thanks*, Cole, you've been a huge help during this—" she shot a glance then at Dale, who was waiting patiently on her "—this whole insane thing."

After a quick peck on my cheek, Emily flagged down a yellow cab. She and Dale got into it. I realized she wasn't heading home, otherwise she would've given me a lift at least.

A long sigh. Then I headed up to Canal Street to the 6 train north.

# 25

I DON'T WANT you to think I'm a total idiot. I can usually figure things out sooner or later, and I was working hard to make sense of what I'd just seen. That Slater wanted to stay in jail … for all he said, that wasn't making sense. The way he kept saying being locked away was in his blood. I thought I had a sense of his blood, that power he brought to Savage Joy, his wild abandon onstage—and, of course, in his life—simply that force that made Slater who he was.

So how could his blood pulse *for prison*? Singing and stinging, as he put it. Did he understand something about incarceration that I and the world didn't? The whole point of jail was that it took *away* freedom. How could Slater find freedom and release there? I really didn't get it and kind of assumed he'd come to his senses soon enough.

That Emily was picking up the lawyer tab? It wasn't news, of course, that there had been a lot going on between them; and I could also get it that she felt responsible because of Harper Hart. She also clearly had the bucks from what Harper had told me.

But who was Sally? What secrets did Slater and Emily hold? And Wendell? Did he have something to do with this? What had really happened to Savage Joy on the road?

I'd been trying to get the answer to that last question since the band had come back to town, but I'd gotten nowhere. Emily, nothing. Slater, just vagueness.

I was thinking all this in my apartment later that night. I was in bed, street clothes still on, brain whirling, certain I couldn't get to sleep so I wasn't even trying. Cole, who didn't really drink, had a glass of the Bourbon I'd found in the back of a cupboard from when I was trying to get somewhere with a girl I'd met my first months in New York. I didn't really like the liquor, but as each splash sparked up the back of my throat, I felt I was one step closer to putting all the mysteries together.

So who else could I talk to? Who else might have something to tell me? Could I really get more out of Emily? And where had she gone with Slater's brother—

That was my last thought before a loud, furious banging shook my front door.

Bed in the back room, the metal door just a few feet from my head; the surprise of the pounding on it jolted me up, spilling Bourbon on my shirt.

"Cole, open the door!"

The high, quavery voice sounded familiar, yet at one in the morning it didn't make sense, so I hung there, not sure what to do. Then in a flash I realized who it was.

"I have to talk to you!" It was Wendell. Wendell Walter from down the hall banging on my door in the middle of the night.

"Wendell?"

"Cole, please open the door." Wendell's voice was as loud as I'd ever heard, but still contained, meek.

I relaxed some, thinking, Thank God, it's just Wendell. Then: But what's he doing here now?

I undid the safety lock and opened the door.

Wendell didn't look good. There was always his moon-glow pale skin and hacked-at hair. He was also always thin, but now he was Biafra skin and bones, as if he hadn't eaten, the snake tattoo up his arm even more pronounced. That extra-long belt he always wore through the silver-cross buckle, its tab actually did clip the top of his left knee. Worse, he looked wrung out, distraught: raccoon circles around his eyes, his nose and cheeks raw and red.

I let him in, and as soon as he'd closed the metal door behind us, he took a swing at me.

In truth it wasn't much of a punch, and I pulled back far

enough that he missed my chin and just nicked my lower jaw. The blow startled me, though, and without thinking I bulled my shoulder into Wendell's torso, caroming him off the wall, then shoving him facedown on my mattress. I jumped on top of him, held down his shoulders.

"What the fuck was that?" I yelled, riled.

"It's your fault!" Wendell shouted this but it still came out muffled from the blankets around his head.

"What's my fault?"

"Everything!" And Wendell erupted in tears.

He lay there beneath me, sobbing. I could feel the tension in his body flow out. He turned into a limp rag.

"Let's talk," I said, getting up. My glass of Bourbon had fallen on the floor, Fortunately the tumbler didn't break, but the liquor was in a puddle. As soon as Wendell got up, he saw the spill. He immediately went and got a paper towel, then mopped it up.

He threw the wet towel in my trash can, then apologized.

"Professor, I'm ... I'm be-side myself," he said. His eyes were still damp. "I'm sorry ... I'm so sorrrrrrry."

"Come on." I took the bottle of Bourbon off my counter, got a second glass, then led Wendell to my eating table and told him to sit.

"Do you want any?" I poured another finger or so into my tumbler.

"I don't really—" Wendell wiped at his eyes, then nodded. "Sure, O.K., yes, please."

I started pouring, looking at him to say "enough," but he didn't say it. I finally stopped pouring with three fingers of the liquor in his glass.

"You hit me?" I said to him after we'd both taken pulls at the Bourbon.

"I'm going out of my mind," Wendell cried.

"I can see that." I half laughed. "But you still didn't have to take a swing at me."

"But it's your *fault*!"

"It's my—" I shook my head, confused. "What did I do now?"

"You got him in jail."

"Slater?"

"You didn't *stop* him." Wendell glared at me. "You could've stopped him and you didn't."

"You mean the fight?" Another shake of my head. "I couldn't have stopped that."

"Why not?" Wendell as fierce as he could at me. "I know you were there."

"I was in the pastry shop. When I got out, he was whaling on the guy. He and Zog—"

At the name of Slater's friend Wendell pursed his lips, tight.

"I yelled at them. Told them to stop."

"I heard you called the cops."

"I ... what?"

"You called the cops on Slater, got him arrested."

"That's crazy." I stared at Wendell. "Who'd you hear that from?"

"It's around."

"Well, it's not true. I was there, I was in Veneiros, I came out, the fight was going on—Harper Hart started it, but Slater and Zog kept it going too long—and I was trying to break it up when the cops pulled up. Slater ran and—"

"Did you give him heroin?"

"Wendell, are you out of your mind?" I pulled my head back. "Me give Slater smack?"

"That's what they have on him."

"And you never saw him use it?" I leaned across at Wendell. "When you were on the van trip with him? You didn't—"

That got him, mentioning the band. Wendell's eyes went dark, spooky.

"Why are you so upset?" I said then. "Is it the band?"

Wendell stayed silent.

"It's not going to be good for Savage Joy, is it? You throw out Emily, and now you've lost Slater. I know you're supposed to be in the studio soon. Is that what's making you so—"

"It's not the stupid band!" Wendell cried, then started crying again.

I got up, walked around the table. I put a hand on his shoulder.

"I love him, professor." Wendell was full-on sobbing now. "I love Slater Martin. I do, I do—" loud whimpering through shivering tears "—God help me, I do!"

I was silent. I didn't know what to say. Wendell loved Slater? What did he mean? What kind of ... then my brain flashed back to that hidden memory, that night I'd knocked on Slater's door and found Wendell there ... the steam ... both of them in their underwear.... That moment had never made sense and I'd buried it away.

Except now I got it. Wendell? Wendell Walter and Slater? Holy shit! Lovers? Slater, pushing all boundaries, together with Wendell? But the church ... they'd been together at the church. And the band tour. Was this love at the heart of what had happened with Savage Joy?

"Wendell?"

"Professor, I ... I can't help myself. I've tried—I've tried ev-er-y-thing—but it's just ... just way too big for me." Wendell kept sobbing, quieter now. "I've prayed. Lord knows, I've prayed. We've both prayed, Slater and me. We have. But nothing changes. I can't live without him. I've asked myself if I could, but there's nothing ... there's not a thing in this world without that man. I ... I was nothing till Slater found me. The Lord? The Lord nev-er stopped me. I begged and pleaded with the Lord to stop me—stop it, stop it, *stop it*!" The wail that rose from Wendell at that moment still chills my soul. "But He never did. I ... I kept loving Slater. It was all I could do. All I could—"

I dove into deep sadness, pitiful and sorry for Wendell. Yet I had no idea what to do, so I pushed his tumbler of Bourbon closer.

This time Wendell stared at it as if it were a snake about to strike.

"Slater wants to stay there," I said softly. "In jail."

"I know! My baby, my baby, I know, I know, I know!"

"I don't understand why."

"*And I do?*" Those three words, ripped from Wendell, soul-searing. "I don't understand *anything*! Any, any thing! I don't understand Slater and I don't understand the Lord and I don't—I don't, I don't, I don't—understand why I ... feel ... this way."

Wendell crossed himself then. He slowly lifted his pointer finger and ran it perpendicular to his chest, then laterally across his chest. Just that: crossing himself once.

"Emily's trying to get him out," I said. "She has a lawyer and they're doing everything they—"

"That cunt."

"Wendell!"

"It's all *her* fault." Wendell started crying again, though they looked to be mostly dry heaves, wracking his shoulders, his thin, spooky head. "She bewitched him. She ... she made him want to do horrible things."

"I doubt that," I said. "I don't think Emily had anything to do with—"

"No, no, it's all that witch's fault. She turned him. Slater was mine and she confused him. Made him have hor-ri-ble ideas." Wendell gulped. "The Lord wept for us. I begged Him to stop us, to stop me, but He didn't. I tried everything but He wouldn't." Another gulp. "I've lost him. Oh, I've lost him—"

"What did you—"

"I'm so a-shamed," Wendell said then. He lowered his head, buried it in his hands. "Oh, Lord, I'm so, so ashamed.

Please don't forsake me like this. Please forgive me. Please, please, please...."

Wendell dribbled out those last words, then stopped speaking. I sipped my Bourbon, tried to will him to drink more of his, but he wouldn't. He simply sat there sobbing, near silent, for another minute.

Then he pushed back his chair and got up and left.

# 26

IT WAS EMILY three days later, again asking, "Have you heard?" Her voice rising slightly. I clearly caught the note of dread.

And flinched. We were in the hall again, I was coming home from work, and Emily was outside her door. She looked as lovely as always, even more refreshed than usual, though as I looked at her closely, I felt a febrile tension radiating from her wide, glorious eyes.

"You'd better come in," she said, standing back to let me pass.

I could count on one hand the number of times I'd been in Emily's apartment, and usually only for a minute or two, so she could change purses or fix her makeup. This was different. This time she poured me some vodka.

I sipped it slowly, in a street-scrounged purple chair between the front windows. Emily was on a coral-pink silk sofa with wooden arms, unexpectedly elegant.

What would she have to say? Nothing good, I felt certain. But what she told me was beyond anything I could have imagined or feared.

"It's Wendell—"
"Wendell Walter?"
"He's dead."

Emily said this flat, no emotion, stunned.

"What're you—I don't," I stammered, all kinds of notions flying around my head. "Emily, is this *true*?"

Even as I said the last words, I knew it was. I even anticipated what she next said.

"He hung himself." She gulped, her Adam's apple bobbing. "In his apartment. With his belt—that ridiculously long belt he always wore, with Jesus on the buckle."

"Holy shit." I shifted in the chair. I felt strikingly ill, something dark and turbid moving in my stomach. It was death … I immediately thought of the ancient Eskimo in what became Slater's apartment. I remembered the putrid, gut-churning smell in the hallway, and that same smell hit me again, though this time wholly in my head. I tried to shake the sensation off but couldn't. I brought my hand to my mouth, fought to hold the bile down.

"Mr. Strump found him. Wendell missed a service. Mr. Strump used his master key." Emily shuddered, a visible shake. The cushions on the sofa jiggled. "I can't actually believe it."

I was thinking of the other night when Wendell accosted me, then broke down in front of me. I thought of what he said about Slater, how he'd gotten so distraught and crazy. A stab of guilt hit me. Should I have known he was suicidal? I couldn't recall any clues. Wendell was just breathlessly upset. How could I know what that would lead to?

Still, I felt horrible, as if I'd let Wendell down. A long sigh. He was dead, gone. I could hardly believe it.

"There's going to be a funeral service," Emily told me. "At that door-front church thing he was part of."

"When?"

"Not sure yet."

"Was there any—" I said slowly, ruminating, but Emily read my mind.

"Any note?" She shook her head. "Just him hanging there. It'd been at least a day." She grimaced. "Poor Mr. Strump."

Should I tell her what I knew? About Wendell coming to me, blaming me for Slater? Did anyone know about that?

"Any idea why he—"

"Not that I've heard." She stood and got the vodka bottle, filled her glass. She walked over and poured more into mine, even though I'd only taken a few sips. "Wendell … Wendell was a strange dude."

"I know." I looked at her intently, burrowing in.

*"What?"*

"I saw him ... he came here three days ago."

"To you?" She fell back on her couch.

"He was upset about Slater. Blamed me for his being in jail. Seemed really, really—"

"Damn!"

"What do you know?" I asked her then.

"What do I—"

"What happened, what really happened out there on the road?" I stared hard at Emily. There was about six feet from the purple chair to where she sat, and I got up and moved over there. I took the cushion next to her. "I keep asking but nobody will say anything. But that's it, right? That's where this—"

"I don't know what you mean." Emily pulled away from me, deeper into her cushion.

"Of course you do. Wendell was ... he told me he was in love with Slater. And you ... *you* were in love with Slater." I nodded, it all falling together. "All roads lead to him."

Emily stayed quiet.

"And Slater, he loved it all ways. He was ... we were at this party, he was trying to tell me all about this. 'No limits.' 'Whatever feels right.'"

"He had his ideas," Emily said softly.

"The idea that he could be loved by *both* of you. You and Wendell—that it wouldn't make any difference."

Emily, by not speaking or moving, told me this was true.

"And you wouldn't take it, right?"

Nothing.

"That's what happened with you. Slater chose Wendell over—"

"No he didn't!"

"Didn't what?" I leaned in at her.

"Choose *him*."

"No, he couldn't do that, could he? Choose some clueless

guy over Emily Prosser of the Connecticut Pross—" Even as I said this, I knew I was going too far. I was letting my own jealousy out and....

Emily slapped me. It was clean, her palm flat and sharp against my cheek, the blow Wendell couldn't land.

"You shit."

"I'm sorry," I said quickly. "I—"

"You should be."

"I am, I am." I meant it. I *had* gone too far. This was not about me. And in truth I just wanted to know—*needed* to know.

"But you're right," Emily went on. "Slater thought he could have both of us ... thought he could have both of us together—"

"Togeth—"

"There could *not* be any limits! Those were his words, his fuckin' mantra. 'Emily, child, you have to let it all go. You have to go just where it takes you. You can't—'" She shook then, not the baffled shudder over Wendell's death but a shiver of boundless fury. I felt the sofa buck and crumple. "Well, ass fuck, I can do just whatever the fuck I need to."

Those words spoken past me, to Slater, who was of course not there.

"It wasn't right. He didn't—he never understood me. He never—"

"You loved him," I said, clearly stating fact. "Wendell ... the poor soul loved him too much. But did he love you?"

"What?" Emily, startled by my question.

"Did Slater love you back?"

A long moment's thought, then a vague shake of her head.

"No?"

"I don't know, Cole." A more vivid shake. "What does it matter? Slater's in jail, Wendell's dead. What the bloody fuck does it matter?"

It didn't, I guess, except that all the feeling I once had—

oh, *still* had—for Emily was percolating under the surface here; and the jealousy of Slater was there, too. How wrong I'd been. Everything that I'd been burning up over while Emily was on the road with Savage Joy sounded like little but a huge fractured mess. Learning this was kind of a victory, even if a sad, pathetic one, and it emboldened me.

"Who's Sally?"

That hit Emily out of the blue. Her head jerked to the side.

"What do you mean?" she said warily.

"I'm asking who Sally is. Just that."

Emily didn't say anything, only glared at me. These were sharp knives flung across the sofa. I sat there, not backing away. Everything was coming out, and I had a right to know. Emily looked at me, looked at her vodka bottle, then back at me again.

When her eyes dampened, I knew she was going to confess.

"Sally's—" Emily looked ready to slip into tears. "She's my daughter."

"Your what?" My words burst out. Emily had a daughter? She was just a kid, like me. How could she—

"My daughter." She swallowed hard. "Not mine ... but *mine*."

"I don't—"

"I had her ... it was this mixed-up thing. I was just seventeen. A boy in Hartford, we took off, and—" She looked down. "I got—well, it happened. My family was insane. I was ... I didn't know what was going on, I was such a child, and ... and I had to give her up." Emily's tears were full on now, tracing her cheeks, messing with her makeup. "She's adopted by a ... well, I guess they're nice enough. But not a day ... oh, Cole, I miss my little girl so much."

Her cry wrenched my heart. I was also thinking back to lunch with Harper Hart; so Emily's daughter was what he wouldn't tell me. It took me a moment to say anything.

"At the jail, Slater said she was the reason you didn't—"

"Sally's the reason I do *everything*, Cole!" Emily let this out with a shout. "I want her so much." Huffing breaths, almost hyperventilating. "I just can't have her."

"You can't—"

"I gave her up. I was a fuckin' child, and it was 'in my best interest' "—fingers flicked in the air "—and I legally gave her up for adoption. She ... she belongs to—"

"So what do you do?"

"I go ... sometimes I go to Maryland, where she lives, to watch her play in the park. I'm not supposed ... well, I can't help it. I yearn for her. I cry for her. I'd do anything—"

"And Slater wouldn't—"

"That selfish prick couldn't, wouldn't ... he didn't even try to imagine what he could do for *me*." She kept breathing hard, puffs I felt across the sofa. "I'm *glad* Slater's in jail—I hope he stays there and fuckin' rots!"

All I'd heard, my head swam. I felt close to bursting. All this had been going on around me and I hadn't a clue. What an idiot! What a fool!

"Your lawyer, Finnegan?" I said, trying to at least sound useful.

She shook her head.

"And your money—I hear you have a lot of money."

"There's nothing I can do to get Sally back." She shook her head again. "We've looked at every—"

"Is there anything I can do?" I said this softly. With a suddenness that spooked me, I was thinking of the most ridiculous, romantic, quixotic ways to help Emily. That somehow *I* could make things better. That maybe *only* I could make things...

"Like what?"

But any vain notions butterflying through my brain looked wispy and stupid the longer I looked at them.

"I'd do anything I could," I got out.

"That's sweet, Cole." Emily smiled. "I always think of you that way, that you have my back." She reached out and touched my shoulder, then leaned further and kissed my cheek. I smelled her perfume, that citrusy, musky scent that always made me crazy. It had stayed with me for days after she'd slept with me that one night. Smelling it now, all of that flooded back.

"But there's really nothing," she said. "Nothing anyone can do." She grimaced again, tight lines off her pretty mouth. "Just ... just one foot in front of the other, right? Through the daily horror?"

I had no answer, and no words came out even when Emily kissed my cheek again. Then with a determined flourish she got up, took one last belt of the vodka, walked to her apartment door, and disappeared.

I didn't get it. What, Emily just walking out of her own place, leaving me there?

I sat on the sofa for a while, thinking she'd return, but she didn't. Finally I threw back the vodka and followed into the hall.

Her door was wide open. God, what should I do? Had she taken a key? Where had she gone?

I stood there a long minute staring plaintively at the gray metal door, then finally pushed it shut. I heard it click. I realized I liked being that guy who was there for Emily—who always had her back—and I took a gamble she'd have a key or at least another way to get herself back in. This was the East Village, and there was crime everywhere. Shutting her door would be keeping her safe, wouldn't it? The smart thing to do? You couldn't just leave somebody's door swinging open, could you?

I ran up the stairs two at a time, trying not to think of any of this.

As I walked through my own gray metal door, I don't think my three rooms ever seemed so empty and dead.

# 27

THE FUNERAL ... well, it wasn't technically a funeral, some city rule about the Church of Jesus Christo not being licensed to take a corpse made it a memorial service. Wendell Walter was already in the ground, back in Kentucky, family I wasn't around to meet escorting the body back there.

There were about a dozen people in the small storefront. All were church members except for Emily and me. We'd both dressed up, me in the suit I'd bought after a month in town, a big-city fella now. Emily wore a smart wool suit from Bendel's with a string of perfect white pearls.

As we sat there, I kept looking around for anyone else I knew.

I felt strongly Slater should be there. I mean, he could get out of jail anytime thanks to Emily's lawyer, and if once bailed out, he had to stay out, well, wouldn't that be good for him? If he wanted prison so much, he could always plead guilty and be shipped upstate to Sing Sing or someplace. Maybe he'd change his mind sniffing real air.

And for Wendell? The boy loved Slater. They'd been lovers. Even if their intimacies were mostly Slater's own doing, for his own unknowable reasons, that seemed to be fact. He and Wendell had been together all through the Savage Joy tour. Emily, too, though she'd left the band because of that.

Yet Slater wasn't there.

Neither was Chet the bass player, though I doubted if he even knew about it. Since Slater had been arrested, and now Wendell dead, the band looked to be totally kaput. The record company, who knows, it could've been good publicity for Savage Joy, all the turmoil. But you couldn't do much with the band leader–singer choosing to stay in jail and the guitar player dead.

I also wondered about Sailor, why she wasn't ... and then, a couple minutes before the services were to begin, she pushed in through the double doors from the street.

I was looking toward the altar, but I felt the wind of the doors opening and I turned, having a suspicion it was Sailor before I saw her. I'd just been thinking of her. I hadn't seen Sailor since that day she'd come by and tried to talk me into writing *Savage Joy*. Not much had come of that. I had the crazy thought that if she and I had come up with the *Savage Joy* song—had written it well and true enough—and Slater had been ready to take it into the studio, somehow none of this would have happened. Yes, crazy. And now there wasn't even a band to write anything for.

Sailor looked good. Her deep red hair, a little longer now, flipped over her ears. That severe stage look, it had mellowed. She was more just a pretty girl you might glance at a little longer than usual on the subway. She was wearing a robin's-egg blue skirt under a lavender coat that fell to her knees. Sleek black boots. A bone-white blouse, pulled tight across her chest.

Sailor also looked healthy. Emily still looked haggard, though as always her deep beauty shone through. Everything was weighing on her, I guess. I hadn't seen her around the building since she told me about Wendell. I didn't know where she'd been. Wherever it was, it hadn't done much for her.

But Sailor was fresh, full of energy, sad under the circumstances, of course, but under that, sparkling with vitality.

I waved to her and she came and sat on the other side of Emily, who was on the hard wooden pew by the narrow aisle.

"Hey," she said. "God, this is such a drag."

"Yeah," both Emily and I said at the same time.

"I couldn't believe ... I mean, after Slater." Sailor shook her head. "It's all too much."

"Where've you been?" Emily said. "What're you doing?"

"Home and nothing special." Sailor whispered this as Mr. Strump was walking from the first pew to the wobbly wooden lectern.

We all nodded to each other: *We'll catch up more later*. Then we turned to face the front of the church.

Two sentences out of Mr. Strump's mouth and there were tears in his eyes.

"Wendell, he was a good boy," he said, starting out in his storefront church voice, but it broke immediately. His thin silver hair was combed up, his fully lined face cracked like old leather. "He ... in God's truth, Wendell was a son to me." A deep nod. "A true son."

I choked up, too, as the old guy's hands shook. I could see Emily dabbing her eyes and Sailor using a white handkerchief to wipe away her tears.

"But the Lord's seen fit to take Wendell. His mysterious ways, unaccounted for here, but my son is gone.

"And I am furious!" Mr. Strump's hand flew off the lectern, shaken at the ceiling. His eyes funneled dark. "There is *no* reason for this. Wendell was ... he might've wavered from time to time ... might've had his deeee-mons ... but at heart he be a *good* boy. At *heart*. Deep, deep, deep faith. He beeee-lieeeeved!"

The old preacher took a couple steps back, composed himself.

"I stand here now and ask, Is that all that remains, the Lord's mercy? For peace for His son. Should we cel-e-brate the end to ... to Wendell's torment? That it had to end like, like—" He swallowed hard, his eyes tight and angry.

"But I don't know *why*." His palm pounding on the lectern. "Why, why, why?"

Mr. Strump's eyes, hooded and rank, glared through the makeshift church. His tears were dry. At that moment he was all malevolent fury, searching, beseeching.

"I can't—. If I think too...." His tongue out, red between

his blood lips, his parchment skin. "There be no ... not a soul in the ... I call and I—"

Stammering now, head tilted back, eyes fireworks.

"I mean, what did Wendell *do*? Laws crossed, sins beholden ... but what amounted to *this*? His sordid fate! Hanging there, dangling, dangling.... Can You explain ... can You—"

Another shake of his fist, then his hands opened, palms out, beseeching.

"I know You hear our cries. You're up there, and You know all and You ... You can forgive all. Oh, I believe! I believe it still! You sonofabitch, I believe it, I believe it, I believe it!"

That's where he ended, the final line a hearty cry; then Mr. Strump was in tears again, a ragged white cloth to his face. He stepped back, unsteady. A needle dropped on a record player, *shhhpppp, shhhhhppppp*, a single male voice singing: *Amazing Grace*.

People around me joined in. Emily joined in. Sailor joined in. I joined in. *Amazing Grace*. How sweet the sound? *"Yes, when this flesh and heart shall fail / And mortal life shall cease / I shall profess, within the veil / A life of joy and peace."*

A life of joy and peace. Tantalizing, yearned for, visible out there before us, so close, so possible to embrace ... yet not for Wendell. Not for Slater. Not at that moment for any of us.

＊ ＊ ＊ ＊ ＊

THAT WAS the service. No one else spoke. There were no homilies, nothing soothing. Just Mr. Strump's furious cries and our mournful song.

Emily, Sailor, and I stood out on 11th Street, normal daily business whirling along.

"That was ... odd," Emily said.

"I'll say." I stood next to Emily, Sailor next to her. I didn't mean to make light of Mr. Strump and what we'd all just seen, his outburst had seared and confused me (and I've often found it whipping through my 4 a.m., wide-awake thoughts);

but all I said then was careless and dismissive. "At least it was short."

"Were you guys thinking Slater should've been there?" Sailor said.

Both Emily and I nodded.

"I guess this is it for the band." Sailor smiled at Emily. "Hey, you want to start a folk duo?"

I guffawed; Emily laughed, too. It was a cloudy day but was quickly turning bright. Visible shafts of sunlight sliced the sky. Wendell's funeral, as disturbing as it had just been, seemed miles away.

"I mean, look at us." Sailor nodding at my suit, Emily's pearls. "Some wild rock and roll band now. Maybe we should go all the way, shoot for the Café Carlyle uptown."

"You know about the Carlyle?" Emily said, eyebrows rising.

"Hey, I get around." Sailor winked.

"I think it's a great idea," I told them.

"No, no." Emily shook her head. "I'm done with music." Then softer, to herself, a sigh floating away from her. "Done with every—" Her voice trailed off.

The sadness in her at that moment, I wished I could have done something more than reach out and softly touch her shoulder, which I did. Emily gave me a gentle, abashed look. I nodded, to buck her up.

"Are you playing with anyone?" I said, turning to Sailor.

"Nope." She too sent Emily a sympathetic look, then bounced up on her toes, irrepressible. "As I said, just laying low, staying close to home."

"You know, we never finished our song."

"You never called me back!" Sailor's eyebrows flew up, in disdain, mock, I hoped.

"I know, things were really—"

"Crazy." Sailor nodded. "I can see." She stepped back, raised an eyebrow, and said with a knowing nod: "So, how *are* you guys?"

A long pause. The way her words came out carried powerful meaning, yet I wondered what she was getting at. Was she picking up some couple vibe coming off Emily and me? I couldn't imagine it. I mean, I'd pretty much given up any hope of being with Emily Prosser. Forever I'd be her friend ... have her back, as she said. Maybe in twenty years that might be enough. I knew it wasn't close to enough now.

Yet as I smiled and said we were fine, I kept wondering exactly what Sailor was picking up on? Could I be missing something? Was what Emily had been through, with Slater, with Wendell, with whatever was going on with her daughter, Sally—was it all somehow changing her? Did Sailor get that even though I couldn't?

Like so many times before, my heart leaped. What was it about Emily Prosser? My first friend in New York. That everlasting mystery around her. Her sophistication yet her trashy vibe, too. Or simply the bone-deep blonde loveliness that as thrashed out as she looked today still glowed pure.

My hopes—my soul—lifted on the implications of Sailor's question, but I shut it all down. Nothing would happen with Emily, ever. I'd done everything I could, and there was no getting past that. Love is either there or it isn't, right?

*Riiiight?* Oh, I was still so young, the romantic in me would not hear of this. *Why won't Emily love me?* That midnight cry that so often sent me off to harsh sleep. Why isn't Emily here in *my* bed? Where is she? Doesn't she know I'd be so good for her? That I'd always, always have her back....

Oh, I was so hopeless. The curious thing, as I stood there mooning one final time for the woman I'd been obsessing about all year, I had the sense that Sailor got it. The way she looked at me, with kindness, empathy—it was so much the way *I* looked at Emily....

Was there even a faint yearning there?

I didn't know, I didn't know. On that sun-blasted East 11th Street sidewalk I was so wrapped in my final swoops and swirls of desire for Emily that I wasn't sure what I was picking up on.

All I know is that the three of us stood there a minute longer, silent, a little awkward, until we all bid each other good fortune and headed off, Sailor toward First Avenue, Emily toward Second, and me upstairs to my apartment.

# 28

WHAT NEXT?
That was the question haunting me. After Slater and Wendell, after getting nowhere with Emily—who wasn't anywhere; as far as I could tell; she had abandoned her apartment, just as she had her fancy publishing job—and at work, after all my writing and the encouragement (even after my poem was published), I was still getting each new story rejected, not just from Dan down the hall but in those accusatory manila envelopes that after nearly every other lunchtime lay heavy on my desk.

I wanted to get away. Needed to get away. Then I cooked up a plan.

Did I mention that I was the second male ever hired in *The New Yorker* typing pool? There had been one guy before me, and he'd sold a very long short story to the magazine, then quit and used the money to travel around Europe. From the moment I heard about him, that was my ambition: Sell a major piece to *The New Yorker* and spend the money traveling.

I kept writing stories, and Dan kept calling me down to his office to tell me they weren't going to take this one.... "Close, Cole, be sure to try again."

Finally I decided I couldn't wait.

I didn't want to leave the magazine, just get away for a while. And I didn't want simply to go to Europe but all the way around the world.

I proposed a six-month leave to Mrs. Walden. Think about it: some chutzpah, huh? to ask for a half-a-year leave from the best entry job in publishing, a joint I'd only worked at for a year or so. But it *was The New Yorker*, which understood eccentricities (and personal drive); and I was hungering to embrace a whole globe's worth of experience; felt my writing cried out for it ... my soul, too.

It took a few days but Mrs. Walden agreed. In three weeks I was going to be sprung to go anywhere I wanted.

My mood brightened. I couldn't wait to get going. Turned out my old L.A. friend John had his own world trip in mind, and before I knew it we were on our way to JFK to catch a Laker Airways flight to Gatwick, outside London.

We both went straight to Oxford, John to see an old friend, me to stay with Mary, my friend from Spain, now happily back in school and about to graduate. A week in the old city, then I wanted to go to Paris, John didn't. Very simple: different agendas. The split was amicable and off I went.

After a few days in a hostel I was invited to move into Shakespeare and Co., the cluttered expat bookstore then run by George Whitman (no relation to me; if you believed George, a direct one to Walt) right off the Seine. George let budding writers crash on the second floor (never mentioning the mattresses were infested with bedbugs). During the day he'd take off and ask guests to tend the till, selling used Penguin paperbacks and other volumes to anyone who straggled in.

That's what I did—I ran Shakespeare and Co., at least for brief periods. One night I met a guy named David, also crashing there after a stint teaching literature to sailors on a Navy destroyer, and we hit it off. He was planning to go to Greece. I'd never been and couldn't think of anything better.

I flew, David took a train, ended up stuck endlessly in Yugoslavia. He missed our meet-up day. But I liked him and wanted a travel companion, so I hung on in Athens till finally a note from him appeared at American Express.

Off we went. David taught me rule No. 1 of Greece travel: When you hit a new island, immediately head to the back side, where the lodging was cheap and daytrippers never made it.

We bounced around islands till we got to Crete, hiking through the Samariá Gorge and ending up in Agia Roumeli, a village unreachable by road. Now this was truly the other side of the island, and we stayed there, swimming, sunning, happily eating squid some barefooted boy would leap out into the sea to spear for us.

A week later David met an American nurse and went off with her. I headed back to Athens.

A great thing about the capital was it was an airline-ticket bucket shop, with great deals to everywhere in the world. I strolled around Syntagma Square, trying to figure out where to go in Asia ... in truth, trying to figure out if I had the guts to fling myself all the way out there.

I wanted to see the world, but halfway around the globe on my own? A lot of hesitation. A lot of second guessing. A lot of—

Finally, the Eagles solved it for me. Slater would've been appalled; hell, *I* was appalled. The Eagles? The band was inescapable but hard to take seriously.

Nonetheless, their song *Take It to the Limit* started looping through my brain. Over and over, Randy Meisner singing just that: *Take it to the limit.*

It only took me a day or so to realize this was my subconscious sending me a message. Right then I booked a flight through Rome to Delhi.

Ah, India. I'd traveled a lot in Mexico and refused to live like a middle-class American, so in that spirit of being like a native I ended up in a crumbling joint on the Main Bazaar, a few blocks from the central train station. In the thick of it now. Elephants, lazy cows, snake charmers, gaily dressed women in thousand-mirrored saris, legless men on skateboard-like platforms, white-clothed businessmen lifting their noses, smoke-belching three-wheeled tuk tuks, and always the host of women beggars clutching children (who I saw they passed among themselves), hands ever out, whispering, "Help me, help me, help me...."

It was a lot. I got kind of overwhelmed; I got sick. The usual, stomach, but odd fevers and other alarms, too. Met an Indian drug seller and his beautiful German junkie girlfriend, ate dinners with them. Met a British guy, Nigel, who wanted to go see the Taj Mahal, then head to Benares (now Varanasi). I loaded up on Lomitil and took the train to Agra. Glorious.

Still living like an Indian, Nigel and I crashed at a 50-cent-a-night place in Benares. It was a good three blocks from the leper corner, yes, the street corner where those with leprosy lived. More personal illness but I pushed on through. Dawn boat trip on the Ganges, smoke drifting off of funeral pyres, mongrel dogs chasing bones from corpses freshly burned on the riverbank, lamentations crushing the sky. (A quick thought of Mr. Strump; a silent prayer of my own.) Fevers, rashes, eyes looking suspiciously yellow....

Deeply worried but ... *take it to the limit.*

I was out walking, turned down a narrow, five-feet-across alleyway. Mud and goop slurping at my shoes. Dank, shadowed, hard to make out much. No side alleys.

I kept on walking. Another test. Do I turn back? Darker, danker. But, no. Take it to the limit. You keep going and you'll be fine—somehow prevail.

Dogs gathering. Shadowy figures in doorways. Smells, rotten fruit, urine, feces, overwhelming. But ... keep going.

I did. Finally to the end. A way back to the main road, skirting the leper corner (erupting lesions and pustules, limp arms, curled backs) to our hotel. A sailor's shower from the pipe poking out from the wall: fully dressed, washing my clothes at the same time as my body. A fine curry at a vegetarian restaurant with Nigel. I'd done it. I had not turned back.

Off on my own again. More towns, more adventures. Bangkok. Hong Kong, Taipei. Seoul. Then I was in L.A., pulling myself back together at my parents'. Another three weeks before I was expected back at *The New Yorker*.

A lot had changed at work. The union movement was resolved: No union, but an employee bargaining committee and much better wages. Right away I was earning nearly twice what I'd made before I left.

The typing pool was different, too. There were four new hires, all younger than me. Two more men, Craig and Rob, and two women, Betsy and Christine. The place had a whole different feel: Less Mary Elizabeth Tea Room and much closer to CBGBs.

It took me a while to get it. I remember Craig, my second day back, asking if I was into Elvis. I blinked, thought he was asking about Elvis Presley (then only months away from an ignominious demise on his toilet seat). What, has the typing pool turned into a '50s nostalgia crew?

"Um, not really," I said. "I mean, he's not really my genera—"

"Elvis Costello? *My Aim Is True?*"

"Um, I don't know who—"

Oh, the look on Craig's face. Was this a huge stumble? I had been out of the country, but the look he threw me made me feel like I was forty years old. How odd. *The New Yorker* had gotten young and cool since I was away.

Turned out Craig had seen Savage Joy at CBGBs and dug them, so I immediately got points by saying I had known the band—that their name was my idea.

Then I was invited to an Upper West Side party for Saturday night.

Seems that this new group of typing poolers had been having huge, almost-anybody-can-come parties at Christine's sprawling apartment at Broadway and 93rd. She had four roommates and they invited people; by 3 a.m. you couldn't move through the narrow halls.

That first party was great. I talked to a gazillion people, spun stories of Asia, drank too much, and stumbled back to 11th Street at 7 a.m.

Then back to work. Even with the new blood it was the same job: mostly sitting around, Ved Mehta stuff in the afternoon, an occasional Andy Logan column, the daily sheaf of letters, then a lot more sitting around. I began to spend most mornings plotting out where I'd have lunch. Yes, that's what I was doing every day: planning lunch.

I wanted to get back to work on my own stuff but was having a hard time settling into a groove. I'm a big believer in just sit there and write, but even in front of my Selectric at home, I found I was staring out the window, remembering my trip, trying to ground myself in NYC again, embrace the daily-job boredom and use it for my own purposes.

Doing that had worked before, and I was sure it would work again. I just couldn't get started.

Thank goodness, another uptown party the coming weekend.

This one was at somebody else's sprawling West End Ave. apartment and on Friday night. The new kids in the typing pool were going, and I was happy to be asked along, even though I had no idea whose place it was.

In the New York way, the party was to start at 10, which actually meant you showed up around midnight. That's when I got there, and it was pretty sparse. Half an hour later I had to press and squirm to move from one room to another.

I was heading to the kitchen to get a refill of red wine when I felt a tap on my shoulder. I turned, saw a good-looking strawberry redhead in a simple black dress.

"Hey?" She smiled hugely. She sure seemed to know me, but I couldn't place her.

"Hi," I said tentatively.

She kept looking at me, with her spectral green eyes, her brow raised in disbelief, then annoyance ... and finally a jab at my shoulder.

Her poke was far from even Wendell's blow that night before he died, but it startled me just as much. A stranger just punching me in the middle of a party?

"Jesus, Cole, what's with you? Are you pretending you don't remember me?"

The voice was starting to come clear but she didn't look like ... ohmigod! It was Sailor.

But not the Sailor I remembered at all. The black dress was expensive, and now I saw a string of pearls around her neck. She had on heels, black, high. Her hair was far longer than before, layered, stylish, and clearly cut uptown; her nails were manicured. She looked stunning ... way, way different from the cab-driving East Village drummer chick.

"I know, I know," Sailor said with a light laugh as I kept looking at her. "I had a business thing, and, well ... I'm usually not silly enough to wear my premature matron clothes to a party that starts at midnight, but—"

"Your premature ma—"

"Come on, Cole, I can see what's in your eyes." Sailor smirked.

"I think you look great!" This just came out of me, and as soon as I said it, I blushed, half wished I could pull it back.

Light danced in Sailor's eyes.

"Well, I'm not as far gone as I appear, though ... hey, it's been how long since that horrible morning with Wendell's funeral?"

"Seven, eight months," I said. "I've been off traveling."

"I heard."

"You did?"

"Oh, I keep up with all my old friends, best as I can." Sailor looked down at herself again. "It might look like I've changed, but I'm not *that* different."

"So what is going on?" I felt my eyes go wide and round. "What's the deal?"

"You ready for this?" A bounce on her toes, heels clacking the wood floor as she lowered them. "I've got a job—a straight job."

"That's what you look like."

"Right, I know, I know. But it's a good one. Christie's. An assistant in their photo division. Did I ever tell you I love photography?"

"I don't think so," shaking my head.

"I studied art in college—art history."

"I didn't even know you went to—"

"Vassar." Sailor laughed. "Class of '73."

"Wow."

"Yeah, wow!" That sexy smirk again. "Am I blowing your mind, Cole?"

"Um—"

"By the way, I'm Laura now. My birth name. Laura Pershing." She stuck out her hand, and I shook it. A firm grip, determined, sure of herself. "Glad to meet you, Mr. Whitman."

"So the ... the music thing with Slater and Savage Joy, that was just—"

"Something I gave all my heart and soul to, yeah."

"Right." The way she threw this at me, with both pride and as a challenge, I wasn't sure how to respond. Instead I just let my head spin. This was ... well, Laura. Tonight Sailor looked more like a Laura, though I couldn't get the old figure out of my memory. I really liked Sailor, felt we were good buddies, but this Laura....

"So who do you want to hear about?" she asked.

"What?"

"Aren't you curious?" That mirthful, just a couple beats ahead of me snicker. "Aren't you *dying* of curiosity?"

"About—"

"Well, Emily."

I swallowed. Of course I'd thought about Emily. My first day back I'd knocked on her door, only to hear a scramble of Spanish and have it open on a Dominican couple in their forties.

"O.K." I nodded half-hearted, a little anxious.

"She's gone. Out West." A lift of Sailor's—I mean Laura's—pretty nose. "You'll never guess with whom."

I noticed that, her perfect grammar; and suddenly I saw this stunning strawberry blonde woman as a cute strawberry blonde girl gamboling through Vassar, rushing to classes, soaking up art history—before somehow she dyed her hair blood red, clipped it into a violent bob, became Savage Joy's wild drummer.

"Is it Slater?" I said, half holding my breath.

"No, no, that idiot's still in jail. He wasn't fooling." Quick, dismissive shake of her head. "Jerk meant it. Pleaded guilty to assault and possession. Slater's doing five to ten in a prison up in Watertown. What I hear is he's saying he has a lot of things still to learn there." A short, dark chuckle. "God help us when the miscreant gets out."

"So who—with whom?"

Sailor laughed. Sorry, that's how I kept thinking of her. My friend Sailor. But I had to stop. She was Laura now, glowing, classy, splendid Laura.

"Slater's brother! You remember Dale, right?"

"Of course."

"I don't know the gory details, but Emily took off with him. Got a postcard from Jackson Hole, Wyoming, of all places."

"Jackson—" My head was spinning over this. What, it's not enough to get messed-up by Slater Martin, you have to go for Dale Martin? All in the family?

"Probably just passing through, though I think I recall hearing Dale has a standing job cutting timber up in Montana."

"Wow!" O.K., the news was settling in some. Emily ... just one more adventure, I guess. Or maybe not. As Sailor told me this, I remembered a distinct fizz between Emily and Dale; and he was also hardly his brother, far more sane, competent, real. Whatever Emily was after, maybe she could find it with him. Another kid? That thought pierced me out of the blue, but the more I thought of her and Dale, the more I saw it happening. Mitigate the pain of her daughter Sally's loss with her own family. (Years later, I found out my speculation was spot on. Six kids, big house in Wyoming, by all accounts she and Dale were all good.)

"So who else?" Sailor, no, Laura said, musing. "I'm trying to think of who else we knew. Slater, I told you, Wendell, that was so sad. Hmnn. I can't—"

"Um, me?"

"What?" A slight blip, quick recovery. "Oh, sure, what about *you*, Cole?" She laughed, bore down on her next sentence almost facetiously. "What's new with *you*?"

"Hey!"

"Come on, I'm just goofing. But, really, tell me. I'm all ears."

"Sailor!" She was teasing me, and her old name just leaped out.

"Come on, Laura."

"O.K., sure, Laura. Laura, Laura, Laura," I said over and over. "Miss Laura Pershing—"

"Come on, Cole—" a hand on my shoulder "—talk to me."

"Well, I'm back from my ... my amazing trip." I shrugged. "Settling in. Still in my apartment, still at the magazine—" a sigh "—and, well, I hope to get back to work on this novel I'm—"

"Do I know about a novel?"

"You knew I was always writing."

"Yeah." She lifted her chin a bit. "What's it called?"

"Oh." I took a deep breath. I had been learning it was never smart to talk to anybody about what you were working on, even if it was going splendidly. One twitchy eyebrow, one awkward cough, you can only assume they think you're an idiot—and that'd kill three, four days of work ... even if you were sure you were writing well. If you were brimming over with confidence. If you....

"Come on, Cole, I want to know. I really do."

"I don't like to talk about—"

"Cole!" Her sharp, demanding tone made me jump. That same tone came to always make me jump. And laugh.

"I'm calling it *Negative Space*," I blurted out.

Emily lifted her lips, tasted the two words. I half held my breath.

"That's great." She was nodding; my heart was ... *bippity, bippity, bippity* ... slowing. "You have a way, you know. I like the way the title hits you hard, almost makes sense, yet—"

"Well, you know—" I swallowed hard "—I kind of borrowed it, and—"

"Sure, negative space, from artspeak."

"No, this was from this terrific book of movie criticism, guy named Manny Farber, and—"

"So you have a good eye." Laura shrugged. "Good ear. No reason you can't use it as your title, and it's great." Beat, beat, my head whirling at her compliments. "I love it."

"Thanks."

She was silent then, her sweet button-mouth lips close against each other.

"What?" I said.

"You know, *we* have some unfinished business," Laura said. "You and I."

"We do?"

"Don't you remember?" Lips parting, wry smile, teasing.

"Um—" I stood there, quickly uneasy. Unfinished business? What was I forgetting? I suddenly didn't want to forget anything with Laura.

"Savage Joy."

*"The band?"*

"No, stupid, the song! Remember? We were going to write *Savage Joy* together. I kept trying, and you—"

"I know, I wasn't there."

"You're here now."

"I am."

"So let's do it, Cole." She lifted on her heels again, waggled her shoulders, shook her strawberry hair. "Let's write that song."

She was so strong, so abrupt, I pulled back a touch.

"But you're not doing music anymore, right?"

"Who says?"

"I don't know, I thought that—" My gaze coursed her oh-so-proper black dress and stockings, fitting tight, fitting just perfect....

"I know, I know." She shot a dagger down her own person. "Sure it looks like I, well, that I'm some kind of whole new person. But I'm not. It's still just me." A light shrug. "Sailor, if you wish."

"I'm kinda getting used to Laura—"

She smiled.

"And I'm still doing everything—any friggin' thing that intrigues me. And 'sides, if we write a good song, Cole, I still have that Sire connection. Who knows?"

Laura was standing there simply shining, her hair flipped up, her forehead beaming. She blew out an inexhaustible enthusiasm, and I was catching it.

"O.K.," I said. "Sure. Let's write it." A sudden anxious look at her, but no, she was still beaming, not goofing on me or pulling back at all. "When do we start?"

"How about Tuesday night? Tuesday's a light day for me, and—"

"Light for me, too." I shrugged. "I'll just have my daily dose of Ved Mehta drivel." This just came out. Yes, there I'd be, back in the typing pool, back pounding out the Vedette's hasty scrawl, back spending the morning wondering where to go for lunch, back to....

"Come on, it can't be *that* bad. It's the friggin' *New Yorker*."

"It's not India. It's not Thailand. It's not—"

Sailor held up a hand, killed my stupid whining. She was

looking hard at me, right at me, her gaze sharp against my face, almost like fingernails, against my eyes, my cheeks. It was some way she had, her quick intensity, her sureness. I liked it. I liked it a lot.

"You're worried the adventure's over?" Sailor put a hand on my shoulder, leaned in close to my ear. Her voice was between a whisper and a purr. "Sweetie, believe me on this. The adventure's just beginning."